HOLLYWOOD CEMETERY

LIAM O'FLAHERTY

Introduction by Jenny Farrell

Afterword by Tomás Mac Síomóin

NUASCÉALTA

Introduction©Jenny Farrell, 2019.

Afterword©Tomás Mac Síomóin, 2019.

www.nuascealta.com • info@nuascealta.com

Cover Illustration and Design:© Karen Dietrich, 2019.

Typesetting: Nuascéalta Teoranta.

ISBN: 9781795055512

ACKNOWLEDGMENTS

The publishers would like to thank the family of Liam O'Flaherty, especially Máiréad Ní hEithir, and Cumann Liam agus Thomáis Uí Fhlaithearta (The Liam and Tom O'Flaherty Society).

INTRODUCTION

Liam O'Flaherty spent the best part of a year in the United States, from late April 1934 to June 1935, mostly in Hollywood. It was the year his cousin John Ford made the famous film adaptation of O'Flaherty's 1925 novel *The Informer*, premiered 1 May 1935. It was also in California that O'Flaherty met his future partner Kitty Tailer.

Hollywood Cemetery is O'Flaherty's sardonic fictionalised account of his encounter with an industry that is emblematic of the American Way of Life. The disclaimer "All the characters in this book are highly improbable for obvious reasons" — sets the tone. The entire novel continues in this riotous manner, telling the story of the Irish writer Brian Carey working with American producer Jack Mortimer, his companion-secretary Larry Dafoe and cameraman Shultz, to make a film of his novel *The Emigrant*. What unfolds exposes the core of Hollywood film-making. It is hardly surprising that experiences related here are not so far removed from O'Flaherty's observations in the filming of his own novel.

O'Flaherty had left his native Aran in pursuit of an education in Dublin, joined the Irish Guards in World War I and was wounded, discharged with shellshock, having travelled the world extensively before he returned briefly to Ireland to take part in the very early days of this country's incomplete independence. By 1922, he had moved to London and begun to write. One of his close associates was Carl Lahr, a German socialist, who ran Progressive Bookshop, in Red Lion Street, London, and whose circle included many progressive writers, among them D.H. Lawrence and Aldous Huxley. This circle of friends around Lahr was O'Flaherty's political home in many respects. It was Lahr and his wife Esther who supported O'Flaherty and published some of his works for the first time, including his expressionist play *Darkness* (1926) and in 1931 the only recently republished *A Cure for Unemployment* (Swift, O'Flaherty, Mac Síomóin: *Three Leaves of a Bitter Shamrock*, Nuascéalta, 2014.)

The Informer was written in the years when O'Flaherty moved in this circle. Film and cinema were becoming a major art form and industry, dominated by expressionist silent film, not only in the US, but also in Germany and the USSR, among other places. *The Informer* is written in a visual, cinematic style and was first made into a motion picture in 1929, by German-US film director Arthur Robison for British cinema. This movie has much less in common with O'Flaherty's novel than Ford's version and its greatest interest lies in its enacting the transition from silent to sound film. Half of the film is silent, with intertitles; the second half is with sound. There is no suggestion of slums, prostitution, or ugliness of any kind—indeed the plot is reduced to a tale of jealousy. Its only claim to honour is that it was banned in Ireland. O'Flaherty was present for some of the shooting of the British venture and one can only imagine his disappointment when the second attempt in Hollywood also proved not to be a true reflection of his novel. As the reader is reminded in *Hollywood Cemetery*, the American film industry had similar 'decency' stipulations, which imposed sugary anti-realistic movies on cinema-goers. In fact, O'Flaherty arrived in Hollywood just as Joseph I. Breen, a prominent Catholic layman who had worked in public relations, was appointed head of the new Production Code Administration (PCA). Under Breen's leadership, enforcement of the Production Code became rigid and his power to change scripts and scenes incensed many writers, directors, and Hollywood moguls.

The Informer is set in the Dublin slums; its main characters are the lumpen proletariat, prostitutes, a paramilitary communist organisation, working class people. It is very similar to the world portrayed by Sean O'Casey in his Dublin plays. O'Casey and O'Flaherty are among the great Irish working-class writers of the early 20th century.

O'Flaherty's characters are real; they are starving, consumptive, yet full of life. They speak in the voice of the Dublin slum dwellers. Katie Fox, one of the main female characters, is known as a prostitute, "drug fiend", her "young face, old before the years had time to wrinkle it, sad, hard and stupefied". Mary, on the other hand, has managed to come up in the world to an office job, dresses the part, but her mouth is "a product of the slums". Enter Hollywood. The celluloid manifestations of these two characters could hardly be further from their literary models. Sophisticated, elegant and photogenic, they seem to mock their originals. Instead of making a film based on the Dublin working-class experience, Ford and his script-writer Dudley Nichols, along with the entire machinery, cleansed the novel of its deeper political texture to make a film that presents stereotypes as seen by those who have no interest in the inhabitants of tenements beyond their monetary value. As an insider joke in *Hollywood Cemetery*, the Hollywood crew who discover a suitable beauty in Ireland for a film around whom a script will be written, rename her 'Angela Devlin'. Heather Angel is the name of one of the two female leads in Ford's *The Informer*.

Just how Hollywood operates, the allure of incredible salaries and resulting prostitution of its employees for money, is exposed in *Hollywood Cemetery* by the Communist Party newspaper, *Proletarian Power*: "Hollywood is a cemetery where the remains of present-day bourgeois intellectuals are buried, after being fattened like the sacrificial victims in ancient Mexico on enormous salaries, only to have their hearts plucked out and eaten by the Moguls of modern mammon." O'Flaherty contrasts this prostituting culture with that of the USSR several times in the book.

Proletarian Power's assessment not only gives *Hollywood Cemetery* its title, it suffuses the entire text. This acknowledgement of the US Communist Party, of which Liam's brother Tom was a founding member and regular columnist to the party paper, is of particular interest. O'Flaherty had travelled to the USSR in 1930 and written a book entitled *I Went to Russia*, published in 1931. In it, he employs the voice of an unreliable narrator, a Gentleman with a vague interest in socialism. This narrator is by no means a radical, and harbours many of the general Western stereotypes of the first socialist state. The narrator cannot be identified with Liam O'Flaherty, and it is interesting to tease out where O'Flaherty's actual views come into the tale, as they do, for example, in his portrayal of the absence of hierarchy amongst his ship's crew, whose first mate is a woman.

Ever since this book was first published, Western readers have a gloated over O'Flaherty's apparent disillusionment with the USSR, supposing to find their own thinking confirmed in the text. Despite the many references in the text to it being 'a book of lies', these readers prefer to believe the unreliable narrator.

Apart from its addiction to money and glamour, the exclusion of reality, Hollywood has also a propensity for violence, and gunmen lurk throughout the novel — this lifestyle comes at a price. In addition to the philosophy of anti-realistic, sentimental and glamourous celebrity-based fiction, Hollywood transports an ominous indication of things to come, reminiscent of Huxley's *Brave New World* (1932). 'Angela Devlin' is drugged into compliance and held against her will. Male characters too are bribed and manipulated. There is no space for culture or art. This is a dystopia. *Hollywood Cemetery* is a greater metaphor for a ruthless industry and society that deals in illusion, whose god is money and whose abject slave is the mainstream media.

However, it would be wrong to think that O'Flaherty is simply lampooning his cousin Ford. Indeed, leaving the US, he wrote him a letter stating: "Well, Jack, I'm very glad I came out to Hollywood. Looking back now, it's been a marvellous year and I thank you very much for all your kindness, particularly for *The Informer*, but perhaps most of all for yourself. During the past year I have learned to admire you as the great man you are. If I have gone away three thousand miles to say so, that is the Irish way."

In the letter to Ford quoted here, O'Flaherty also mentions work on his epic novel *Famine*. He writes: "I wanted to get back home myself to put *Famine* on the stocks (…) I think *Famine* is going to be great, and you need never feel ashamed, I assure you, that it's dedicated to you. I'm going to hammer out every word from the depths of my soul." *Famine* is the first major artistic grappling in Ireland with the nation's 19th century colonial holocaust. O'Flaherty presents a differentiated panorama of the starving peasantry, the money-grabbing famine-profiteering gombeen men, clergy with and without a spine, and deeply inhuman British colonialists. Significantly in this novel, the people fight back. Resistance is a key theme in O'Flaherty's work and *Hollywood Cemetery* is no different. In the context of dystopias, this resistance is noteworthy. In this respect, O'Flaherty anticipates authors such as Alan Moore's *V for Vendetta* or Margaret Atwood's dystopian fiction. Another theme that links the authors is O'Flaherty's high regard for women, their intelligence and capacity for defiance.

O'Flaherty hoped that Ford would make *Famine* into a film after it appeared in 1937. Had Ford taken on this material, and resolutely portrayed this liquidation of a large part of the Irish nation, along with their resistance, it could have made a significant contribution to a cultural acknowledgement of colonialism in all its inhumanity.

In the 1930s, O'Flaherty was one of the most censored authors in Ireland, in fact his Galway novel *The House of Gold* was the very first book to be banned (*The House of Gold* was published by Nuascéalta and officially launched in Ireland for the first time in 2013.) In other writings, he had made clear his class understanding of the new Irish state as one that kept its people in continued ignorance and poverty. He wrote against this, by revealing the shameful role of the Catholic Church in usurping the ideals of Independence, depriving the Irish of their freedom and by exposing the fact that the gombeen men of colonial days had now taken the seats of power and emulated their former master.

Seven US publishers refused publication of *Hollywood Cemetery*. O'Flaherty had started the book while still in the US and finished it in France in the summer of 1935. His first draft was returned to him by his London publisher Gollancz as too outspoken. It was revised and finally published on 18 November 1935.

Dr Jenny Farrell
Oranmore, Co. Galway
Ireland
January 2019

*All the characters in this book are highly improbable
for obvious reasons.*

TO
S. P.

CHAPTER I

AT THE LAST MOMENT I find myself unable to introduce my heroine in the manner I had intended, owing to the universal prejudice entertained in this age against describing a certain human function. Sterne, in his *Tristram Shandy,* managed to elude this prejudice by discoursing on the manner of his own conception with such subtlety that the prejudiced mind did not know what he was writing about. I lack Sterne's wit and in any case his parents were properly churched, making their nocturnal athletics not only salutary to the species by the production of genius, but also legal; whereas the antics of my heroine were nothing of the kind.

And yet I am forced to mention the act in which she was discovered by Mr. Mortimer, since it was the intensity of her passion that roused that gentleman's interest.

It must be understood that he had just burst into fame as a motion-picture producer. While the rest of Hollywood was staggering under the clerical attack on indecent films, he had hurriedly produced a picture called *Little Virgin,* which was a colossal success. Within three months it had flooded all the capitals of the world, outside of pagan Moscow, with the tears of the multitude. It had poured a profit of four million dollars into the bank account of World Films Inc. But it also placed Gentleman Jack Mortimer in a quandary, for he was well aware that, in Hollywood, success is a trull that rarely spends two nights in the same bed. He must follow up his colossal success with one still more colossal, or else the "velvet knockers" would soon take the place of the sycophants.

He had another, as he said himself, practically in the bag, a script called *The Widow's Mite*, dealing with a small boy who became the millionaire head of a great corporation by being kind to his widowed mother. However, at the very moment when he was ready to begin work on his new masterpiece, with the same director and the same star as in *Little Virgin*, they both ran out on him. Lily Valentine, the star of *Little Virgin*, had completed her contract with World Films and refused to sign for another picture unless she got a medium suited to her position as the Countess Krasnov, since her fifth husband had just given her that title. Bud Tracy, on the other hand, was the director, a man of really great talent, without whom Mortimer knew very well that he could produce nothing of consequence. Tracy insisted on directing a story called *The Emigrant*.

"I'm sick an' tired o' directing tripe," he said to Mortimer. "I've made enough money to last me as long as I live. Unless I can direct what I want, I ain't goin' to stick around. I'm for the South Seas."

"Okay with me, Bud," said Mortimer. "If it's a choice between you and the script, it can go, although I'll lay five grand to a nickel there's big dough in it. Give us the dope on this emigrant guy."

Tracy explained that it was the work of a European writer called Carey.

"Never heard of him," said Mortimer.

"Why, he's a big-shot intellectual," said Tracy, who prided himself on being well informed about current literature.

"That don't worry me," said Mortimer. "Have you got the book?"

Tracy produced the book and Mortimer gave it to a secretary, who made a synopsis, which another secretary read to Mr. Mortimer while he was having his bath. The story, even in the synopsis, was a very gloomy one, entirely unsuited for the masses of screen addicts, as it dealt with the adventures of a young Irish girl, who was brought to America by her parents, after being evicted from a farm in the county of Galway. The young girl grew up into a ravishing beauty, amid the sordid environment of the Irish quarter in South Boston and then led a life of sin, which ended in the electric chair with her gangster paramour. However, Mr. Mortimer became wildly enthusiastic about it, both because he must do it in order to retain Tracy and because he also knew that the screen writers in his employment could turn even *King Lear* into a merry comedy. He had, furthermore, an inspiration that was worthy of his genius.

"Bud," he said to Tracy, "it's a knock-out. Listen, pappy, I've got the swellest idea of my whole career. I'm goin' to find a new star. This is an Irish story. Well! I'm goin' over to Ireland and I'll pick up a kid..."

"Jees!" cried Tracy. "Do that, you old son of a gun. The country is lousy with them. One of those wild, red-headed, blue-eyed, Irish broads..."

"Why, it's a cinch," shouted Mortimer. "Listen, Bud, I'll transport a colleen over here that could put sap in the trees of the petrified forest."

"Do that, goddam it," yelled Tracy, " and get hold of Carey while you're over there. He hangs out in London. Just slip him a couple of grand and he'll come. He's one of these highbrow guys that knock the movies. Be good publicity having him around."

"Okay, pappy," said Mortimer. "I'll haul him along. Meanwhile, you get hold of Sam Gunn and start in on the script."

So Mortimer came to London, with his companion secretary and a cameraman. He easily collared Carey, who succumbed to the offer of five thousand dollars for the screen rights of his book and a salary of five hundred dollars a week for three months, helping with the scenario. Then the party went to Ireland, which they scoured for a suitable girl. After wandering about the country for some time without success, they at last came to the village of Ballymorguttery in the county of Cork.

An extremely pretty river flows through the outskirts of that village, along the edge of a wood, in which Mortimer and Carey went for a stroll, while Shultz, the cameraman, was taking shots of the village from the wooden bridge that spans the river. As they walked in silence over the lush grass beneath the trees, they heard a series of low cries nearby. They halted. To their astonishment, they found that it was a girl making a most intimate appeal to her lover. Mortimer pressed forward on tip-toe, in the direction of the voice, followed by Carey. Presently, from behind a tree whose overhanging branches concealed them from view, they saw a girl sporting with a young man on a grassy slope in a clearing. For a few moments they watched in amazement. Then Mortimer clutched Carey by the arm and pointed towards the lovers in great excitement.

"What magnificent abandon!" he whispered.

"Boy! It's colossal. She's got something on the ball, that kid. Whoever she is, she has the elemental quality that goes to make a screen star. Look at the primitive savagery of her expression and yet her movements are as delicate and as graceful as... Say! Doesn't she remind you of Pavlova? She has the same..."

"Don't be silly," said Carey gloomily. "She's just some common little slut having a romp with a yokel."

"The hell she is," said Mortimer. "I have an unerring instinct for possible screen material. I don't mind telling you, son, that I've a strong hunch this young dame is going to go places. Within a year, if my hunch is correct, her name'll be flashed on electric signs across the continents. Say! Will you look at those outstretched arms shivering like the delicate leaves of some tropical plant? Oh! Boy, I'm a pushover for that young dame."

"Bunk!" said Carey, in a tone of absolute disgust. "I must say, Mortimer, that I'm beginning to have a sordid opinion that you are slightly insane."

Mortimer looked at Carey in sudden anger that brought a flush to his sallow cheeks. His monocle, the constant use of which gave him the nickname of gentleman, fell from his eye on to his puffed-out stomach. In fact, he presented a ludicrous appearance, with his bald forehead, his fat perspiring face, his short round body dressed in a check plus four suit, bright blue golf stockings and black and white brogues. He was a type that does not get angry with dignity.

"Listen, buddy," he whispered, "your goddam superciliousness is beginning to get my goat. I've hired you to help me out and not to make ritzy remarks about my sanity."

Suddenly he raised his voice from a whisper to a shrill shout and continued:

"I'm paying you big money to turn your lousy story into suitable screen material and not to..."

He was interrupted by a cry from the girl and he turned

around just in time to see the lover leap from the grass and run towards the trees on the other side of the clearing. Mortimer waved his arms in despair.

"See what you've done?" he shouted at Carey. "You've ruined the goddam scene. Hey!"

He held up his hand to the girl. She was also getting to her feet and arranging her dress, preparatory to following her lover in flight.

"Hey! There," he called. "Hold on a mo'. We ain't going to bite you."

He hurried into the clearing towards her, while Carey shrugged his shoulders and muttered viciously:

"My God! My God! To think that poverty could make me suffer this humiliation! "

He was a young man of thirty, of rather attractive countenance, but so slovenly in carriage and dress that he looked almost repulsive. It is an impression that is given to the average, sane, bourgeois person by most intellectuals of a certain type. Either their hair is too long, or they slouch, or there is a button missing somewhere, or they have the furtive expression of the fellow who is out to borrow money. In all these respects Carey was capable of giving offence to the respectable. His fair hair needed trimming at the back. He slouched, with his hands in the pockets of his shabby flannel trousers. There was a button missing from his tweed coat. His eyes showed that he had a grievance against society. The grievance was his novel *The Emigrant*. Led astray by the critics, who over-praised it on its publication four years previously, he had become afflicted with the mania of genius and got to hate humanity for buying no more than four thousand copies of his masterpiece. Of late he had become so embittered that he could scarcely write anything at all and he was living precariously on hack journalism when Mortimer rescued him.

The girl had halted on seeing Mortimer approach. She stood with her back towards him, looking at him over her shoulder, while she stooped to fasten her stockings to her girdle.

"Sorry to butt in on you," said Mortimer, putting his monocle to his eye and assuming his normal, jovial expression.

"My friend, Mr. Carey, and myself were resting under the tree there, having a little discussion, when we suddenly heard a scream. Anything wrong? Is there anything I could do? "

He was very shrewdly giving the girl a chance to put a good face on her conduct of a few seconds previously, and at the same time he was making a test of her ability as an actress, as well as of her intelligence.

"If she jumps to it," he thought, "then I'm certain she's got the goods."

Our heroine did, in fact, jump to it with remarkable ability. She stood erect and turned towards him slowly. At the same time, her face assumed a helpless expression. Tears came to her eyes. Her lips quivered and her chin sank down towards her bosom, on which she placed her outstretched fingers, as if to protect herself from shame.

"I was just sittin' there," she mumbled through her tears, "when he rushed at me, a young fellow that's always annoying me, though I have nothing to do with him. He started gettin' rough and I was so afraid that I couldn't say a word, until at last, when he began to...I screamed. That terrified him and he ran away. Thanks very much, sir, for helping me. It's very kind of you."

"Marvellous," thought Mortimer, as he looked in rapture at the coquettish glance she gave him through her tears, a glance that wandered from his face and became foxy, when her eyes appraised the visible signs of wealth on his body, his magnificent wrist-watch, his diamond tie-pin, the quality of his clothes. "She knows what's what, that kid. She ain't got much to learn."

"Aw!" he said aloud. "I wouldn't worry about a little thing like that. Let me tell you, Miss..."

"Murphy," she said with a smile. "Biddy Murphy."

"My name is Mortimer," he countered. "Ever hear the name?"

"Yes. I know a boy called Mortimer, but he's not a bit like you. He travels in underclothes."

"He what?" cried Mortimer.

Carey, who had come up just at that moment, burst out laughing and Mortimer turned on him angrily once more.

"What's biting you now, my foul-smelling friend?" he shouted. "Excuse me, Miss Murphy. This is Mr. Carey and he has a very peculiar sense of humour, of which he possesses the sole monopoly."

"Pleased to meet you, Mr. Carey," said our heroine, glancing at Carey in a rather contemptuous and hostile fashion.

She could see by Carey's eyes and lips that he was not inclined to play Mortimer's charming game of pretending not to have seen her gambols. Therefore, she sensed him at once to be her enemy. Furthermore, she sensed his poverty, since he had not troubled to spend on his person any of the money he had received from Mortimer. Her sneering eyes, wandering pointedly about his clothes, made him feel uneasy, but he could think of nothing biting to say, so he just bowed.

"Well! Now, Miss Murphy," said Mortimer, "it may happen that this little inconvenience you suffered ... she was attacked by that guy we saw running away," he said hurriedly to Carey. "It may happen, Miss Murphy, that this little adventure was the luckiest thing that ever happened to you."

"How is that, sir?"

"Did anybody ever tell you that you had screen possibilities?"

"Really, Mortimer," said Carey, raising his eyebrows, "you don't mean to tell me that Hollywood has descended to *that.*"

He had been on edge to say something biting, after the humiliation of Mortimer's remarks and the glance which our heroine had given him, but he was startled by the effect of his words. Mortimer went white with fury and our heroine got no less angry, although she did not very well understand the meaning of what he had said.

"Good God!" thought Carey. "Now I've done it."

"I think you had better take a little walk, Carey," whispered Mortimer in a sinister tone.

"I think so, too," said our heroine.

Then she began to barge Carey, waving her arms and using the language that fishwives at Billingsgate are supposed to use. The effect of her outburst on Mortimer was astonishing. He was enraptured by it. He stood back and gazed at her with folded arms, nodding *his* head now and again, as if she were acting a scene at his request.

"Boy! She's got everything," he muttered. "She's a gold mine."

Our heroine certainly did look beautiful at that moment. She was a little above the average in height, full bodied and well-moulded without being plump, with a gorgeous mass of red-gold hair and a pair of dark-blue eyes in which her recent tears still glittered. She had teeth like a negress, short and white and even. But it was through her lips and the whole contour of her mouth, from her sensitive open nostrils to her dimpled chin, that the demon, whom Mr. Mortimer called "the great come on," manifested himself.

However, beauty like hers, which affects the senses like an exhilarating drug, is beyond the power of mere description. In fact, I am convinced that beauty of this sort must be seen, either in reality or on the screen, in order to be felt. Measurements of bust, hips, thighs, arms and ankles are inadequate to give a vivid impression of a beauty that depends on personality rather than on form for its subtle quality. As she stood there on the greensward that had been trodden flat and pale by her recent tumbling, in her wrinkled cotton frock, with heaving bosom, she looked like a perfect statue of the Goddess of Desire, come suddenly to life.

"That will do now," said Mortimer at length. "That's fine. Let's talk business."

She paused and looked at him, panting. Then she pointed to Carey.

"I'll talk nothing," she said, "until that big stick of misery either apologises or gets out of my sight."

"He'll do both," said Mortimer. "Now, Carey, like good man, do what the lady tells you and then take that little walk I suggested."

Carey bit his lip, bowed and said:

"Sorry to have offended you."

Then he tumed on his heel and left the clearing. As soon as he was out of sight, he took off his hat and tore at his hair, cursing bitterly.

"Now what have I done?" he cried aloud.

As he walked towards the car, which they had parked near the bridge, he accused himself violently of being a cad, for behaving in the way he did.

"Good God!" he thought. "A month ago, I would have been happy to have this job, but no sooner have I escaped from my predicament than I begin to despise the man who saved me.

Why can't I keep my mouth shut? After all, I should have refused in the beginning to have any truck with him, or else accept the situation with a good grace, no matter how repulsive it may be. The best thing to do, under the circumstances, is to resign."

He got into the car and sat there, with his head in his hands, trying to make up his mind. He was interrupted by Shultz, the cameraman, who came around the comer from the bridge, mopping his brow.

"What's biting you now?" said Shultz. "Had another row with the chief?"

"Nothing in particular," said Carey curtly. "Why?"

"No why," said Shultz, "only you look as if you'd just got a balling out."

"Oh!" said Carey in a superior tone.

He did not like Shultz, for the reason that he thought the man impertinent. That is, Shultz treated Carey as a human being and not as a man of genius. In fact, Carey thought that Shultz, owing to his free and easy manner, did not think that Carey was a gentleman. Shultz, on the other hand, being a jovial sort of man, with a heavy body, a thick neck and a square head, did not give a damn what Carey or anybody else thought about him. He had no idea what the word gentleman meant, except that it was one of those "goofy Limejuice words" that had no meaning for an American.

"Where is the boss?" he said, absolutely indifferent to Carey's sneering tone.

"Over in the wood," said Carey. "We eavesdropped on some young woman making love and Mortimer is persuaded that he has found a new star."

"The hell you did," said Shultz.

He spat out a cud of chewing gum, threw his camera into the front of the car and laughed heartily.

"I miss all the good things," he said. "Is the boss on the make for her?"

"I don't exactly know your meaning," said Carey, "but if you're asking what his intentions are, I can tell you that, at the moment, he intends taking her to Hollywood."

"On the strength of ..." laughed Shultz.

"Precisely," said Carey.

Shultz laughed as if he would never stop. Carey bit his lip and thought:

"Good God! There I go again, making offensive remarks. That sot, I'm sure, reports everything to his employer. Why can't I keep silent? What does it matter what these perfectly awful barbarians do?"

"Well! I'll be goddamned," said Shultz. "The chief is the greatest artist in the business and no doubt about it. After three weeks in this lousy country, I came to the conclusion that ole pa stork did the necessary for bringing people into this world, judging by the difficulty I experienced with the local dames. If the boss has found proof that I'm wrong, I'll say he's some explorer. Isn't it just my luck to miss a thing like that? Hold on, though, I'm going to look-see. Show might have a second act."

With a mischievous wink at Carey, he was about to set out towards the wood, when Mortimer appeared, shouting and leading our heroine by the hand.

"Hey! There, Carey," he cried. "That you, Shultz? Listen, fellahs."

"Shoot, boss," said Shultz. "We're listening. What's on your mind?"

Mortimer approached, panting with excitement.

"I've just had the greatest inspiration of my whole career," he cried.

"You're telling me," said Shultz, as he gloated over the ravishing beauty of our heroine.

"Listen," said Mortimer, as he came up to the car. "This young lady here has lived to this day with the unsuitable name of Biddy Murphy. I started out to figure on a proper title for her beauty and I worked it this way."

He put one foot on the running-board of the car and his arm round our heroine's waist. Then he cleared his throat, glanced in triumph at the two men and whispered in the melting tones of a bond salesman:

"A beautiful woman is the rarest thing in the world. She has that quality of tenderness which appeals to the mother love in all of us, the angelic quality that gives us a fresh angle on what is meant by Heaven. But at the same time, she is a combination of good and evil, for she has that beauty of body, that sex appeal, that rouses the demon in us and prevents us gettin' tired of her angelic quality. Well! Now for the angelic part of it, Angela is sticking out a mile. But for the demon part, that's where I consider I've done a swell job. For it had to be an Irish name. D'ye see, Shultz, it had to be a Mick name with the devil in it? For that part can you beat Devlin? Angela Devlin. Can you beat that, Shultz, you old rum hound?"

"I couldn't beat it, boss, with anything short of Cleopatra," cried the sycophantic Shultz. "You've gone an' done it this time, boss."

"Think so, Shultz? "cried Mortimer delightedly.

"Think so?" cried Shultz. "Why, those eyes could set fire to an Eskimo's igloo."

Mortimer fairly danced with delight, for he thought highly of Shultz's opinion, as an indication of what the masses demanded of a female star. He struck Carey a resounding whack between the shoulder blades. Carey flared up in anger for a moment, regarding as an impertinence this familiarity from a man whom he considered his inferior. But his anger changed almost at once to delight, as he realised that his inferior was also his employer, whom he had recently insulted in a way that threatened dismissal.

"That's splendid," he thought. "He's forgotten about our unpleasant scene. Now I don't have to resign."

"Boys," said Mortimer, "I have another inspiration. This occasion may very well be historic and it should be recorded for the Hall of Fame. Shultz, I'm going to stand here on this rustic bridge with Miss Devlin. No. Wait a minute. I know something better. She'll be leaning over the bridge here, her chin in her hand, looking into the lazy stream, dreaming pensively of Hollywood. Then I come along, I see her, I step back, take off my hat and bow to her. She curtseys to me, know what I mean, Shultz, and then...say, Carey, can you work out a bit o' snappy dialogue for this scene?"

Carey again got furious and his wild blue eyes shot fire at his employer.

"I can't see what this has got to do with *The Emigrant*?" he said.

"Wha-at?" shouted Mortimer. "Who the hell said a word about *The Emigrant*?"

At this moment, our heroine saved the situation. She had been standing in the loop of Mortimer's arm, smiling in a most charming fashion. Now she leant towards Carey and whispered seductively:

"Please, Mr. Carey, won't you do this to please me?"

She shot such an alluring glance at Carey that he flushed and became embarrassed. Then she touched him gently on the arm and he surrendered completely.

"Very well," he said. "What do you wish me to do, Mortimer?"

"Thank God!" said Mortimer. "At last I've found the Open Sesame to your brains. Now, Shultz, let's go."

They all moved down to the bridge to enact the historical, as distinct from the actual, discovery of Angela Devlin by Gentleman Jack Mortimer. Having done that, they all got into the car and drove into the village of Ballymorguttery, to interview the guardian of our heroine.

CHAPTER II

IT WAS SATURDAY AFTERNOON and the village of Ballymorguttery was crowded with people, as the luxurious car rolled down the Main Street, glittering in the brilliant June sunlight. As we all know, there is only one street worthy of the name in Ballymorguttery, which street is easily the dirtiest and most sordid thoroughfare in western Europe. Of one hundred houses inhabited by human beings on that street, thirty are licensed for the sale of intoxicating liquor. Of these latter, Mary Ellen Hynes, the aunt of our heroine, occupied one of the most popular.

Its popularity, however, did not depend on the superior quality of the liquor sold there, or on the fixtures, for the house was as squalid as any on the street, but on the fact that Mary Ellen's character was very liberal in the moral sense, so that a fellow could enjoy himself on her premises. On this particular afternoon, she was doing an exceptionally brisk business from behind her sloppy counter. When Mortimer's car drew up before her establishment, she was drawing a gallon of porter for some young fellows who had just finished a game of handball in the alley at the rear of the house.

"Whose car is that, Paddy?" she remarked to the young man who was buying.

"Divil a bit o' me knows," said the young man, "unless it's a car from Dublin."

"It's from Cork," said another man. "I saw it a while ago comin' in along the Cork road. I saw what looked like Yanks in it, be the cut o'them."

"Bad cess to them," said Mary Ellen. "Them same Yanks are everywhere, but there's whiskers grows on their money, they're that shy of partin' with it."

"Yerrah, will ye look at who is with them in the car?" said a ragged old woman, who was peeping out the window. "It's Biddy, be the hammers o' hell. Janey Mac! There's a toff beside her an' he with one spectacle in his eye. Now he's helpin' her outa the car and the diamonds shinin' in his front, God forgive me, like a priest's vestments. Now, would ye believe it?"

"Oho! Bad luck to her," said Mary Ellen, "she'll get hung yet, pickin' up with every strap she meets on the road. It would be a load off me mind if her holidays were over and she back at her job in Cork. Fitter for her to give me a hand here behind the counter than to be gallivantin'. Yanks, did ye say?"

At that moment, Mr. Mortimer entered the shop, sweeping off his hat and crying with the heartiness of the born showman:

"God save all here."

The rogue had learned that much during his tour of the country.

"You too, sir," said Mary Ellen genially, carried away by his manner.

"Pleasure to meet you, Miss Hynes," said Mortimer, coming forward with his hat in his hand, "and all you ladies and gentlemen here present. Your niece told me all about you, Miss

Hynes. A very remarkable resemblance. Well I Now, Miss Hynes ...”

He continued to talk at such a rate that Mary Ellen, as she said afterwards, did not know whether she was standing on her head or on her heels. The upshot of it was, that he took complete charge of the establishment, as if it were a set in his studio at Hollywood. He put Angela and Shultz behind the counter to look after the customers, whom he asked to drink his health as many times as they pleased, at his expense, in the best liquor that the place afforded. Then he led Miss Hynes into her private sitting-room. Then he fetched Carey, to whom he whispered:

“You're a Mick, Carey, so you'd better stick around while I'm putting over this deal. You'll be able to give me a psychological slant on how to deal with any difficulties the old dame might make. See?”

When the three of them were seated in the parlour and they had toasted one another in Mary Ellen's best sherry, he began:

“Now, Miss Hynes, I've come here to-day to offer your niece the opportunity of making a brilliant career. In other words, I am Jack Mortimer of Hollywood, California, and I want to give your niece a screen career, if she passes the test I intend making in Dublin to-morrow. Of course, as you are her guardian and she is still under age, we must have your consent, but I feel sure that a woman of your understanding and fine business instincts will put nothing in the way of her climbing to a paramount position in the motion-picture industry.”

Mary Ellen had stared at him confusedly while he was talking and then, realising the purport of his speech, she gradually broke into tears. She was very fat, with dirty auburn hair that was turning grey at the temples, several gullets like a turkey and an *embonpoint* that was quite enormous. She overlaid the chair on which she sat, making Carey's sensitive nerves revolt at the sight of her loose, blubbery body, shaking with sobs and slithering down on either side of her. When Mortimer had finished, she began tearfully to extol the virtues of her niece.

"She's my sister Mary's only child," she said. "Mary was a wild thing, God forgive her, as pretty a creature as you ever laid eyes on, but she was that wild it was impossible to hold her, until in the end she up and run off with a corporal out of the Lancashire Fusiliers. Off she went to Liverpool with him. Faith, it was love at first sight and no doubt about it, over on furlough he was in the first year of the war, they met and she ran away to England with him, for her mother would never hear of her marryin' a fellah like that, an' he only a cattle-drover before he enlisted, though a good looking boy sure enough in his uniform, an' then the war an' all turnin' the girl's head: I'm with ye tonight love an' to-morrow I'm dead. That kind o' thing. Well! Lord have mercy on him, he was soon dead right enough and a short while afterwards Biddy was born. Poor Mary's troubles weren't over. She went to work in·a munition factory and got blown to bits. Then Biddy was brought here and I raised her."

She paused, wiped her eyes with a comer of her apron and took a sip of sherry. Then she began to retail all the expense she had incurred raising our heroine, with a view to getting as much as possible out of Mortimer for relinquishing her rights in our heroine's body. After a great deal of haggling, Mortimer finally offered her five hundred dollars. Mary Ellen affected to consider this sum insufficient. Then it was that Carey came to the rescue with his "psychological slant."

"Of course, Miss Hynes," he said icily, "we should have to make a few enquiries as to her moral character among the prominent local people, the parish priest for instance, before ...”

“You needn’t bother, then, young man,” cried the aunt in alarm. “I can give her all the character that the gentleman needs. Who has a better right to give her character than her own aunt, that has known her since the cradle? If there are people that say she is a bit flighty like her mother, sure it’s only the high spirits of her nature, and what harm is there in that? So, if you’ll be so kind, Mr. Mortimer, as to transfer the sum you named into my keeping, I’ll be ready to sign any papers you may wish.”

“Done,” said Mortimer, shifting his cigar from one side of his mouth to the other and smacking Macy Ellen’s outstretched palm with his own. “It’s a bargain and I hope it’s a gift.”

And it was in that way and exactly under those circumstances that Angela Devlin, late Biddy Murphy, was sold to Mr. Jack Mortimer, for the term of one year at two hundred and fifty dollars a week and a consideration of five hundred dollars in American currency paid to her aunt and guardian, Mary Ellen Hynes, for relinquishing her legal rights in the aforesaid Angela Devlin’s body. This being agreed, drawn up and signed, the party left the house, bearing Angela with them, attended by the wild cheers of the customers, who gave Mortimer the title of the Finest Gentleman That Ever Struck Ballymorguttery.

Indeed, to this day, events in that foul village are dated “Before or After Mortimer” and reminiscences are prefaced with: “It was about the time the showman bought the drink.”

CHAPTER III

I DARE SAY THAT, nowadays, nearly every pretty girl like our heroine sees, in her day-dreams, a gentleman like Mr. Mortimer appear with an offer of a screen career in Hollywood. These day-dreams do not affect the consciousness to any great extent. The average girl just dreams, sighs and goes about her business cheerfully until the next time she goes to the movies. Therefore, when a gentleman like Mr. Mortimer does appear to one of them, it is a profound shock.

So it was only natural that Angela was shocked. As a barmaid in a small hotel in the city of Cork, she could not possibly develop any great conceit. The most she had ever expected to get out of life was to marry a bank-clerk and even that was highly improbable. And now when she found herself in Mr. Mortimer's luxurious car, with her one shabby suitcase at her feet, she fairly dithered with excitement.

Not a tear did she shed, as she bid good-bye to her aunt. The aunt wept copiously, good woman, but they were tears of delight at having received one hundred pounds sterling for what she had always believed to be a worthless relative.

"May God watch over you, *a stór*," she said, "and be sure and write to me."

"I will, Aunt Mary," said Angela. "Good-bye."

She waved to the crowd of people that lined the dung-strewn Main Street of her foul village as the car purred into movement.

"God bless you," the people cried.

As the car came to the cross-roads outside the village, where the sign said Dublin one way and Cork the other, Mortimer said to Shultz, who was at the wheel:

"Drive straight to Dublin, son, and step on it, for we're in an almighty hurry."

"Okay, chief," said Shultz, as he shot the car at an alarming speed around the corner in the Dublin direction.

"Dublin?" said Carey, when he had recovered his balance after the jolt. "I thought we were going on to Galway to find a primitive village suitable for the initial scenes in my book."

"We may have been," said Mortimer, "but I can tell you right here and now that we have changed our minds. All that is dead and gone. And furthermore, I'm going to give you, Carey. a little lecture that may be useful to you, if you mean to play ball with me and make some big dough for yourself. If you don't mean to play ball, then we part company when your three months' contract is finished, without any ill feelings on either side. Get me? "

"Quite," said Carey, with a feeble effort at being superior.

Angela gave Mr. Mortimer an adoring look and that gentleman settled himself more comfortably against the back of the car, at the same time getting his arm so far around Angela's waist, that he could touch the firm apple of her port bosom. Then he took a long puff at his expensive cigar, blew out the smoke and continued:

"I'm in this business, Carey, for all the dough I can get out of it. No more, no less. And after all these years, I've come to the conclusion that there ain't no money in primitive villages on the screen. At least, not in the natural born villages I've seen in this country. If I want a primitive village as a background for my star, why, my scenery expert, Sam Goldberg, can rig one up in a couple of hours, far superior to the original, which was not built in the first place for the screen, but to accommodate the lousy inhabitants. Get me? So drop this idea of your primitive village. All of them in this country are the bunk as screen material. They're too improbable. You couldn't get an American audience to believe that a primitive Irish village is like what it is. No, sir, they want the real thing and the real thing is the genuine Hollywood product, made by the most highly paid expert in the business. Hey, Shultz, how many villages have we shot on this trip?"

"About fifteen," said Shultz.

"Was there a single one of those villages," said Mortimer, "that looked like an Irish village?"

"Not a darned one, chief," said Shultz. "The only Irish village I ever saw previous to this trip was at the Chicago Century of Progress. That looked pretty bum compared to the Swiss and French villages, which were real snappy and had a big drawing power, running into several grand a week. But these punk Irish villages are just too sordid for anything. Why, they wouldn't even look convincing in a news reel dealing with a goddam revolution. Why, the best actor in the business would look a ham against a background like that."

"What did I tell you ?" cried Mortimer, waving his cigar and looking in triumph at Carey.

Carey flushed, sat forward and glared at his employer, with his wild eyes shooting sparks of hatred.

"It's too much, Mortimer," he cried out. "It's far too much. I can't stand it."

"Can't stand what?" said Mortimer in a slow, sinister drawl. "The truth?"

"No," said Carey. "But I'm beginning to realise, what I should have realised in the beginning, that you have no interest in the screen as an art medium."

"As a what?" shouted Mortimer.

"Here you have the power," cried Carey passionately, "to do what you please with a wonderful new invention, to guide it in the direction of becoming a great medium for the expression of human genius and you are dragging it in the dung of your own ignorance."

Mortimer was stung to a frenzy.

"Cut it out," he yelled. "I won't allow you to use language like that in the presence of this lady. You've been looking for trouble since we set out on this trip. I've had enough of your snarky remarks. You think you are a better man than me. Well! I don't agree with you. See? My dough is good enough for you but I'm not. We'll see about that. Let me tell you what you are. You're a goddam Irishman that turned his back on his own country. You're a has-been, a washed out highbrow scribbler that couldn't sell dirt to a tabloid newsrag. Shut up. You asked for it and you're going to get it good an' hot."

He paused for breath and glared like a fighting cock at Carey, who cowered in his corner, gathered like a tiger ready to leap. Shultz, at the wheel, uttered a yell of delight and pressed on the accelerator so that the car went into the seventies. Angela, also delighted, pressed close against Mortimer's body and dug her finger-nails excitedly into the soft flesh of his thigh. She felt certain that the quarrel between the two men was, as usual in such cases, on her own account; and she took sides, of course, with Mortimer, since he was the man with the wallet and the key to fame.

"Art medium!" roared Mortimer, as he squeezed Angela within the loop of his arm. "Art has always appeared to me to be the greatest bunk on earth. I never met anybody who could give me a clear definition of what it means and I never met an artista who wasn't a two-timer. They go round shooting off their mouths about art for art's sake and then grabbing all the dough they can get. I grab the dough, but I give value for it. I create stars. That is the purpose of the screen, to create stars. Listen, Carey."

He leaned across Angela towards Carey and suddenly changed his tone to a gentle purr.

"Aw! What's the use of balling one another out?" he said. "I'm a sport. Let's forget it. Play ball, son and you won't regret it. Only you've got to get the right slant on this racket, or else leave it alone. I'm not a fool. I could go round talking like Gertrude Stein as well as the next."

"But hardly like Shakespeare," said Carey viciously.

"That cap fits you, too," said Mortimer, "even though you may think yourself a big shot. If Shakespeare were alive to-day, he'd probably be the greatest box-office attraction in the motion-picture industry. There was a guy that went after the dough in the modern American style, if there ever was one. Why, I once paid two an' a half dollars for a book that proved he was a moneylender. A slick merchant. He gave the public what it wanted. He was the first historical example of the barefooted emigrant that got to the top by brains, pluck and go-getting. And you take it from me that I'm in his line more'n you are, you an' your highbrow friends. He gave the public *Midsummer Night Dreams* and I give them stars. See this little girl here ?"

He drew Angela forward, threw his cigar out the window

and held up her chin.

"Here was this wild Irish rose," he cried in his most melting tones, "blooming unseen by a wild Irish river, when I come along and see her. What do I do? I take her along to Hollywood, teach her screen technique and offer her to the world as a modern goddess, as a film star. That's what I do. And she becomes a goddess, for the modern film star is a goddess, worshipped by the multitude, as they worshipped Venus of old. She is the ideal of beauty and luxury and magnificence of every man and woman, toiling away on farm and in town, big or little, all over the world. She is the ideal of what every man and woman would like to be, in other words, the star in each one's firmament of life. And I make her. Mine is the hand that plucks that rose from its hiding-place in the valleys and places it among the constellations in the firmament."

He paused, waved his free arm, wiped his forehead and then said, in a different tone, as he affixed his monocle with difficulty:

"A swell spiel that, Shultz."

"You're telling me, boss," said Shultz.

Carey growled and muttered to himself:

"I can't stand it any longer. I quit as soon as I reach Dublin. By God! I will."

Angela, on the other hand, looked up at the perspiring Mortimer with enraptured eyes. It must be admitted that he was by no means a handsome fellow; indeed, to the unprejudiced mind he was positively ugly. Yet Angela thought he was the most wonderful man she had ever seen. He had something, she told herself, that "stirs you right in here." She meant her heart, the region where vulgar, spontaneous passions are supposed to originate; not the shrewd little brain, which governs the passions of the wise person. He had a glamour about him, she felt, that made her "all of a dither." She thought the way he spoke was marvellous and it gave her intense delight to see him annihilate the supercilious Carey. And how gentlemanly he was, never once letting her feel that he had seen her with that awful boy, Tony Silke, manager of the Ballymorguttery Creamery! Now all that was millions of miles away and the generous, magnificent, wonderful Mr. Mortimer was going to make her a goddess. Virgin Mary! How wonderful it all was!

So she dug her finger-nails deeper into the soft flesh of Mr. Mortimer's thigh and, as he bent down to press his cheek against her red-gold hair, she whispered in his ear:

"I think you're wonderful."

"Not half as wonderful as you, kid," he answered her thickly.

The passion in his voice thrilled her from head to foot and he could feel her body trembling beside him and he thought:

"She's on. Better let her have some more."

He straightened himself, cleared his throat and continued to talk in the same strain as before, about the role of the modern film producer. Wise devil that he was, he was "selling himself" to Angela. Not, mark you, "on the make for her," as Shultz would say, but with the deep purpose of binding her to himself by the closest bonds, so that she would be pliable to his design in moulding her. What was she, after all, in spite of her beauty and her immense power to excite passion, more than the crudest of raw material for the manufacture of screen goddesses? It was he, Mortimer, who would give her the necessary temperament, guile, subtlety, carriage, all the godly female star-traits. So he talked and Angela listened, fascinated.

Shultz in the meantime drove the car at such a pace and with such dexterity that they simply devoured the road without killing more than two roosters, which had chosen the centre of a Tipperary road for a fight. They made one halt for a drink and another to shoot some clouds and then they reached the outskirts of Dublin, *en route* for the Shelbourne Hotel. On finding that the Shelbourne was their destination, Angela protested.

"What's the matter, kid?" said Mortimer. "Don't you like the joint?"

"Look at the way I'm dressed," she said, "going to a posh place like that. I'd be ashamed of me life."

"Don't you worry," said Mortimer. "Leave it to pappy. You'll have a swell time."

When they drew up before the hotel and the hall porter threw open the door of their car, Mortimer grabbed Angela and her shabby suitcase and hurried with them through the hall to the registration desk, where he barked at the clerk:

"Get a room for Miss Devlin as close as possible to my suite."

Then he dragged her with him upstairs.

CHAPTER IV

ASHE THREW OPEN THE DOOR of his suite and strode into the sitting-room, Mr. Mortimer uttered an exclamation of astonishment, which was occasioned by the sight of his companion-secretary, Mr. Larry Dafoe.

"Larry," cried Mr. Mortimer, "are you gone mad?"

"Ha! Ha! Ha!" cackled Mr. Dafoe. "I'm not mad, Jack. I'm Queen Victoria."

He was preening himself before a full-length mirror, twisting about like a woman who has just put on a new frock. His costume consisted mainly of bed-sheets, that were wrapped cunningly about his handsome, pampered body, with pillows arranged fore and aft to give the impression of a middle-aged woman of generous proportions. A bath-towel was wrapped around his head. Around his neck hung various ornaments. In his right hand he held a black fan, which he tried in different attitudes as he twisted before the mirror. With his left hand he held up his great train of bed-sheeting. Not at all embarrassed by the position in which he was discovered, he smiled on Mr. Mortimer with his great, wide-open, limpid, blue eyes. Then, waggling the after part of his costume, he came forward, curtsied and said:

"We are pleased to see you back again, Mortimer."

Then he leaned back, dropped his train and his fan, laughed uproariously and shook his body in such a way that all the pillows and the sheets fell to the floor, leaving him in his shirt and trousers, which latter were turned up about his knees.

"So you've broken out again, Larry," said Mortimer. "On the loose again, eh ?"

He looked angry for a moment, but then the humour of the situation got the better of him and he joined in Dafoe's outburst of laughter. He threw himself into a chair and continued to laugh, with his hands clasping his capacious belly, as Dafoe, still laughing, tripped to a little table on which stood a bucket, containing some ice and a bottle of champagne. He filled a glass from the open bottle, bowed to Angela who stood by the door watching the scene in amazement, raised the glass to his lips and said in a solemn tone:

"To a new star that has just risen in the firmament."

Whereupon he smartly tossed the contents of the glass down his throat, sighed deeply and plumped into an armchair that stood behind him. His words had an astonishing effect on Mortimer, who leapt to his feet and whispered in a tone of awe:

"How did you know it, Larry ?"

Dafoe, staring gloomily at Angela in the manner of a seer, shook his head several times and said:

"That is something I can't tell you, Jack. I just feel these things. All morning I felt that something tremendous was going to happen. At last, the emotion got so strong that I simply had to break out. Witness."

He waved a hand towards the champagne and the remains of some caviar on a plate.

"It's marvellous," said Mortimer, with the rapt expression of a devotee on his sallow countenance.

He trotted over to Angela, pointed to Dafoe and said:

"He's a prophet. Now I'm certain. I wanted him to see you first before I could be certain. That ole drunken son of a gun is the greatest prophet since Moses."

With tears in his eyes, he came back to Dafoe and said devotedly:

"God, Larry, I'll never forget this. I don't mind you drinking champagne and eating caviar at Jack's expense. You're worth it, son."

He stooped and kissed Dafoe on both cheeks. Looking over Mortimer's shoulder, Dafoe said to Angela:

"Won't you take a chair and make yourself comfortable while Mr. Mortimer recovers from the effects of his long journey."

"Aw! Hell," said Mortimer, as he straightened himself, flushing. "Can't you ever be serious for more than a second?"

Like a flash, he became violently angry. He pointed to the wine and cried:

"Champagne, eh? Doing yourself well at Jack's expense? Well! Son, you have to snap out of it now. Your drunk is over. Declare to God, I don't know the hell why I put up with you. I suppose you've been drunk all the time I've been away. Smart guy! Pretending to have visions so I wouldn't ball you out."

Dafoe got to his feet lazily and drawled:

"What must your humble servant do?"

"Plenty," yelled Mortimer. "Sit up and listen."

"I'm all ears," said Dafoe.

As he cuts rather an important figure in this story, I had better give some account of him. He was about thirty-three years of age and of unknown origin. He appeared in Hollywood

31

four years previously from Honolulu, as valet to an Englishman, who deserted him owing to financial difficulties. He drifted about the studios for some time, earning a precarious livelihood as an extra. Then he began to practise telling fortunes, through his association with an extra girl, who had been the mistress of an Arab Messiah. He also developed his natural aptitude for private entertainment. In other words, he became the kind of man whom people going on a rout of any sort want to add to the party. In Hollywood, where dullness and lack of imagination are prevalent human characteristics, such a man is sure of constant employment, if he has real charm of personality. "Let's get hold of Dafoe," became a popular cry among the roustabouts. It was in this way that he met Mortimer. As Mortimer was the biggest fish that had ever come within range of his hook, he made a special effort to land the fellow and succeeded brilliantly; with the result that he was added permanently to Mortimer's person at a fixed salary.

"You've just got to make me laugh when I'm in the blues," Mortimer said. "That's all you've got to do. Except now an' again, when I'm planning something big, you might give me a slant on the future. See?"

"Fine," said Dafoe and he lived in the lap of luxury ever since, making Mortimer laugh and peering into the future on request.

Mortimer, however, was no fool. He had arrived at his high position in the motion picture industry, from a poor start as newsboy in New York, by getting the last ounce of value from every human contact that he made. So that, from time to time, he used Dafoe as a reserve contact man, private secretary, travelling valet, general information clerk, expert on etiquette, deportment, clothes, food, drink and the more subtle methods of passing spare time amusingly. In all these respects Dafoe was a most marvellously useful man.

"Have you got all that, Larry?" said Mortimer, when he had finished giving orders.

"All," said Dafoe.

"Okay," said Mortimer. "Now, there's one thing more. Get hold of this guy, Carey, and stall him off. Calm him down. I had to ball him out, but I don't want him to run out on me before we get to Hollywood. I promised Bud to bring him dead or alive, so I have to deliver him, though I'd rather travel with a skunk. Anyhow, I've sunk ten grand already in his goddam story so I have to get something out of him. Butter him up. You know what to do, Larry."

"Thy will be done," said Dafoe.

"Okay," said Mortimer. "Get going. While I'm looking over my mail, Angela, slip into the bathroom and freshen up. You'll find everything there. Show her what to do, Larry: perfume, dressing-gown, pyjamas, you know what I mean, son, just a little dinner, free an' easy style, relaxed, know what I mean? God! I'm all in."

"I get you, chief," said Dafoe. Then, turning to Angela, he added with a smile: "Come, follow me, to prepare thyself for the banquet of thy lord."

CHAPTER V

WHEN DAFOE ENTERED Carey's room, the latter was packing his bags.

"Hello!" Carey said gruffly, as he disliked Dafoe.

"What's the idea ?" said Dafoe, opening wide his eyes in pretended astonishment. "Packing? What for?"

Carey shrugged his shoulders and hurled a shirt into the bottom of a suitcase.

"I see," said Dafoe. "I don't blame you."

He dropped idly into an armchair and took out a gold cigarette-case, which he flicked open.

"Yes," said Carey. "I've had enough of what you facetiously call the art of motion pictures. I'm taking the morning boat to London."

"I see," said Dafoe once more, in a very friendly tone.

Carey bored him, but his peculiar nature made him ambitious to be on friendly terms with everybody. After all, from the point of view of an adventurer, everybody is potentially useful some time or other, except an enemy. And therefore the hostility of even the most humble and apparently least useful person, for the moment, must be overcome as a point of principle. So that, apart from his employer's orders, he was anxious to remove the coldness that existed between him and Carey from the moment they first met in Carey's shabby flat on Finchley Road, Hampstead.

"Lucky you," he said gloomily. "I wish I could do likewise, but alas I'm not a genius. I have to take what I can find, no matter how bitter the pill. May I offer you a cigarette?"

"Thanks," said Carey, as he came to take a cigarette from the gold case.

As Carey bent to take the cigarette, Dafoe moved the case, so that the gems with which it was studded sparkled. Carey noticed the sparkle and his forehead wrinkled.

"Charming workmanship," said Dafoe, as he closed the case. "A present from a Hawaiian princess. I'm very attached to it. In a hurry to start another book, I suppose?"

"Er … not exactly," said Carey, "but I … look here, Dafoe. The point is…I…"

He threw his cigarette to the floor and stamped on it. Then he held out his clenched fists and cried:

"The whole thing is too sordid. That's the plain truth. I couldn't stick it."

"I know the feeling," said Dafoe sympathetically. "At the same time what are you going to do about Tracy? He relies on you, you know. After the way he has fought to get Mortimer to do The Emigrant it would be sort of…Well! I don't want to interfere, but I can't see how he is going to do the picture properly unless you come to Hollywood and help."

"But I…" began Carey, waving his arms and twitching his forehead nervously. "After my experience with Mortimer during the past three weeks…"

"Ha! Ha! Ha! " cackled Dafoe mirthlessly. "You don't know

Mortimer. That's just his way of liquidating his inferiority complex. I mean what irritates you in him. He's a shrewd fellow in spite of that. He'll make no mistakes, provided, of course, he is dealt with properly. For that reason I think you should swallow your disgust and come to Hollywood. You see, he feels that you despise him and... You know what I mean? If you could only...sort of...Oh! Just smile at his silly remarks. It would make him feel so happy. For the sake of the book you should try."

Carey's vanity was flattered. He smiled vaguely and said:

"That, of course, is a different way of looking at it."

"Ridiculous ass!" thought Dafoe, as he cunningly watched Carey pace the room. "For years he has been crawling on his belly, trying to get his wretched books accepted for the screen. Now when he succeeds in selling one, he pretends that it's beneath his dignity."

"Puts one in rather a difficult position," said Carey, after taking a few turns about the room. "I don't want to let Tracy down. At the same time, I can't have *The Emigrant* bowdlerised to make a movie holiday."

"Of course not," said Dafoe. "Don't you see that you must positively be on the spot to prevent that happening? You must fight tooth and nail. Tracy and you could manage Mortimer. Without you, Tracy would find it impossible. Of course it's none of my business, except in so far as I'm interested in seeing a marvellous book like *The Emigrant* being the first work to give the screen its chance to show what it can do as an art medium."

"Dash it, Dafoe," said Carey, cracking his fingers, "I believe you are right. One should swallow one's pride for the sake of one's work. But it's so discouraging. I expected him to choose one of the better actresses for the principal female part and now he seems intent on using a young trollop we picked up in a Cork village."

Dafoe got to his feet and said:

"Let's go and dine, shall we? We can talk over this better at table."

"Good idea," said Carey. "I like you, Dafoe, and I want to get to know you better. You must forgive me for being so cool since I ... "

"Ha! Ha! Ha!" said Dafoe, slapping Carey on the back. "I'm Irish, too. I understand."

"Are you really?" said Carey in astonishment.

"Keep it under your hat, as we say in America," said Dafoe. "I find it useful in Hollywood to remain a man of mystery, but I feel that I can trust you with my secret."

The secret of his origin was one of Dafoe's favourite tricks for establishing confidence. He had a remarkable talent for discovering new birthplaces; always coinciding with the nationality of the person in whom he was confiding.

"Indeed, you may," said Carey. "That explains everything. I felt there was some strong attraction between us, and as usual that made me feel hostile. We Irish dislike deep emotions, although we are extremely generous with the surface ones."

"Let's go," said Dafoe.

They went to dine in the hotel restaurant. When they were seated, Dafoe grabbed the bill of fare and said:

"May I choose for both of us? Food is one of my favourite hobbies. In the meantime, please tell me how you found this girl. I'm very interested, as I really think she is something above the ordinary."

While Dafoe very deliberately chose the dinner, Carey related the story very vividly and bitingly, stressing the more sordid aspects of it.

"She sounds like the real thing this time," said Dafoe, after he had given the order to the waiter.

"How do you mean ?" said Carey rather angrily.

"You're not going to tell me that you, too, believe she has acting talent on the strength of..."

"Acting talent has very little to do with starring for the screen," said Dafoe. "The minor characters supply the talent in the average picture. They act as setting for the star, who must just be physically attractive. The director and his crew are really the important factors. Excepting, of course, the writer, without whom there would be nothing...naturally."

"I see," said Carey. "Then you think..."

"If I were you I wouldn't let the girl worry me," said Dafoe. "Judging by her appearance and the way you discovered her, she seems to have the necessary quality. Mortimer is going to prove that definitely to his satisfaction this evening. In the morning she may go back to Cork, or she may come with us to Hollywood. Who cares? I don't. Why should you?"

"You mean that Mortimer is going to ... "

"Precisely," said Dafoe. "He is going to give her a screen test. I have ordered dinner and made the preliminary arrangements for the test. I have acted Lord Chamberlain, or whatever it is, on many similar occasions; few of which, I must say, looked as promising as this." He sighed. "There are times, Carey, even in the life of the most wise, when a feeling of envy disturbs that harmony which Aristotle admired so much."

Carey could no longer resist Dafoe's seductive cynicism. He leaned back and laughed uproariously, the first time he had laughed in three weeks.

"By God! Dafoe," he said, "you are an astonishing fellow. Damn it, I like you. Do you mind if we shake hands as friends?"

"It's done," thought Dafoe, as he reached for Carey's hand and clasped it.

Carey's face had changed in an unbelievable fashion. It

seemed that he had, as if by a miracle, become a radiant young man once more, fired by enthusiasm for life. His whole body had become vital, electric, to such an extent that even Dafoe was carried away into a feeling of enthusiasm.

"Marvellous," Dafoe said. "Thank God that the flower of your genius has at last consented to open."

Carey leaned forward and said in the excited voice of a little boy:

"Let's get drunk, Dafoe. What's your first name? Larry. Good. You must call me Brian. God! This is great. What shall we drink?"

"Champagne," said Dafoe.

"Hell! No," said Carey, striking the table. "Champagne is for women and foreigners. Let's drink claret. The mind becomes idiotic on champagne. Paper caps, Rotarians, old men with chorus girls. Claret, Larry, is the only drink that feeds the imagination. It wraps itself like a gorgeous silk dressing-gown around the intellect, which leans back and cavorts among the subtle images of poetry. Its honey loosens the tongue. Can we get any here, though? Waiter!"

His yell startled the other diners, mostly composed of foreign trippers and destitute Irish noblemen on the lookout for an American heiress. While the waiter hurried towards him, he cried to Dafoe:

"You may know about food, but I know about drink. It's my hobby. Ha! Ha! You magnificent swine, I like you. I'm going to Hollywood with you. Hey! Waiter, have you got a good Haut Brion, or Chateau Margaux, or Mouton Rothschild? It must be good or I'll make you drink it as the Aztec topers drank. Bordeaux, damn you, not Burgundy. Be quick. We'll get roaring drunk, Larry, not in body, but in mind. We'll get viciously drunk and write bawdy verses on this cloth in wine."

His plump, pale cheeks glowing with satisfaction, his large, limpid eyes rolling like the eyes of a negro, Dafoe cackled mirthlessly as Carey spoke. When the latter had finished and the terrified waiter had gone to fetch the wine, Dafoe drawled:

"I'm very glad you're not going to miss the opportunity of getting a close view of the most insane phenomenon in the whole history of mankind. Hollywood!"

"Insane," whispered Carey, leaning across the table and looking quite like a maniac, his eyes glittering feverishly. "That's the idea. Brilliant! Periodic insanity is as necessary to the artist as water to a flower. But is it really insane? Tell me. Don't lead me astray."

"Ha! Ha! Ha!" cackled Dafoe mirthlessly. "You have already entered by its door. You are as insane as the rest of us."

"Yes. By God! I feel it," cried Carey. "Rejuvenation. I had grown stale, impotent. A man can't live always on a mountain-top. Nietzsche was a liar. He was a gelding. Let's go down into the pit and wallow like pigs. Is it really foul, Dafoe? Is it as foul as I think? Is Mortimer typical, or are there more swine like you there than dogs like Mortimer? I like swine but I hate dogs. Dogs are fawning, vulgar animals. Swine are fierce, unfriendly animals like cats. They are disgusting but they are exciting. No offence, damn you. If we are going to be friends, let us begin by being frank. I too am a swine, so there. Let me tell you."

He pointed at Dafoe and recited:

"To give a kingdom for a mirth; to sit
And keep the turn of tippling with a slave ;
To reel the streets at noon, and stand the buffet
With knaves that smell of sweat: say this becomes him
As his composure must be rare indeed
Whom these things cannot blemish."

Then he dropped his hand, closed his eyes, bowed his head, drew his palms down along his cheeks and sighed deeply. Dafoe, watching him, muttered:

"What an actor!"

Then the waiter brought food and they began to eat, both of them ravenously and in silence. Not until the claret arrived did Carey revert to his exalted state. Then he bared his teeth, sucked in his breath and said, his eyes almost closed:

"Blood an ouns! Do you believe in God, waiter?"

"Beg pardon, sir?" said the waiter with a start.

"Never mind. Take it out of that basket and stand it up."

"Very good, sir."

He stood the bottle on the table and hurried away at Carey's command.

"I hate servants," said Carey, as he poured out the wine. "I love people, though. For the moment we are people, you and I; you not altogether, because you really hate me; just partly, because you are an adventurer. That is what is good in you, being an adventurer. You adventure on earth. I adventure in heaven. Hey! I asked the waiter did he believe in God. Do you believe in God?"

"Anything to please you," said Dafoe, with his mouth full of food. "Which do you prefer? My preference is for Allah."

"Don't talk nonsense," said Carey. "Here, drink with me, top and bottom ; to God, I drink adieu."

They clinked and both drained their glasses.

"Now God is dead," said Carey gloomily.

"My only chance is to get him drunk," thought Dafoe.

CHAPTER VI

ANGELA PASSED HER TEST with flying colours. While in her bath, she did a great deal of shrewd thinking. To suppose that she remained overwhelmed for long by the sudden change in her position would be to form a very false estimate of her character. What little embarrassment she felt, or pretended to feel, on approaching the hotel, disappeared on contact with the luxury of Mr. Mortimer's suite.

"Here I am," she said to herself, "and here I stay, if I break my neck in the attempt. But I have to watch my step."

The paramount characteristic of great cunning is a childish simplicity and that was the mask that Angela decided to wear. Once before, she had had an opportunity of bettering her position, when she attracted the attention of Patrick Aloysius Finnerty, choice wine importer, of Cork. In her eagerness to compromise his affections to the extent of marrying her, she had behaved with reckless abandon and warned off the worthy fellow, who took her for a loose creature.

"Larry," said Mortimer to Dafoe on the following morning, "she has got everything. I don't have to teach her a goddam thing except a proper accent."

"Figure?" said Dafoe.

"The best I've seen."

"Brains?"

"The right sort. Not too much. Not too little."

"An actress?"

"Of the first water. A born mummer. You shoulda seen her do her aunt. I put her through the ropes all right."

"Sounds swell," said Dafoe.

"Fix Carey?" said Mortimer.

"He's drunk in bed," said Dafoe. "He was easy. It's a waste of time, though, taking him to Hollywood, and in fact, it might be a dangerous business. With a fellow like that, you never know what may happen. I advise you to drop him."

"Nerts," said Mortimer. "I'm taking him to Hollywood dead or alive. He fits into my plan. Listen, mug, I think I've got the biggest publicity stunt of the century."

"Spill it," said Dafoe.

"It's this," said Mortimer. "I'm going to take Angela along as a mystery woman, veiled, know what I mean, secret. Last night I thought of it, seein' she was a bit raw, know what I mean, couldn't spring her right now, and then…I thought…Hell! Mystery woman. Might catch on. Never know…"

He paused and looked at Dafoe searchingly.

"Get me?" he said.

Dafoe opened wide his eyes and nodded.

"Everything has got to be done quietly," whispered Mortimer. "Get her passport, clothes, berths on the boat, keep her hidden on the trip across, rush her from the boat to the train, across country to Hollywood and then out to the ranch. Get the idea?"

"It might work," said Dafoe, as he cackled mirthlessly.

"What are you laughing at?" said Mortimer.

"Rumours," said Dafoe. "What about Shultz and Carey? They're in the know."

"How d'you mean?"

"If we give her a romantic background," said Dafoe, "they might, either one of them, spill the beans out of spite."

"Nope," said Mortimer. "Don't worry. We'll get there first. First come first believed. The public believes what it wants to believe. Get busy, fellah."

CHAPTER VII

FOUR DAYS LATER the party sailed from Southampton. Dafoe had done his work very well, so that there was quite a little excitement attached to their departure, with the newspapers trying to discover the identity of the veiled lady whom Mortimer of *Little Virgin* fame was exporting from Europe in the utmost secrecy. Even Carey, whom no reporter in London had thought worth a paragraph for years, became a man of importance and was besieged for information. In reply, Carey, who had remained raving drunk during the four days, used all the expressions for which barrack rooms are famous.

"Don't annoy him," Dafoe whispered to the reporters. "It's the one malady for which there is no cure."

"What is it?" said the reporters.

Dafoe put his hands on his heart and looked upwards as he whispered:

"Love."

Then he cackled mirthlessly and tore himself from the importunate fellows. They, of course, had to print something, so they gave rein to their imaginations, with very amusing results, all of which gratified Mr. Mortimer. To my mind, the most amusing of the lot was a cable to a New York tabloid from its London correspondent, running as follows:

"HOLLYWOOD MAGNATE TURNS TURK"

"Gentleman Jack Mortimer, monocled movie executive, left Southampton to-day on board the *Aquitania*, accompanied by members of his staff and a veiled lady, whose identity was kept a close secret. The celluloid tycoon reversed his usual practice and pulled the Garbo act when trailed by newshawks. Also in Pasha Mortimer's entourage was gloomy Brian Carey, Irish highbrow writer of international repute, whom rumour links with veiled colleen. Fatty Dafoe, the monocled tycoon's henchman, hinted that love-sick Carey was the bait that enticed the veiled lady to take the Hollywood trail from her Hibernian castle."

Neither Carey nor Angela, of course, knew anything of these reports. Carey was too drunk and miserable to take any notice. Angela did not get the opportunity to learn anything, owing to the close guard under which she was kept. She was, however, in such a state of ecstatic happiness that she asked no questions and made no protests about the manner in which she was treated, accepting everything that was done for her and obeying every request, with the manner of a queen performing some public function.

Already, even before she sailed, she had changed out of all recognition. Mortimer, Dafoe and Shultz crowded about her, like working bees that have elected a new queen. And when they dressed her in a veil and in a sombre, virginal costume and shielded her from all human contacts, she felt like a girl being convoyed by relatives to a convent, which she was to enter as a nun. Her nature was so plastic that she adapted herself, body and soul, to her "part"; in other words, she was the perfect actress. This admirable quality annoyed Mr. Mortimer a great deal on the first night after leaving port, when he hurried to her room at a discreet hour, from a quiet game of bridge in the lounge.

After glancing along the corridor furtively, he tried to open her door and found it locked. A trifle angry. he knocked smartly. He heard her voice, crying out in a startled fashion:

"Who is that?"

"It's me. Jack. Open quick."

"But I'm in bed."

"Aw! Come on. Hurry."

"Anything wrong?"

"For the love o' Mike, will you open this door?"

He heard her move and then cross the floor. Casting another furtive look along the corridor as the door opened, he dived into the room, to see her rush back into bed, clasping her dressing-gown about her.

"Thought you'd never open up," he panted, as he put his back to the door after closing it. "Ships are worse'n hotels. You never know who's goin' to crawl around a corner. What's the matter, kid?"

Angela, with the bed-clothes drawn up about her chin, was staring at him in a startled fashion. She did not speak. Mortimer strode over to her bed and sat down on the side of it.

"What are you lookin' at me like that for?" he said sourly. "Got a pain? Are you sea-sick?"

She put both her forefingers between her little teeth and shook her head violently. Mortimer burst out laughing.

"Well! I declare," he said. "You're up to the damnedest tricks. You little marvel."

He leaned forward and pinched her cheek. Angela drew

back, hid herself completely under the clothes for a moment and then thrust out her head, now looking absolutely terrified.

"Aw! Cut it out," said Mortimer. "That's enough. Let's be natural."

"But I am," said Angela in a trembling voice. "You scare me."

"Why? What the hell is the matter with me?" said Mortimer. "I just had one high-ball."

"No, but..." Suddenly she burst into tears, covered her face with her hands and added: "I don't understand."

"Now what the...?" said Mortimer. "What's come over you?"

"You want me to be one thing one minute and something else the next," she sobbed.

"You mean...?"

"Yes. How could I be what you want me to be if you come in like this and...?"

"Aw, I don't let that worry you," he said, putting his arms around her magnificent body, that thrilled him from head to foot. "Day time is the time for work. Night time is play time, know what I mean, when you can be natural. Can't you see I'm nuts about you, kid? Honest. I've fallen for you in a big way. Aw! Listen, baby, I'll soon dry those tears. You leave it to pappy."

He jumped up and began to undress in a great hurry.

"Mr. Mortimer, what are you doing?" cried Angela in alarm.

He paused in the act of undoing his collar and stared at her.

"What's bitin' you?" he said angrily. "Didn't I tell you to quit? For goodness' sake, we're not shootin' a scene. This is genuine."

"No, no, no," she cried in alarm, as she got out of bed. "You must leave me alone."

"The hell I will," said Mortimer furiously, as he slipped his braces off his shoulders. "You can't pull that stuff on me."

Thereupon Angela screamed and ran for the door. Mortimer dived after her, caught her in his arms, put a hand over her mouth to prevent her screaming again and then hauled her back to the bed, where he threw her down with some violence. In the meantime his trousers had fallen about his heels and he presented a most ludicrous spectacle. He was also very short of wind and the effort had made him pant and he became so confused that he quite lost control of himself. He stood for several moments looking down at her, clenching his fists and trying to say something abusive, until Angela sat up with an expression on her face that showed she had finally stopped acting. She looked the same shrew that had barged Carey in the wood. She did not speak, however, for she became aware of his ludicrous appearance before she had time to open her mouth. At once she pointed a finger and then leaned back, giving voice to a riotous peal of laughter. Mortimer looked down at his shanks and blushed to the roots of his hair. He stooped and pulled up his trousers.

"You'll be sorry for this," he blurted out and turned to the door.

As invariably happens, her laughter had turned his passion into a vicious desire to hurt her.

"Jack, where are you going?" said Angela.

"None o' your business," said Mortimer, opening the door.

"But you can't go out like that," she called. "Your clothes..."

He had got as far as the corridor in his fury, but dived back again into the room and closed the door behind him.

"My God!" he muttered. "Am I gone mad? Goin' out like this. Wonder did anybody... ? Say, listen Angela, what d'you mean by it?"

"Oh! I'm so sorry," she said, coming up to him and putting her arms caressingly around his neck. "I didn't mean it."

"Mean what ?" he said, taking away her arms roughly. "Let me get my clothes on. You make me behave like a goddam fool. I've had enough. Get me ? You can't fool around with me. I'm no sucker."

"No?" said Angela in a menacing tone.

"No," cried Mortimer furiously, as he grabbed his collar from a chair and shook his fist at her.

Her expression, however, gave him a rude shock. She looked like a wild cat. Her red-gold hair seemed to stand on end and her eyes blazed. A magnificent sight, but one that struck terror into Mortimer at that moment. God's blood! It is enough to strike terror into braver hearts than Mortimer's, the sight of a red-headed Irish woman in a temper and that temper directed against a helpless man, who is dressed only in his shirt and trousers.

"You try to behave like that to me," she hissed, "and I'll tear your heart out. You dirty, old, bald..."

For three minutes he bore it, trembling from head to foot, his lips shaping inarticulate words and then he slid to his knees and held up his clasped hands begging for mercy. Then she spat on him and subsided. With her bosom heaving and her arms folded across her breasts, which had become bare in the tussle, owing to her nightdress being torn, she sat on the bed and glared at him. Mortimer rose to his feet slowly.

"Aw! Honey," he whined, "will you forget it? Will you, honey ? I'm on the level. I swear to God I am. I'm just nuts about you. Can you blame me for trying to pull a ... "

"Shut up," she said. "You promised me a career as an actress and I'm going to hold you to it. Get that into your pipe and smoke it. You've got to treat me with respect. Otherwise... Well! You wait and see. Get your clothes on and get out of here, before I lose my temper again."

Meekly, without another word, Mortimer got dressed and stole out of her cabin. Then he hurried to his own quarters, where he really lost his temper, stamped about the place, cursed, tore his hair and vowed vengeance, until he was finally taken with a nervous attack as a result of his choler. He sent for Dafoe, who came and massaged him and administered various medicines. It took nearly two hours to calm him down. Then he fell asleep. He awoke in the morning burning with rage and determined to have his revenge; but after some thought, he decided that he could not afford revenge.

"Listen, pappy," he said to himself, "don't be a fool. You've got a swell property in this young dame, so why go an' spoil it for a little thing like that? Naw! You're crazy, lad. If you feel sore, why not work it out on Carey?"

He jumped to his feet and cried aloud:

"Yeah. Carey. That's the guy. Hangin' around, just swillin' booze at my expense. Here's where that guy starts to work. Betcha life he does."

Barefooted, with his portly stomach straining the buttons of his striped silk pyjama jacket, he rushed into Dafoe's cabin, which lay on the far side of his drawing-room. He hauled the sleeping Dafoe out of bed and cried:

"Hey! Wake up. What's the game? Goin' to sleep all day. Go get Carey. Here's where we start to work. Get hold of that guy and bring him here. Tell Angela I want her here, too. Get my breakfast. Where's Shultz? Wake up, damn it. Everybody's got to get to work."

At times, the insolent Dafoe got really afraid of his employer and this was one of them. Meekly, he got into his clothes and went to rouse Carey. To his astonishment he found Carey's room empty. The bed was still made up. He looked at his watch. It was nine o'clock. The first thought that came into his head was that Carey had committed suicide. He remembered parting with the man at midnight in the lounge, leaving him in the company of a rather plain lady from Buffalo, who was returning home for a holiday from Soviet Russia, where her husband was an engineer.

"Can't remember her name," said Dafoe aloud. "Lounge steward might know."

At that moment Carey entered the room. Except that he shook visibly and that his eyes were hollow and somewhat bloodshot, it would be difficult to imagine from his appearance that he had been drinking for four days.

"Many happy returns," said Dafoe. "How do you feel?"

"I have a marvellous idea for a short story," said Carey. "You were quite right, Larry. I'm glad I came. I'm bursting with ideas."

"Splendid," said Dafoe. "They couldn't have arrived at a more opportune moment. The boss wants you."

"What about?" said Carey.

"*The Emigrant,*" said Dafoe.

"Oh!" said Carey, "I had forgotten all about it."

"It happens to be the reason for your presence on this ship," said Dafoe.

"Fine," said Carey. "One must make sacrifices. What do the French say? *Tout s'arrange. Tout se paye.* I feel that I'm going to get out of myself. Europe is dead. Europe is a fathead. A sick head, like mine. Fresh air. I must have a wash. How is Mortimer?"

"Better come and see for yourself," said Dafoe with a cackle.

"Amusing fellow," said Carey, as he washed his face in the basin. "I must get to know him better. The mind is confused and everything appears in a false light and then suddenly..."

"One wakes up," cackled Dafoe.

"What do you mean ?" said Carey, drying his face.

When Carey had finished his toilet, they went to Mortimer, who was having breakfast in his drawing room. He received them very coldly.

"Sit down, Carey," he commanded. "Get Angela yet, Larry?"

"Just going to," said Dafoe.

"Well! Be quick about it. Hustle. Jump to it."

Dafoe obediently fled from the room. Carey sat down and watched his employer nervously. This was a new Mortimer that confronted him. The amiable buffoon was gone. So was the hail-fellow-well-met, the glad-hander, the ignoramus, the bumptious self-made man and all the other masks under which Gentleman Jack hid his ruthless cunning and his capacity for governing men. It seemed as if the Great Mogul, returning to the scat of his despotic power, had resumed the cruel dignity which he had flippantly discarded during his tour abroad. Returning to his lair, the jungle cat had begun to show his claws. Carey was astonished and not a little terrified. He was also ashamed of himself for having made the mistake of despising this fellow as an inferior.

"Now, Carey," said Mortimer, after they had sat in silence for some time, "about this story of yours. Let me see, what's the name? Something about a barefooted emigrant, ain't it? "

Burning with shame, Carey whispered in a voice that surprised him by its meekness:

"*The Emigrant* it's called, I think."

"How do you mean, you think?" Mortimer flashed back viciously, as he pushed away his devoured grapefruit and raised his napkin to his mouth.

Carey's eyes flickered venomously, but he made no retort. His eyes met Mortimer's for a moment and then they dropped defeated. For the first time he hated this little fat man, whom he had hitherto despised. He hated himself, too, and became conscious of being unclean and he saw the bed in which he had spent the night and the words of love he had whispered into the ignorant ears of a stranger and away beyond that vision stood the glorious panorama of the past, a winged poet singing on the mountain-top, and dewy sunlit dawn upon the earth. Now the poet lowered his eyes in shame before two little eyes, dark as sloes and sneering with the vicious triumph of a female that has humiliated a male, stuck in a coarse, ugly face. He saw the fat, pampered, diamond-ringed hands, the luxurious dressing-gown, the little feet, in gaudy slippers, peeping from beneath the little table. And he felt himself coiled in the grasp of a serpent that he had thought a croaking frog.

"What do you mean by, I think?" repeated Mortimer, in a still more sinister tone. "Can't you remember the name o' your own story? Or are you too drunk?"

Still Carey did not retort. His bluff had been called. He smiled weakly and said:

"I dare say I have been drinking too much."

"You said it, kid," muttered Mortimer. "However, I'll overlook it. Only it must stop. Get me?"

"Very well," said Carey, almost inaudibly.

Mortimer belched and began to break an egg into a glass.

"Well! Now," he said, "about this story of yours. Have you got it all worked out in your mind, I mean a screen treatment of it?"

"I...I thought I..."began Carey.

"Never mind," said Mortimer. "You haven't done a goddam thing about it and maybe that's all to the good. Well! This is a lousy ship. This egg is...Never mind. Well! Better leave Ireland out of it altogether."

"What?" said Carey, sitting forward tensely. "But half the book is placed in Ireland, the whole background, without which ..."

"Never mind," snapped Mortimer. "I'm talking, not you. This picture, if I do it, is going to cost four hundred grand at least and it's going to be a Mortimer production, see, so I can't monkey around with a setup like Ireland. Ireland isn't front page since the skids were put under Tammany Hall. Christ sake, haven't you heard yet that prohibition is repealed, or that there are Jews nowadays on the New York police force? You're behind the times, son. Get this slant. Ireland has got no box-office appeal outside of a few highbrows. Unless we tear up the book and write another about sweepstakes. Can't do that, seein' as how I've sunk ten grand already in the goddam thing."

"Allow me to tell you," began Carey, re-capturing for a moment his insolent tone.

"Cut that out," snapped Mortimer. "I want no more o' that Limey drawl. You're a Mick ain't you ? You're Irish, huh?"

"Yes. I'm Irish."

"Well! Then, why can't you talk like one? Wrap a chunk o' the brogue around your tongue an' I'll think you're a good guy like myself. Whoever heard a harp talk like a Limey?"

Carey was now fuming, but for some reason which he could not explain he was unable to lose his temper on the sneering little man with sloe-black eyes. The serpent's coils were wrapped so close about him that he was robbed of his strength.

"This story," said Mortimer, becoming calm and remote once more, has got to begin on board ship. Emigrant ship, see? Tell you why."

Suddenly, he seemed to change his mind about telling why he wanted the story to begin on the ship, for he proceeded to devour his egg with a rapacious appetite and then Angela entered the room, followed by Dafoe. He looked up and gaped for a moment, dazzled by Angela's beauty. Carey jumped to his feet. Mortimer recovered his self-possession almost at once, scowled and dug his spoon into the egg-cup.

"Good morning," he said. "Sit down everybody. Not you, Larry. Go tell Shultz take some shots of the steerage quarters. I've got an idea. Human interest types. Tell him to lay off the booze, too, or I'll fire him soon as I get home."

Dafoe obediently left the room. Angela took a chair near Carey, who watched her furtively. It was the first time that he had seen her since their arrival at the Shelbourne Hotel. He was astonished at the change in her. She wore a plain, grey, tight-fitting suit, with a white frilled blouse and pretty suede shoes to match her suit. Her head was bare, so that her red-gold hair shone like a fire above this rather austere costume. Her expression especially had changed. Her lovely face wore a gentle smile that was definitely that of a lady by birth.

"Astounding," thought Carey. "First Mortimer and now this ..."

And then, as he stared at Angela, he thought of a plan for taking revenge on Mortimer. The plan excited him so much that he could barely restrain himself from laughing aloud. He was on the verge of hysteria as the result of his bout of drinking.

Angela did not give him a glance. Her eyes were fixed on Mortimer, who did not speak until he had finished his egg. Then he took his cup of coffee in his hand, leaned back and said:

"Get this, you two. Right or wrong, Miss Devlin, I want you to star in this picture, for the moment called *The Emigrant*."

He looked towards Carey insolently and the latter muttered under his breath:

"We'll see."

"Right here and now," continued Mortimer, "you've got to

begin to live the part. What's the girl called, Carey? Rose something or other."

"Rose O'Carroll," said Carey, smiling at Mortimer with equal insolence.

"Okay," said Mortimer. "Now, Carey, you've got to forget the Rose in your book and think of Angela. I mean for that part. Here's the lay-out, as I imagine it's going to be. Rose O'Carroll is travelling steerage to New York as an emigrant. She pals up with a handsome guy, who is also travelling steerage, an Englishman, see, down on his luck, but a member of the old aristocracy..."

"But..." began Carey.

"I know what you're goin' to say," interrupted Mortimer, "but forget it. There's no Englishman in your script, but you've got to put one in, see, because I've got Jerome Broadbent under contract and he's English and he's just the right type to play opposite to Angela. At the present time, male English stars have the biggest box-office appeal in America. Don't know why the hell it is, but the dames like' em. All on account o' the Prince o' Wales, I reckon, bein' such a good guy. Do you know Broadbent's style?"

Carey detested and despised actors. He scowled and said:

"Yes. I think I've seen him on the screen somewhere, as far as I can remember."

"I think he's marvellous," said Angela, rolling her eyes in the peculiar way that girls pay homage to their celluloid gods.

"He's a good actor," said Mortimer. "He knows his job and he's just the right type for the character."

"But what character?" cried Carey, unable to contain himself any longer.

"The character of the landlord's son," yelled Mortimer. "The son of the landlord that evicted this orphan here from her cabin. See? It all comes out in the conversation they have when they meet on the ship. He's the black sheep of the family, though he didn't deserve it, seein' how he only took the blame for a pal. It might be a dud cheque, or savin' the name of the colonel's daughter. Anyhow he has to resign his commission, his ole man cuts him off with a shilling, way they do it in England, or Ireland, or wherever it is. Then he has to leave the country and take passage to America, in the same steerage as Angela. Don't you see it, son? Boy, it's colossal."

Suddenly carried away by a burst of sentiment, he jumped to his feet and with tears in his eyes, he stretched out his hands and said:

"Listen, you kids, with an idea like that you can knock 'em cold. Good lookin' guy, beautiful girl, tragedy on both sides, both flyin' from it to the land of Liberty, that opens wide her arms to the downtrodden of the world, two people from opposite ends of the social scale, hereditary enemies, meet on the same social level on board the ship, see? Carey, it's goin' to make *Little Virgin* look like a flop. Get busy, you two. Get together. It's my way of doin' things. The script writer has got to be nuts about the star before he can write anything suitable for her. The star has got to be nuts about the guy that plays opposite to her. And Jack, good ole pappy, is nuts about you all."

Seizing them both, he drew them together and endeavoured to enclose them in his plump embrace. His arms and his stature were both too short, however, for the purpose. He could only hug them about the waist. But such was the effect of his enthusiasm, his sentimental tears and the frenzy of his foolish imagination, that they were unable to resist, or to offer any objection. In that way, he pushed them out of his drawing-room, telling them not to waste time while the "colossal idea" was still fresh in their minds. Then he closed the door behind them and struck his forehead and said aloud:

"The only thing necessary to do anything in this racket is to make the decision to do it, believe in it, make others believe in it and go through with it, right to the end. Okay, pappy. You've got a wow on your hands, son. Yes, baby, you've got the most colossal and sensational success on your hands since Bell invented the telephone."

Then he sat down in an armchair, clasped his hands on his stomach, frowned and muttered:

"However! I ain't goin' to let her pull that stuff on me. No, sir. She ain't goin' to give ME the run around. Not if I know anything about it. We'll see about that."

Then he jumped to his feet and cried:

"Hey! Larry, how about a little game of chess? Now where is that heel? Hey! Larry."

CHAPTER VIII

"LET'S GO UP ON DECK, shall we?" said Carey, when he and got outside. "I need some fresh air badly."

"Wait until I get my hat and veil," said Angela.

"What do you mean?" said Carey.

Carey had taken two paces forward, swaying uncertainly with the motion of the ship. He was beginning to feel ill as the result of his drinking. Now he turned to Angela, looking very pale at the gills.

"What veil?" he said.

"They told me I mustn't go on deck without it," said Angela.

"Why? Is there something the matter with your face?"

"No, but...he told me..."

"Who did?"

"Mr. Mortimer."

"But what's the idea?"

"I don't know."

"All right. Come to my cabin. I feel too ill in any case to climb up on deck. Come along."

She followed him along the passage.

"Veil," he kept muttering. "What a silly idea!"

When they had reached his cabin and sat down, he said to her:

"Why do you hate me?"

"But I don't hate you," said Angela. "What put that idea into your head?"

"Perhaps you don't hate this me, but you hate the other one. And the other one is the real me. I am going to cheat Mortimer. He has bought the other me, but he can't buy this one."

Angela looked at him in astonishment. He certainly was different from the man she had met in the wood that day. She herself also was different, but she had changed in the opposite direction. She had become refined and restrained, while Carey had become coarse and violent. Yet he was more attractive like this.

"But I don't understand you," she said. "You were very rude to me the first time we met and I gave you a bit of my mind for it, but that's not hating you, is it?"

"And I was rude to you because you were insincere," said Carey, staring at her wildly.

Angela flushed. She had quite forgotten about the incident in the wood. I mean the indelicate part of the incident. She got angry with him for reminding her of it once more.

"How do you mean?" she parried.

"You were doing something that you wanted to do and you were ashamed of it," he said. "That's insincerity or hypocrisy or whatever you like to call it. And then you sold yourself to Mortimer. It wasn't your beauty he bought, but your capacity for insincerity."

Her bosom began to heave with her anger. She looked

radiantly beautiful in her anger. Carey's eyes, as he looked at her, became exalted and almost as beautiful as her own, in spite of their debauched, ugly setting in his face.

"I was ashamed of myself, too," he continued, "but I didn't hide my shame under a mask of insincerity. Listen. We were both given something beautiful. I was given a mind and you were given a body and we were both given something else too, something that we call a soul, the abstract of what is beautiful in each of us. And this dog, who has neither the one nor the other, has succeeded in buying us. I am ashamed and you are not. That is why I was rude to you. I'll hate you if you let yourself be bought. Don't do it."

He stared at her so intently that she felt his eyes boring holes through her. He looked quite mad and what he said appeared to her equally mad and unintelligible; but she was deeply impressed by his face. He was leaning toward her, so close that she could feel his breath, which smelt of alcohol. She could see the stubble on his fair, unshaven jaws stand out like bristles. His face was so ugly, she thought. His lips were cracked and rimed with the lees of the liquor he had drunk. His checks were dappled with unpleasant veins and blots of a sickly colour. Innumerable wrinkles pointed to his eyes like accusing arrows. Yet the exaltation of his eyes counteracted this ugliness and fascinated her.

Carey, with the intuition of the man bordering on hysteria, understood what was going on in her mind and said:

"See what insincerity has done to my face and to my soul? I was once as beautiful as you are now. But I was led astray by the same thing that is now leading you astray. Greed and vanity. More vanity than greed. Just vanity. So take warning. But one doesn't take warning. There is only one way to be saved from the pit. Do you know what it is?"

Angela began to tremble and she looked furtively towards the door of the cabin, as if seeking a means of escape. Carey smiled wanly.

"It's love," he said. "Let's fall in love with one another."

Then Angela shuddered and came to her senses. She drew back and said to him arrogantly:

"You have a neck. Fall in love with you is it?"

She threw back her head and laughed in her throat.

Carey was enraged by her laughter.

"So you laugh at me," he whispered.

Angela got to her feet.

"Go and look in the mirror," she said.

Suddenly jumping to his feet, he grasped her in his arms and kissed her on the lips. For a few moments he remained rigid, resisting, and then she closed her eyes and went limp in his arms, until he suddenly thrust her from him and stared at her, holding her by the shoulders, panting. She opened her eyes and looked at him, startled. Neither spoke. Then Carey began to tremble. The fire died out of his eyes. Now his face was very ugly and Angela, in disgust, pushed him from her and wiped her lips with the back of her hand.

"You beast," she said.

"I know," Carey said. " I am a beast. I'm sorry."

He went over to his bed and sat down on it with his head in his hands. She stared at him angrily, not knowing what to do. She wanted to say something insulting to him, but somehow she could only feel pity for him. He looked so helpless and defeated.

"What's the matter?" she said at length.

He looked up at her pathetically. His eyes were now dim and bloodshot.

"Forgive me for what I said just now," he said, "except

63

when I said that love is the only thing that can save you. I'm ill. I'm a sick man in every sense of the word. Yes. God gave me great talents. I abused them. I sold them for a mess of pottage. He gave me a soul and I lost it. And now I am paying the price. You are right. I should look in the mirror. In the mirror of my own conscience."

Her pity for him increased at these words and she came over to the bed near him.

"You've been drinking too much," she said softly.

"So will you later," he muttered, "unless you draw back while there is time."

"Poor boy," she whispered.

She touched him gently on the forehead with her hand and then drew her fingers gently back over his hair. Carey reached for her free hand and kissed it reverently.

"Blessed art thou among women," he murmured with great feeling. "I have heard your voice before. It's the murmur of a mountain river. The heron flaps his wings and rises from the marsh and in the dawnlight I see his white feathers break beneath like snowflakes tossed."

"You must lie down and be quiet," she whispered gently. "And don't think I hate you, because I don't."

"Your voice is like silk drawn over young grass," he whispered. "He called you Angela. I hate him for that, because I wish it was I did it. The..."

He suddenly became very ill. Very efficiently she put him lying face downwards on the bed and went to work on his back, giving him a massage.

"It's the gas lying on your heart," she said.

"Forgive me," he said, when he got momentary relief.

"Don't worry about me," she said, "I'm used to seeing men like this. All the same you should stop drinking."

"I would if *it* mattered to somebody I loved," he said.

"That's nonsense," said Angela. "It should matter to yourself."

Again he was seized by another attack and this time she could not hold him down. He got to his feet and said:

"My God! I'm going to die this time."

Angela got nervous and said:

"Do you want a doctor?"

"No. I hate doctors. I don't want a doctor. I want love, not a doctor. Please love me."

"Stop your nonsense," she said gruffly, but kindly.

"Take off your clothes and get into bed. Come on now. You're like a child. You should be ashamed of yourself."

"But I am ashamed of myself," he cried.

Without more ado, she took him in hand and had him in bed in a jiffy. There she tucked him under the clothes and said:

"Honestly, you men are all alike."

Carey kept kissing her hands and whispered:

"This is wonderful. When you are near me like this, I no longer feel afraid."

"And what would you be afraid of?" said Angela.

"Mr. Mortimer, is it?"

"Yes," said Carey. "I'm afraid of him. I got afraid of him this morning. We are both in his clutches."

He said this so seriously, that Angela sat down on the side of the bed and looked at him with wrinkled forehead.

"Ye're not coddin' me," she said. "Is he really a bad man?"

"It's not that," said Carey. "I couldn't explain to you. But please don't desert me, Angela. And forgive me for being rude to you that day. I honestly love you and I'll give you everything that is mine and that I abuse, if you love me in return. Don't let Mortimer corrupt you. Promise me that."

"Don't you worry about that," said Angela.

"Nobody is goin' to corrupt me. I know what I'm after. Go to sleep now. Do you think you could sleep?"

"I could if you sang to me," said Carey.

"Honestly," said Angela, with a little laugh in her throat, "aren't you the baby? Now, who'd believe it? And I thinkin' you were a...Never mind. I'll sing for you if you like."

Then she put her head beside his on the pillow and sang to him a crooning Irish lullaby. As she sang, Carey, with his eyes closed, whispered to her:

"With your love and mine, you and I could conquer the world. We could scale the walls of Heaven together, you and I. Love me. Love me. Love me."

He kept repeating these two words as he fell asleep and she, singing softly, was carried away by them into a state of ecstasy, which seemed to her the culmination of all the strange things that had happened to her during the past week, since Mortimer came upon her in the wood. So that, when she ceased singing, she bent over him and framed his face between her hands and kissed him on the forehead. And then suddenly she heard a mirthless cackle in the room. She jumped to her feet and whirled round. She saw Dafoe, his arms folded on his chest, leaning against the wall by the open door.

"Very charming," he said, as he rolled his limpid eyes, like a negro.

Angela cursed under her breath and rushed at him.

CHAPTER IX

MORTIMER HAD JUST FINISHED shaving and he was choosing a tie, when Dafoe came into his room. "Jack," said Dafoe, "give me a drink. She near did, for me."

Mortimer whirled around and stared at Dafoe.

"Well! I'll be burned alive!" he cried. "What's happened? Huh? What you been up to, Larry? "

"She went for me," gasped Dafoe, as he staggered to a chair and dropped into it. "God! What a woman!"
His face was running blood. It had been scratched all over, just as if a wild-cat had got its claws into it.

Mortimer ran and fetched him some whiskey, which Dafoe swallowed at once. Then he finally answered his employer's insistent questions.

"It was Angela," he said.

"What for?" said Mortimer.

"I looked into Carey's cabin," said Dafoe, "and there she was sitting on his bed, her hands around his neck, kissing him on the forehead. I couldn't help laughing. I thought it was such a new way to work on a script and..."

67

"What?" yelled Mortimer. "In bed?"

"He was in bed," said Dafoe.

"In bed," yelled Mortimer. "That lousy son of a Dublin dishwasher got into bed when I told him. She was in bed with him? Huh?"

"No. She wasn't in bed."

"Well! Where was she? Huh?"

"She was sitting on the side of the bed."

"Didn't you say they were necking? Didn't you?"

"Yes."

Mortimer clutched his hair and gave voice to a string of violent oaths. Then he ran to a drawer and pulled forth a revolver. He was rushing from the room with this weapon when Dafoe called after him:

"Where are you going, Jack?"

"I'm going to show that bastard," hissed Mortimer.

"Hold on," said Dafoe. "You don't know the worst yet."

Mortimer halted at the door, looking at the revolver and then hastily went to the drawer and stowed it away.

"Why should I burn for that loser?" he said.

"Answer me that. I know where to hit him. I'll hit him where he feels it most. In the pocket. Yah. These goddam high-hatting bums, that's where they feel it. He's fired."

"Won't you listen to me?" said Dafoe wearily, daubing at his face with a wet towel.

"You shut up," said Mortimer. "What happened to your face? "

"I'm trying to tell you," said Dafoe. "Angela clawed me."

"Where is she now?" shouted Mortimer.

"She went to her cabin," said Dafoe. "Ooh! My God!"

"I'll show her she can't take me for a ride," said Mortimer.

Again he made for the door and again Dafoe halted him

with these words:

"If you take my advice, you'll listen to what I have to say first."

Alarmed by Dafoe's sinister tone, Mortimer came back to Dafoe.

"She said a mouthful while she scratched me," continued Dafoe, "and what she said is going to get you into the ash-can, if she goes through with it."

"Uh?" said Mortimer, and he stared at Dafoe with an open mouth.

"For God sake, Larry," he continued, "what is it?"

"She threatened to sue you for seduction as soon as we get to New York," said Dafoe.

The effect of this statement on Mortimer was extraordinary. His sallow cheeks began to shake as if they were made of jelly. He held out two fat, trembling hands towards Dafoe and blubbered:

"She's goin' to sue me...seduction...goin' to go to court... Say, you can't try to pull...say, listen. Jees! D'you know what you're sayin', fellah? My wife...Oh! Holy God!"

"Now, don't lose your head, Jack," said Dafoe calmly, as he rubbed some lotion on his wounds. "I think you can fix it. This kid has got you in a spot and she knows it. Of course, it doesn't hit me, but I stand by you, no matter what happens. If you go up the river..."

"The river!" gurgled Mortimer. "D'you mean?..."

"All I say," said Dafoe. "That guy, Carey, must have put her up to it. I told you he was dangerous."

"Where's the goil? "said Mortimer in a timid voice. In moments of sincerity, Mortimer, the former newsboy of Manhattan, reverted to the adenoidal murmur of the Bowery slums.

"I said that I imagined she was in her cabin," said Dafoe.

"When she had done with me, she was going in that direction."

"Go, bring her here," said Mortimer. "I'll show her she can't take me for a ride."

"You said that before," said Dafoe calmly. "Why not listen to me, like an intelligent person, instead of behaving like a lunatic?"

Mortimer screamed, tore at his hair and began to barge Dafoe, who took it all quite calmly. The bleeding had now stopped and he was getting his face back to its normal appearance. He seemed to be more concerned with his appearance than with Mortimer's excitement. The latter threw himself down on his bed and shouted:

"To hell with you all. What's the use? I've had enough. I'm going to get drunk."

"Not a bad idea," said Dafoe.

"After all I've done for her," said Mortimer, "to turn around and pass me up for a lousy bum like Carey. Larry, I ain't been so unhappy since the day my mother died. Honest to goodness, Larry ... "

He began to blubber like a child. Dafoe comforted him, just as a mother comforts a naughty child, until he was sobbing peacefully.

"I'm nuts about her, Larry," he sobbed. "She's got something, I don't know what it is, but I just couldn't help it. I went to her room and she put on an act and then...to-day she goes and..."

"I know how you feel," said Dafoe gently. "It's all a misunderstanding. Jack, you've been working too hard. You should lie up for the rest of the trip and keep to yourself. Don't let anybody interrupt you. You have something on your hands here, pal. Something bigger than you thought. Now, listen. Will you leave this to me?"

"Larry, you're the grandest tyke in the world," said Mortimer.

He sobbed aloud and embraced Dafoe, who winked, first one eye and then the other, as the tycoon kissed him on either cheek.

"Here's where Larry begins to get among the big money," thought Dafoe.

"It's all in a day's work, Jack," he said aloud. "Will you let me handle this business?"

"Go ahead," said Mortimer, "as long as she doesn't bring me up before the courts."

"How about a little bribe?" said Dafoe.

Mortimer immediately sat up and said suspiciously:

"Hey! What are you gettin' at now?"

"Quite simple," said Dafoe. "Just double her salary. You're paying her only two-fifty a week. Make it five hundred. It's more money than she ever even dreamed of getting. And it's chicken feed, as you know. Right now, that kid is worth several grand and you know it."

"Too well I know it," said Mortimer gloomily.

"Well! How about it?" said Dafoe.

"Go right ahead," said Mortimer after a pause.

"And ... " began Dafoe, folding his arms and assuming a melancholy expression.

Mortimer looked at him closely and said:

"And what, Larry? What's the big news?"

"Little Larry," said Dafoe in a falsetto voice, "he also gettee small money. Little Larry, he also have mouth. Little Larry likee thousand dollars a week for a start."

Mortimer jumped from the bed and cried:

"You double-crossing son of a..."

"Hush," said Dafoe, holding up one hand and winking

mischievously. "If little Jack has sense, he won't say what he was going to say. One thousand iron men a week for Larry or..."

"Or what?" said Mortimer in a rage.

"You can just imagine," said Dafoe, putting his hands on his hips and doing a little pirouette round the room. "What do you think Larry is in this game for? His health?"

He halted and looked at Mortimer. The tycoon's eyes became very small.

"So you're gettin' too big for your boots, huh?" he drawled in a menacing whisper.

Dafoe was startled by this tone and he halted.

"So what?" he drawled in a tone that attempted to be just as menacing as that of his employer.

"You think you're sittin' pretty, don't yuh?" continued Mortimer.

"I have an idea that I..." began Dafoe.

"Shut up," shouted Mortimer. "Jees! You almost took me in, you louser. You just wait."

He rushed out of the room. Dafoe looked after him, with his head turned to one side and his eyes opened wide. Then he threw back his head and laughed.

"Hold your horses, everybody," he said aloud. "Larry is bound to win. Because he's got it here."

He tapped his forehead.

"Just so," he said. "Because he's got it here."

CHAPTER X

DAFOE WAS RIGHT, of course. In a few minutes, Mortimer came rushing back to his suite in a terrible state of excitement. He found Dafoe sitting calmly in the drawing-room by a table on which there was a bottle of champagne in its bucket of ice. Dafoe was patiently waiting while it got cool enough for his palate.

"What happened?" said Dafoe.

"What d'you think?" said Mortimer. "That goil is a wild-cat an' no mistake. No use tryin' to pull a fast one on her."

"I told you so," said Dafoe, "but you wouldn't believe me."

"I'm goin' to get drunk," said Mortimer.

"Your glass awaits you," said Dafoe.

"Smart guy," said Mortimer sarcastically.

"Smarter than you are, at the moment," said Dafoe, as he poured the wine into two glasses. "I think I have something to say that may interest you."

"Well! This is exactly the psychological moment to shoot the good news," said Mortimer, throwing himself into a chair. "That dame is more'n a mouthful for me."

"She's marvellous," said Dafoe. "Through her, Jack, you're going to get to the top of the tree."

"Say, listen," said Mortimer, after he had emptied his glass, "where d'you think I am? In the jungle? "

"I'm talking about something else," said Dafoe, refilling the glasses. "This is big game. Real big game."

"Let's hear about it, then," said Mortimer. "Jees! Looks like the finish to me, unless we can calm her down. Jees! What a tornado!"

He tossed off his glass once more.

"We didn't come to terms about that small matter of my salary yet," said Dafoe.

Mortimer glared at him with hatred and then he said:

"Okay. You've got me this time. But watch your step."

"That's not so necessary now," said Dafoe suavely, "considering that we have to step together. For the love of Mike, Jack, don't try to come that stuff with me. This motion-picture racket isn't your monopoly. I know how you got where you are. Do you blame me for using the same means in order to get to the top?"

Dafoe and Mortimer now faced one another like bitter enemies.

"Why, I'm a son of a gun," drawled Mortimer "if it ain't hard not to take you for an American sometimes, the way you handle the language. Uh? Pretty good actor? Uh? How come you were only an extra until I picked you out of the gutter? Couldn't get the right break, huh?"

"Don't know the hell what you're trying to get at now, Jack?" said Dafoe. "Whatever it is, it does you no good."

"No?" said Mortimer. "Say, listen. In all my life I ain't let anybody take me for a ride. I ain't goin' to start now. Not for a lousy..."

"Don't say it, Jack," said Dafoe, getting to his feet.

"Let's have another bottle of champagne."

"Yes, I am goin' to say it," said Mortimer, also getting to his feet. "If you make one move against me, I'm goin' to hand you over to the Federal dicks and you know what they've got on you. I've been good to you. Jees! I loved you, you double-crossing louser. Then you turn round and try to hold me up for a grand a week..."

Dafoe suddenly burst into tears and trembled with fear.

"Aw! Jack..." he began in a cringing tone.

"Shut up," shouted Mortimer. "You go and calm down Angela and forget about trying to hold me up. Calm her down, I say, or..."

"I swear, Jack, that I..." began Dafoe.

"Get busy," snapped Mortimer and he emptied the remainder of the wine into his glass.

Dafoe dropped into his chair and sobbed aloud, while he begged for mercy, like a whipped pup. Mortimer put down his glass, went over to his henchman and struck him lightly with the palm of his hand on the cheek. And then, with a laugh, he grabbed Dafoe round the head and shook him, lisping endearments. In a few minutes, nobody would dream that there had been any sort of quarrel between them. They were again bosom friends, the one the master, the other the devoted slave.

"We're a team, see?" said Mortimer. "You ain't worth a goddam without me, Larry, and well you know it. Me, too, I get muddled now an' again. There's where you come in, to give me a slant. But no monkey business. I won't stand for it. Now, what would you do with a grand a week? Just get yourself into a heap o' trouble. Well you know it. Leave it to Jack. What I've got, you've got. So what? Jees! Larry, you're the grandest tyke in the world, but you need me in the saddle. Follow me ? On your own, you're just nuts. Say, wait a minute."

He went into his bedroom and came back with a black pearl ring, which he gave to Dafoe. The latter's eyes opened to almost twice their size, as they gloated over the ring. He fixed it on to his finger and said:

"General, I like your style."

"Betcher life yuh do," said Mortimer. "But say, what was this big idea you had ?"

"It's like this," said Dafoe.

For about twenty minutes he whispered excitedly into Mortimer's ear and then he left the suite to appease Angela. Going along the corridor, he halted and caressed his chin and said to himself:

"One of these days, I'm going to get you on the hook, Jack, so tight that you can't wriggle off, nohow. I'm going to get among the gravy. Ha! Ha! Little Larry is going to feather his nest or die in the attempt."

He rolled his eyes like a negro, waggled his rump and cackled in a sombre fashion, as he knocked at Angela's door.

CHAPTER XI

THERE WAS NO ANSWER to his knock, so Dafoe went into Angela's room and found her lying in tears on her bed, just as he had expected to find her. He closed the door gently, went on tiptoe to a chair and sat down. He took from his pocket a beautiful, gem-studded nail file and pared his nails. The nail-file, according to his own account, was a gift from an Indian rajah with whom he had been friendly in Paris. He sighed now and again, as he worked at his nails.

Angela was lying on her face and she caught a glimpse of him when he came into the room, but she pretended to be unaware of his presence. The poor girl was in a bad state. Her quarrel, first with Dafoe and then with Mortimer, had exhausted her; coming on top of her falling in love with Carey. For in truth she had fallen in love. And love is a disease that assumes many shapes, each different from the other and all of them unreasonable.

At last she had to sit up in bed and look at Dafoe. She saw him shaking his head towards her in a very sympathetic manner. She felt sorry for having scratched him especially as the cunning fellow had put several strips of unnecessary sticking plaster over the cuts. And, in any case, when he wished to look sympathetic and to inspire confidence, Dafoe's countenance was irresistible. As she looked at him, Angela began to think that she had made a fool of herself with Carey.

"Don't worry," said Dafoe at length, in a very gentle tone. "I'm not vexed."

"It's my awful temper," said Angela.

"I understand," said Dafoe, continuing to pare his nails. "Only Mortimer is very angry, I'm afraid. I don't think you need worry about that, though."

"Why should he be angry?" said Angela. "I didn't hit him."

"No?" said Dafoe, raising his eyebrows. "Have you forgotten?"

Here it is just as well to inform the reader that Angela had made no threat whatsoever against Mortimer when she scratched Dafoe's face. She had merely said:

"Take that, you Nosey Parker, an' you can tell old pot-belly that I'll give him worse if he comes breaking into my room again."

That, of course, was a threat, but a very mild one compared to what Dafoe had reported to Mortimer. It had, however, served the purpose of enabling him to blackmail his employer, by the useful information which it imparted. Now he proceeded to persuade Angela that she had threatened to sue him for seduction; knowing very well that a woman in a rage says things which she cannot remember afterwards. And he offered the suggestion so persuasively that Angela believed him.

"Good God!" she said. "Now I'm in a mess."

"You're in no mess," said Dafoe, "but Carey definitely is in a bad one."

"Carey?" said Angela.

"Yes," said Dafoe with a sigh. "I'm afraid he's fired."

"Then I'm fired, too," said Angela gallantly, although she did not mean it. "If he got into trouble over me, I'll stand by him. Anyway, I love him."

"I see," said Dafoe, sighing and nodding his head. "Now would you mind listening to me, while I put the situation clearly to you ?"

"All right," said. Angela.

"Carey is in a bad way and we are trying to put him on his feet," said Dafoe. "As a matter of fact, as the result of drink, I don't think he's right in his head. Mr. Mortimer has been very kind to him and is taking him out to Hollywood as a last chance, to help him make good. We've had a lot of trouble with him and it will do you no good to get yourself mixed up in it. However, if you promise me to leave him alone, at least for the moment, I might be able to persuade Mortimer not to fire him. Otherwise ..."

"Good God!" said Angela. "I never thought..."

"I know, child," said Dafoe. "I don't suppose for a moment that he had any ulterior motive in making up to you, but at the same time, if you play your cards properly, you have a tremendous career in front of you." Here he stretched out his arms wide and continued:

"A magnificent career. You have no idea what it is to be a screen star, to have the world at your feet, to live in a heaven upon earth."

He went on talking with an eloquence that Mortimer himself might have envied, describing the joys of being a screen star, until Angela began to think that she really had made a fool of herself with Carey. And yet, she felt ashamed, listening to Dafoe, for betraying the man with whom she was in love so recently, with whom she was still in love. Even while Dafoe spoke, lisping about the glories of being a screen star, she heard

Carey's soft voice whispering to her that, with their love, they could conquer the world together.

"As a matter of fact," said Dafoe, when he had finished his sales talk, "Mr. Mortimer asked me to tell you that he has doubled your salary, just to prove how sorry he is for having been rude to you last night. He asks you to forgive him and thinks he must have drunk more than he thought he had."

"Double my salary ?" said Angela, opening wide her eyes. "That means … ?"

"Five hundred dollars a week," said Dafoe slowly.

Angela repeated this after him, seemingly unable to believe it. It took Dafoe some time to persuade her that it was not only true, but a very modest beginning.

"Five thousand dollars a week is more like the money you'll be getting later on," he whispered seductively. "One thousand pounds a week, think of it. What couldn't you do with that? If you really love Carey, with that money you could both … what Couldn't you do? It's no use flying in the face of Providence. We all have to live, to earn our bread. No one can afford to quarrel with his bread and butter. For God's sake, Angela, give Carey a break. Let him alone for a while. Let him come to Hollywood and make good, get on his feet, pull himself out of the gutter, get back his self-respect, feel happy again. All this nonsense about love in a cottage is only for romantic school girls."

Angela began to sob and said:

"I will. I'll help him. I'm so sorry for him. I'll leave him alone."

"That's the spirit," said Dafoe. "I knew you'd understand."

Then he went on talking to her for several hours, and by the time he left her cabin, the vision of her exaltation with Carey was very dim indeed. She felt that she was making a noble sacrifice, but a very pleasant one, by denying her love for him.

And then Dafoe went to Carey's room. Carey was still asleep. Dafoe waited patiently for him to awake, which he did not do until four hours later. In the meantime, Dafoe consumed a hearty lunch and drank the major part of two bottles of champagne. He was smoking an enormous and exquisite cigar when Carey opened his eyes.

"What the devil has happened?" said Carey, when he saw Dafoe.

"Plenty," said Dafoe. "I'm afraid you've put your foot in it properly."

Sanity, returning after a severe bout of drinking, has a very disconcerting effect on a nervous person. It comes attended by an alarming sense of insecurity, which grossly exaggerates every sort of trouble. Carey saw the sticking plaster on Dafoe's cheeks and felt that something dreadful had happened.

"What's the matter with your face?" he said.

Dafoe explained all that happened in a very sinister fashion.

"It was only by a trick that I was able to take the revolver off him," he said. "He had the same look in his eyes that I once saw in a woman's eyes in Hong Kong. She shot three men through the heart in cold blood. Had tracked one of them from Jo'burg in South Africa and just plugged the other two because they happened to be with him. Mortimer is bad news when he gets on the war-path. He's just gone crazy about Angela, but not in the way you think. You see it's like this. Have a glass of champagne?"

Carey waved his hands in horror towards the drink and said:

"Never again. My God! Think of it. It's ruin for me now."

Carey saw himself left stranded in New York, penniless, put to shame, thrown back into the pit of destitution from which Mortimer had rescued him.

"Best thing you can do," said Dafoe gently, "is to keep

under lock and key until I calm him down. I may fix it up. Anyhow I'll do my best. Though I'm not in your line, I claim to be an artist also. We artists must stand together. God knows, nobody else will stand by us. We are the insulted and injured that Dostoyevsky wrote about. We have only our dreams and our souls which nobody can touch, to comfort us against the persecution of this bourgeois world. I think, perhaps, that in spite of everything, you and I will laugh about all this later in Hollywood, when *The Emigrant* is selling one hundred thousand copies as the result of the film. You see, Mortimer is convinced that he has found in Angela an actress that is going to raise the art of the screen from its present debauched condition..."

And so he went on for about an hour, explaining to Carey how everything was going to be put right through his, Dafoe's, efforts; so that poor Carey was only too eager to agree with his suggestions.

"Thank God for Dafoe," he said, when he had locked his cabin door after Larry's departure. "There is a man."

The man went to Mortimer and told the tycoon of his success. The tycoon was delighted.

"Well! That's that," said Mortimer. "All over. Let's have a drink."

"Not all over by any means," said Dafoe. Here is where the fun begins. What about that conversation with New York? Have you forgotten my suggestion?"

"Forgotten it?" said Mortimer. "Say, listen, buddy, your suggestion was only an acorn that has grown into an oak tree in my fertile mind. Just watch my stuff. Watch me fire the greatest long-range publicity gun in the history of mankind. Put wool in your ears, fellah. This is going to be louder than an earthquake."

CHAPTER XII

GENTLEMAN JACK MORTIMER speaking over the wireless telephone to Samuel Kruger, Wall Street financier and chief backer of Mortimer Productions, Inc. (Independent Unit of World Films):

"Listen, Sam. I've landed the biggest deal in human flesh since Salome. I've got a dame on board this ship who is going to break all records if you help me to handle her. Here is what I want. In her case, I'm going to revolutionise all previous methods of selling a new star. Instead of publicity I'm going to employ secrecy in order to excite the public appetite. I'll have nobody see her, until they see her in all her glory on the screen. I've got good and proper reasons for doing so, apart from the hunch I've got that this method is a knock-out. Unless I keep her veiled and under lock and key, why, the United States army couldn't keep away the mob. Now here's what I want you to do, Sam."

Mr. Kruger obeyed Mr. Mortimer's instructions to the letter. Satisfied by *Little Virgin*'s success that Mr. Mortimer was a racing certainty in any field; he bought two hundred thousand dollars' worth of publicity right away in the interests of "The Veiled Goddess of Love," who was to arrive on the Aquitania with Gentleman Jack Mortimer. As a result of this, the arrival of the ship caused nearly as much excitement as the birth of quintuplets. A horde of reporters clambered on board. Ignoring all the other notables on the passenger list, they crowded into Mortimer's suite and yelped for copy. Mortimer received them in his best manner, which was one of good-fellowish imperiousness. Having handed out cigars and drinks, he addressed them as follows:

"Listen, you guys," he said. "Take a load of this. I'm going to revolutionise the motion-picture industry. So far, the trouble has been the lack of mystery and dignity surrounding the personality of the stars, on whom the prosperity of the industry depends. It may be news to you fellahs, but the church of the twentieth century is the motion-picture theatre, where the populations of the world come to worship their ideal of beauty and virtue. Now it stands to reason that the objects of their worship should not be ordinary human beings like themselves, but beings that are almost divine like the goddesses of old, mysterious beings that have neither a beginning nor an end."

"Hey! Listen," said one newshawk, "what are yuh tryin' to give us?"

"A new religion?" said another.

"I'm giving you," said Mortimer with great dignity, "a new goddess of love, who, like Venus of old, is going to quicken the slowed-up heart of modern humanity, a woman of such dazzling beauty that it would be sacrilege to look upon. her in the naked flesh. You guys may have heard of the Vestal Virgins of Rome, Italy, and how nobody was allowed to touch them under. pain of death. Well! I have discovered a goddess of the screen who is going to be just as sacred to the masses of the world as a Vestal Virgin. And for that reason, I consider myself, as her high priest, bound by a sacred oath to protect her from all the vulgar publicity to which screen stars have so far been forced to submit themselves. From the moment she signed her name to my contract, she has dedicated herself to the service of humanity, and for that reason she has become unapproachable like a nun. Boys, you can put away your cameras."

At first the newshawks were so astonished that they gaped and said nothing, but finally one of them laughed and said:

"Aw! Come on, Mr. Mortimer, you can't expect us to swallow that dope. What's the idea of this veil?"

"Yeah," said another. "Looks to me like she's covered up while her face is bein' altered."

"You mugs are like Saint Thomas," said Mortimer furiously. "Well! If you must have the whole truth, take this. To get a close-up of this dame's face is tantamount to falling in love with her. I don't want an army following me to Hollywood."

"Yeah?" said one hawk. "How come she escaped her army of followers until you got her to sign on the dotted line?"

"You ask Brian Carey," said Mortimer, "if I'm telling a lie. Ask Larry Dafoe, my secretary. Ask Shultz, my cameraman. They have all seen her face and not one of them has been the same since then. Finally, you can ask me. I'm a married man, gents, and I have had twenty years' experience in this business, but I'm riot ashamed to admit that..."

Here he lowered his voice to a honeyed whisper and his eyes became melting soft, as he continued:

"I felt like a goddam fool the first time that I looked into those eyes. I felt that something struck me and knocked me down and then lifted me up again a different man, with a different point of view, a kind of vision of something beautiful that we all had when we were kids, you know what I mean...Aw! Listen, fellahs..."

Here he shrugged himself and assumed the gruff voice of the honest to God fellow who is ashamed of sentiment as he continued:

"I ain't tryin' to hand you out the usual bull. All I ask is fair play. Give the kid a break. I want Angela Devlin to go before the world on her merits as a screen actress."

Then again tears came into his eyes and he appeared to be overcome with emotion, as he said with hands outstretched in appeal:

"Give her a break, lads."

Influenced by the two hundred thousand dollar flood of publicity which had excited New York during the past two days, the newshawks did not know what to make of this. They were almost half-convinced, in spite of their habitual cynicism, that there was something under contract to Mortimer more interesting than the usual screen-fodder.

"What's the idea of the armoured car?" said one.

"Afraid o' kidnappers already?"

"I refuse to discuss the plans for protecting Miss Devlin," said Mortimer with sudden aloofness. "Boys, I trust you not to ...Get me?"

He looked so serious, as he dismissed them with these words, that the newshawks went away asking one another what it was all about. Had Mortimer gone mad, or was there something afoot that was "real front page?" They got no more change out of the other three than they did out of Mortimer. Carey, acting under Dafoe's instructions and also being oppressed by what he called "the horror of his position," refused to speak to them. They put his rapt condition down to the influence exercised over him by his love for Angela, which had become common property since the cable from England had been published in the tabloid. Shultz was in a state of coma, as a result of having toped his way across the Atlantic. Dafoe himself assumed the look of a seer and merely shook his head in answer to all their questions. And of course Angela was under lock and key. There was nothing for the newshawks to do but to give rein to their imaginations, with the result that the most fantastic reports were printed in the newspapers, to the effect that everybody that looked upon Angela's naked face was brought under a spell that pertained to black magic. One of these reports was destined to get Mortimer into trouble. It was under the following heading:

"Monocled magnate confesses passion for veiled goddess of love. Jack Mortimer claims Angela Devlin's face is dynamite and transports it veiled."

CHAPTER XIII

MR. KRUGER HAD CERTAINLY DONE his work very well. An immense crowd had gathered to watch the landing of the Veiled Goddess, and as the party made their way to an armoured car hired to convoy them to the train, a regular army of cameramen took photographs. They passed through a lane of armed policemen to the strange vehicle.

"What's the meaning of this?" said Carey, when he saw it.

"Never you mind," said Mortimer. "Hop into it."

It was of the type that is used in American cities for the transport of bullion, banknotes and precious stones. It had the customary guard of gunmen, to keep away gunmen not in the same employment. As soon as they got inside, the door was locked and away they went at a great speed. No sooner had they started, however, than an extraordinary adventure befell them, for the gunman sitting on guard with them in the interior of the vehicle proved to be no less a person than John F. Cooney, star reporter for the most scurrilous of the New York tabloid Press. This fellow had reached national importance as a newspaper man in the previous year, when, disguised as a kidnapper, he broke into the apartment of a film star, who was evading interviewers and photographers for the sake of publicity. He managed to get a photograph of her while she was having her bath, by means of a miniature camera that was strapped to his trouser leg and worked by a spring. Since then, he was always disguising himself as one thing or another and interviewing and photographing people that were impossible to interview or to photograph. Thus, for instance, he dropped by a rope from an aeroplane on to the bridge of a ship that was on fire and interviewed and photographed the captain, just when he was giving orders to abandon ship. He photographed a banker in the act of hurling himself from the top story of a skyscraper and he photographed a Labour leader in the act of receiving an enormous bribe from the head of a concern against whom, he, the Labour leader, was conducting a strike. In fact, to Mr. Cooney nothing was impossible.

This gentleman lost no time in disclosing his identity.

"Listen, you folks," he cried, as he laid aside the sawn-off shot-gun with which he was armed, "I'm John F. Cooney, America's number one newshawk. I just want to ask you a few questions and take one or two snappy pictures while this heap gets us to our destination. Okay with you folks?"

"Why, I'll be goddamned!" said Mortimer. "How did you get here?"

"Influence, fellah," cried Cooney. "Just influence."

He stood up, crouching against the roof, pulled a flash from his pocket, planted his leg on the seat and pulled up his trousers. There was his camera strapped to his leg.

"Hold it," he said, raising the flash.

While the party gaped at him in astonishment in the interior of the darkened car, he fired the flash and the picture was taken.

"That beats hell," said Shultz.

Nonchalantly chewing a stick of gum, Cooney threw aside the used flash and sat down.

"I guess this is going to make history," he said.

"Now for a few questions. Which of you guys is the bird that's nuts about the dame?"

"Say, this is too much," cried Mortimer, pretending to be angry, although he was really lost in admiration of Cooney's technique and fully conscious of the publicity value of the adventure. "How d'you think you're going to get away with this?"

"Take it easy, brother," said Cooney. "Anything you say will be used as evidence against you. Monocled executive froths at mouth on being trapped in armoured car by our representative while rushing veiled *houri* through city."

"You got a noive," said Mortimer, now angry in earnest.

"Play ball, brother," said Cooney. "Play ball. Nothing is sacred to the great American Press. We unlock doors, tombs and memories. Let's have the story."

There was no gainsaying Mr. Cooney. Handsome, in a fresh-complexioned beefy sort of way, he radiated energy, callousness and the mental alertness of the street Arab, so often mistaken for intelligence.

"You'll get no story from me," said Mortimer. "Well! How about you?" he said to Carey.

"You goin' to open up?"

"Ha! Ha! Ha!" cackled Dafoe. "This is amusing."

"You shut up," shouted Mortimer. "I'm boss of this outfit. There is no story. This is an outrage."

"Love birds sing dumb, huh?" said Cooney.

"Are you referring to me?" cried Angela, speaking for the first time.

She was on the point of raising her veil, in order to speak her mind with greater ease, when Mortimer lurched across the car and grabbed her hand. She tussled with him. Like lightning, Mr. Cooney again leaped to his feet, produced a flash and pulled up his trouser leg. He was on the point of firing his flash, when Carey rushed at him and struck him a violent blow on the side of the head. The interior of the car became at once a scene of the utmost confusion. Cooney got to his feet and grappled with Carey. Shultz, rushing into the fray, to give the interloper a finishing blow, hit Dafoe instead with his wildly swinging right hand. Dafoe went down on top of Mortimer. Angela began to scream. Mortimer yelled at the driver to stop the car. The car halted. The other gunmen came to the assistance. Mr. Cooney was thrown out into the street, after receiving brutal treatment from Shultz. The camera and the photographs were smashed. Then the car proceeded to its destination without further incident.

When they were getting on the train, however, a still more unpleasant adventure befell Carey.

CHAPTER XIV

H ERE IT IS NECESSARY TO EXPLAIN that Carey had written a novel, three years previously, that had been considered somewhat too matter of fact by the authorities and suppressed as a result. Owing to its suppression and the nature of its subject matter, it found an enthusiastic group of followers among middle-aged, unmarried, intellectual women, consumptives, political cranks, dyspeptics and various other types of faggots with maggots in their brains. The most fervent of these was a woman called Margaret Nemo, who, after an extraordinary career, had reached the mature age of thirty-seven without being satisfied that she had discovered the proper mode of expressing her personality. On the book being suppressed, she gathered round her eleven other women of the same type as herself, more or less. The twelve formed a society called "The Carey Circle," for the purpose of studying and modelling their lives on the philosophy adumbrated in the novel.

What philosophy the novel expounded, if any, I am unable to say, not having had occasion to read it; but I gather from reviews that it dealt with some sort of mystical worship of the human body, so current nowadays among intellectuals of the decadent type. There was, I believe, also, some balderdash about "dark blood streams" and the "unexpressed dream consciousness" and various other extraordinary theories usually found among the pseudo-scientific work of Germans. I don't suppose that Carey himself had any idea what it was all about, the novel being probably an impotent outcry against his disordered condition. But to disordered minds disordered thinking appears to be the clearest truth. So the book became a sort of bible to a few cranks.

At the instance of Margaret Nemo, the twelve disciples invited Carey to New York, in order to lecture to them on the philosophy of the novel. They had taken a house in Greenwich Village as their headquarters, a house that had been successively a Dutch church, a speak-easy and the rendezvous of some obscure sect of Communist revolutionaries. Carey arrived, but he stayed only a week, and during that time he delivered no lecture. When he left for Europe, nine of the disciples abandoned the Circle. They went to a town in New Mexico and conjointly wrote a book, which was published privately, proving in no uncertain way that Carey was a fraud and a mountebank. Nothing daunted by this schism, Margaret Nemo and her two friends remained faithful to the author. Indeed, they had been mainly responsible for his maintenance during the lean years that elapsed before the appearance of Mortimer.

Having got wind of Carey's progress towards Hollywood in the company of Mortimer and "The Veiled Goddess of Love," and infuriated by the reports of his being in love with Angela, they determined to take action. They tried to get at him on the pier, but were prevented from doing so by the guard of policemen that surrounded the approaches to the armoured car. By means of bribes they discovered that the car was conveying the party to the train for Chicago. Forthwith they drove madly to the train in Margaret Nemo's car and reached the culprit, just as he was about to pass through the gate on to the platform.

With one eye blackened and his clothes disordered as a result of the fight with the newspaper man, Carey cut a poor figure, but he looked an exquisite compared to the three enraged worshippers. Like the Christians of old, they had adopted a common uniform, which consisted of hair cropped close over the forehead and half-length at the back, a loose white gown like a nightdress, held together at the waist by a monastic cincture, bare legs and Haitian sandals, which they were forced by a rule to make themselves.

Furthermore, they believed in what they called "the body primitive," which meant they were bound to make no attempt to stay the march of time, or the ravages caused by the human appetites, with the result that they resembled dropsied Amer-Indian peasant women.

Miss Nemo got at Carey before he was aware of her presence. She seized him by the shoulder, whirled him round and gave him a resounding slap in the face.

At the same time she cried out in a loud, shrill voice:

"You traitor, was it for this we dedicated our lives to you?"

A tall, heavily built woman, with high cheek-bones, she was by no means a frail creature and poor Carey on seeing her and feeling the power of her open palm on his face was manifestly afraid. The other two women also joined in the cry of traitor and threatened him with their fists.

"Deny it if you can," continued Miss Nemo. "Can you deny that you are going to Hollywood with that wretched woman?"

"Prostitute," screamed the other two disciples.

On hearing the word prostitute, Angela, who had already

94

entered by the gate, rushed forward and cried out in a shrewish tone:

"Who are you calling a prostitute, you old tub o' guts?"

"For the love o' Mike," cried Mortimer, grabbing Angela, "what's this? Come on, Carey. Let's go. Hold her, Larry. Hey, Shultz."

By main force, Mortimer, Dafoe and Shultz dragged the screaming Angela with them along the platform, leaving Carey at the mercy of his disciples. The three women seized the poor fellow and tried to haul him with them, in the same manner that the three men were hauling Angela in the opposite direction. At the same time, a group of cameramen, with exclamations of joy, were photographing the ridiculous scene.

"Let me go, damn you," shouted Carey, struggling in the clutches of his admirers.

"Prostitute," they yelled.

They had hauled him several yards before two policemen managed to rescue him and hustled him within the gate on to the platform. Then he found tongue and turning towards his disciples, he cried out:

"Yes. I am a prostitute, but I prefer being one to being..."

To being what, nobody will ever know, as he was struck at that moment on the mouth, by a small clay idol, which Miss Nemo had snatched from her bag and thrown with a good aim. The idol was a naked replica of what they believed the philosophy of the novel to represent. It drew blood from Carey's lips and then fell on to the platform, where it broke into three parts. Bleeding, Carey hurried away to the train, while the policemen herded Miss Nemo and the other two women from the depot.

The affair caused quite a sensation in New York and I cannot forbear quoting from an article that appeared concerning it in a Communist newspaper called *Proletarian Power*. The article read as follows under the title:

"HOLLYWOOD CEMETERY"

"The cry that was uttered by a member of the so-called bourgeois intelligentsia, when attacked on the way to Hollywood by female admirers of his work, is an unintentional indictment of the whole content of present-day capitalist literature. They are all prostitutes, the whole tribe of bourgeois intellectuals.

"Hollywood is a cemetery where the remains of present-day bourgeois intellectuals are buried, after being fattened like the sacrificial victims in ancient Mexico on enormous salaries, only to have their hearts plucked out and eaten by the Moguls of modern mammon. Proletarian Power sheds no tears over their fate; whether their hearts are plucked out by the sandalled old maids of Greenwich Village or by the monocled Mortimers makes no difference to the march of the world's working class towards the realisation of its historical role.

"As soon as any writer in the present world economic crisis abandons the class position, then his doom is inevitable. The more bourgeois traitors that are engulfed in Hollywood Cemetery the better it is for the working class. "Out of their own mouths they are now condemned as prostitutes."

CHAPTER XV

PHEW! IT WAS ROASTING HOT and yet the sun was going down. Shultz stood at the window of his compartment, looking out at the Arizona desert. It was the first time he had got out of bed since he left Chicago. He was as tight as an owl.

"Oh! Boy," he cried aloud, "ain't it good to see that desert again?"

A great stretch of barren country, studded with low hills, cactus and yucca trees, wandered away aimlessly to the horizon. Shultz stuck his arm through the window and waved it.

"Hoo-ee! You old son of a gun," he shouted, "here I am. It's good to set eyes on you again. Hoo-ee! Here's what I think of Europe."

He spat through the window and then, waving both arms, he addressed the desert, stray Indians, herds of cattle grazing on the ranges, jack rabbits and even advertisements. These latter were scattered in abundance, either painted in great white letters on eminences or else written, phrase by phrase, on little crosses that lined the railroad tracks. Shultz read them aloud, as if they were quotations from a Koran or a Bible.

"Why, there it is," he cried, "the old Honduras Shave. *Noah forgot, going into the ark, to bring his razor, when the dove, brought the twig, he had bugs, in his beard, so don't forget, to buy your, Honduras Shave.* No, sirree. Not me. First drug store I get to. Ho! There's the old Morgan Dairies sign. *Drink Morgan's Milk. It Comes From Contented Cows.* Okay, Morgan. Well! What d'you know? The Eucalyptus Crematorium still goin' good. *Don't Burn In Hell. You Got To Burn Some Time. Why Not Let Eucalyptus Crematorium Do The Job And Leave Your Ashes To The One You Love Best In A Eucalyptus Casket. Cheat The Devil.*"

He was so intent on this amusement that he failed to notice Dafoe's entry into the room until the latter tapped him on the shoulder and said:

"Boss wants you."

Shultz whirled around and said:

"Gee! What's up? I made a mug o' myself, I know, on the trip across. A little Swiss dame, she was so cute. Honest I meant to get those shots he told me to get, but...I got so tanked up, and this little dame, Larry, you shoulda seen her..."

"Listen, you mutt," said Dafoe, giving him a friendly punch in the chest, "it's nothing to do with those steerage shots. That was all a gag in any case. You know what the boss is at times. It's something else."

Shultz clutched Dafoe by the shoulders and cried excitedly:

"He ain't sore at me?"

"Why, no," said Dafoe. "What put that idea into your head?"

Shultz uttered a wild yell and lifted Dafoe in his mighty arms.

"Why, that's swell," he cried. "I thought I was going to get the sack."

"Looks to me more like a rise," said Dafoe.

"Why, what's happened? What have I done?"

"Nothing you've done. Get dressed and come along to the boss's room. Hustle."

Shultz got dressed and followed Dafoe to Mortimer's compartment. The magnate was seated at a table which was littered with newspapers, telegrams and writing-pads. Carey was also in the room, looking very gloomy.

"Sit down," said Mortimer, as the two men entered.

They sat down, while Mortimer continued to write two more telegrams. One was to his wife and it ran:

"You and Junior meet pappy at Pasadena to-morrow." The other was to Bud Tracy, as follows: "Well! You old rum hound. I've gone and done it at last. Meet me at Pasadena." When he had finished, he sighed and looked up.

"Well! You're all here now," he said in a very grave tone, "all that have been associated with me in this great adventure. I have something very important to say to you. To-morrow we arrive in Hollywood. I want you to remember what I'm going to say."

He paused, coughed, and fixed his monocle in his eye. Then he continued in a tone that was still more grave:

"In the past, I am sorry to say that I never had much time for religion. It's a racket that hasn't appealed to me, somehow or other. I always thought there was something phoney about it and I ain't a man to have any truck with something that's phoney. But right here and now, I'm going to tell you guys that I've changed my mind. Religion has got something and it's got me and I want it to get you guys, too. Listen."

He pointed a fat finger in the direction of Angela's compartment and whispered: "In that room there's a girl who is going to change the whole face of modern history. And if that ain't a miracle, then I don't know one when I see it. And I'm reckoned to be pretty smart. Ain't I, Shultz?"

"You said it, boss," said Shultz. "You can give 'em all a start. And how!"

Carey raised his head and his nostrils began to twitch. Dafoe smiled, stuck out his tongue and began to cackle silently. Mortimer looked round the room and then, drawing his elbows into his sides, he fluttered his hands as if he were being strangled and with his head forced back so tightly on to the back of his neck that his sallow face got florid, he whispered with great farce:

"Even I had no idea what she was when I saw her first and gave her the name of Angela. I only saw what was apparent to everybody, even to you, Shultz—her great beauty. I didn't realise all she had, or that she was an angel sent to save mankind."

Carey jumped to his feet and cried:

"What's the idea?"

Mortimer, as if he had been waiting for this interruption, suddenly changed his whole attitude. He turned on Carey and snapped:

"The idea is this, Carey, that you had better watch your step. You gave a guarantee to Larry on board the ship, that you'd lay off Angela, that you'd stop annoying her. But since we left New York, I'm fully aware that you've been watching for an opportunity to get at her again. I've seen you slinkin' around like a dog, looking for an opportunity to slip into her room."

"That's a lie," said Carey in a rage. "I just wanted to explain."

"Oh! Yeah!" said Mortimer insolently. "Explain what?"

"The incident at New York," stammered Carey, flushing.

"What incident?"

"You may be my employer for the moment, but you've no right...Damn you, Mortimer, I hate you."

"Oh! Yeah!" drawled Mortimer still more insolently. "That ain't likely to make me lose any sleep. So you wanted to explain, huh? Swell way of putting it. Ain't it, Shultz? "

"Damn right, it is," said Shultz, looking at Carey aggressively.

Carey looked from one to another of them and saw Dafoe winking and making signs with his hands.

"Sit down," they said. "I'll tell you later what to do."

He sat down and said in a low voice:

"All right, Mortimer."

Mortimer leaned back in his chair, put his thumbs in the armholes of his waistcoat and drawled:

"Would it hurt you very much to say mister when you speak to me?"

Carey glared at him and then he became rigid, as if he had been stabbed. He seemed on the point of jumping on Mortimer, who flinched and glanced hurriedly towards Shultz. Carey also shot a quick glance towards the burly Shultz and then, changing his mind about attacking Mortimer, he rushed from the room. Shultz got to his feet, nodded with his head towards the door and winked, as he said to Mortimer:

"How about it, chief?"

"Sit down," said Mortimer in an evil tone. "He's fired."

"But, Jack..." began Dafoe.

"Shut up," said Mortimer, "I'm boss of this outfit. That guy has a bad reputation. See what the Chicago papers said about that affair at the railroad depot in New York? Huh! We don't want any scandalous publicity of that kind. Whatever use he was to us is now dead and gone. I might overlook that, if he'd consent to play ball, but he obviously has no intention of playing ball. I put up with him too long. You know that, Larry."

"I'm sorry about this," said Dafoe, with a melancholy expression, which was, however, entirely unconvincing.

"What's Bud going to say?"

Mortimer jumped to his feet and put his hands to his hair.

"Ain't I done all Bud asked me to do?" he cried.

"Ain't I brought the guy to Hollywood? Bud can do what he likes with him. But I'm not having him round my lot. I ain't goin' to stand for him messin' round with Angela. Not after bein' connected with those crazy dames in New York. It ain't good publicity. Get this, Shultz, if you know what's good for you. I've always treated you on the level, ain't I?"

"Betcha life," said the sycophantic Shultz, enthusiastically.

"Well! You're goin' places with me, Shultz," said Mortimer, "on one condition. You've got to get religion."

Shultz opened wide his eyes in amazement and licked his lips.

"What's that, boss?" he whispered.

"You heard me," said Mortimer. "Get religion. From the first moment you set eyes on Angela Devlin you saw the light. Get me?"

Shultz leaned back and drew his great hands over his knees and along his thighs.

"Why, sure," he said slowly.

"Ha, ha, ha," cackled Dafoe mirthlessly.

"None o' that, Larry," shouted Mortimer. "Now, listen, Shultz. In consideration of getting religion your salary is doubled from this day. How is that?"

"Why, boss," cried Shultz, almost inarticulate with delight, as he jumped to his feet, "I'll turn Mormon, Mahomedan, Buddhist, anything you like..."

"You'll turn nothing," said Mortimer. "You're a believer in Angela Devlin, see? She saved you, Shultz. You're a different man. You've seen the light. You worship her. You're prepared to defend her with your life."

He approached Shultz and stood over the man, as he

continued with great vehemence:

"She suddenly appeared to you, me leading her by the hand, you don't know where, but the moment you laid eyes on her, you were struck to the ground and then lifted up..."

"I get you, boss," said Shultz.

"And if at any moment you might be inclined to forget that you're saved, your pay check will help to remind you," cried Mortimer, catching the man by the shoulder and shaking him. "And furthermore, remember this. Carey was fired because he tried to make her. See?"

"I get you, boss," said Shultz.

"Now go and celebrate your doubled salary," said Mortimer.

With cries of joy, Shultz left the room. Then Mortimer turned to Dafoe and said in an ecstatic whisper:

"How about it, son? We're sittin' pretty, huh? Glad I got rid of that bum."

"You were wrong, though," said Dafoe quietly, "when you said he had served his purpose. Not yet, by a long shot."

"What d'you mean?" said Mortimer, with his mouth wide open.

"Let me explain," said Dafoe.

Then he began to whisper to his employer. Mortimer listened intently. Now and again he looked with furrowed brow at Dafoe and said, waving his hands, as if warding off something dangerous:

"Impossible. You couldn't work a stunt of that kind."

But Dafoe went on, whispering cunningly and at length Mortimer stroked his chin and said:

"Gee! Larry, you think of everything. Gee! That would be some stunt. But listen, fellah, I know nothing about it. Get me? I know nothing about it. Get me?"

"Don't worry," said Dafoe.

CHAPTER XVI

IT **WAS ALMOST MIDNIGHT** and Angela lay on her bed, tossing about. The heat was terrific. She felt dazed and miserable. Since her arrival in New York she had been stupefied by the extraordinary things that had happened to her, the drive to the train in the armoured car, the women trying to seize Carey, and then on the train, Mortimer continually flattering her and reading extracts from newspapers and telegrams. Flowers at every stopping-place, delivered by messenger boys of the Western Union, all addressed to Angela Devlin. What was it all about? Who was Angela Devlin?

At times she sat in a swoon of delight at being the centre of all this fantastic excitement. It was like a fairy story. But like all dreams it was exhausting and she recovered from these swoons with a feeling of horror and disgust. Her nerves were on edge. At times she wanted to scream. The loneliness was awful. She never saw anybody but Mortimer and Dafoe. She was under lock and key except when they were with her. It was like being in prison.

Sometimes, when she was alone, she burst into silent tears

working in the little hotel, where it was always amusing in the evening, with young men saying pretty things to her over their drinks. Of course, she was of no account back there and she used to long for something wonderful to happen, like this for instance, to have her name in the papers and to wear beautiful clothes, but...Now that it had all happened, she longed for her former life of obscurity and hard work.

So she thought, as she tossed on her bed, while the train roared through the night and the summer heat of Arizona made it difficult to breathe and impossible to sleep. And then a knock came to the door. She sat up in alarm. Was it Mortimer? From that night on the boat, he had treated her with exaggerated respect. In fact, since they left New York his attitude towards her had been that of an inferior paying homage. He kept calling her a goddess and all sorts of fantastic things. But at the same time, she thought, a girl couldn't trust these men. They adopt all sorts of tricks to attain their wicked ends. For now it appeared wicked to her, that sort of thing, since she had fallen in love with Carey. She burst into tears and called out in a quaking voice:

"Who's that?"

"Hush," whispered Dafoe outside. "Open the door. I have something important to say to you."

She got up at once and opened the door. Dafoe, with his finger to his lips, came into the room and closed the door behind him.

"He's asleep," he said. "Don't make any noise."

"Who?" said Angela.

"Mortimer," whispered Dafoe. "I want you to do something for me."

"What is it?" said Angela suspiciously.

"I want you to come with me to Carey's room," whispered

Dafoe. "Be quick and make no noise."

"To Carey's room," said Angela in surprise. "But you told me ... "

"Hush," said Dafoe. "Hurry. We're taking a chance."

Angela pulled on her dressing-gown and followed him. They tip-toed along the corridor of the Pullman and knocked on Carey's door. The door opened and Dafoe pushed Angela into the room. Then he entered and closed the door. Carey, in his pyjamas, stared at them.

"Brian," said Dafoe, "I knew you wanted to be alone with Angela. He's asleep, so I managed to arrange it. I'll come back in half an hour to take her to her room. So long."

And before Carey could utter a word, he slipped out of the room and closed the door behind him. In the corridor, he put his hands on his hips, leaned back his head and laughed without making any sound. He returned to Mortimer's drawing-room and sat there for an hour, now and again throwing back his head and laughing without sound. When the time was up, he went and knocked once more at Carey's door. Angela came out, looking radiantly happy. Carey looked equally happy.

"I'll be back as soon as I see Angela to her room," Dafoe whispered to Carey.

"Thanks, old man," whispered Carey excitedly, as he grasped Dafoe's hand.

On the way back, Dafoe was pleased to see that Angela wore the rapt expression of a girl madly in love. She seemed unaware of her surroundings and did not reply when he whispered good night to her.

"Ça y est," whispered Dafoe to himself, returning once more to Carey.

"How can I ever thank you for this?" Carey said.

"Before you brought her here, I don't mind telling you that

I was seriously thinking of throwing myself out through the window."

"I see," said Dafoe, with a smile. "It's got you badly."

"Not now," said Carey. "Now, it's wonderful. Everything happens for the best. I was cursing myself for having come, but now I see that it's going to be my salvation. She loves me. Can you imagine? That wonderful creature loves me. She loves me, a ridiculous individual like me. It's incredible, but wonderful. To my dying day, I'll thank you for this."

With the ridiculous enthusiasm of a man in love, he seized Dafoe by both hands and swore undying friendship.

"Let's talk," said Dafoe, when Carey had grown a little calmer. "Sit down there. I have a lot to say to you."

"I'm not in a fit state to talk sense," said Carey. "It's all too wonderful. I didn't think I could ever again feel like this."

"One never does," said Dafoe with a sigh. "Now, what do you propose to do?"

"What's that?" said Carey, opening wide his mouth. "What? I hadn't thought...It was all so wonderful. There wasn't time to think. I...What do I propose to do? Why, of course...Hadn't thought of that."

The light went out of his countenance and he slumped down on the side of the bed. Dafoe nodded his head and smiled.

"Shall I tell you?" he said.

Carey looked at him and said:

"I wish you would."

"Okay," said Dafoe. "Then don't bein' a hurry. Take your time. You may spoil everything by doing something rash at this moment. Mortimer is a dangerous man. He has me in his power, but one of these days I'm going to get even with him. I'm telling you this, Brian, because I feel I can trust you. We're both Irish."

"You can trust me to the last drop of my blood," said Carey with enthusiasm.

"Thanks," said Dafoe. "I know your wish is to run off with her at once and I don't blame you. But this is a funny part of the world, and Mortimer is not a man to stop at anything. That's impossible. But in a little while, if you do what I tell you, I promise that she'll be with you, and in your pocket you'll have enough money to provide for the immediate future. Money is not to be despised, you know. Alas! We can't live without it. Not even if we are geniuses."

Here he laughed heartily and Carey joined in the laugh.

"You're right," he said. "You're quite right, Larry. But how am I going to get it. I mean apart from..."

"Leave that to me," said Dafoe. "Don't stay at Tracy's house. Go straight to the International Hotel. And don't worry about Angela. I'll look after her out at the ranch. I'll get in touch with you at the hotel. Now have a good sleep and keep your hair on. Keep cool. That's the important thing."

Carey thanked him profusely and then Dafoe left. Carey, however, was unable to sleep. All night he strode around his little room, wild-eyed, smiling, wondering. And then dawn came, bringing with it the glory of the Southern Californian landscape and he felt that he had really been transported into an earthly Paradise on the wings of love. All round the rushing train stretched a Lotus Land of the imagination, a vast garden, luridly bright with the refreshing moisture sprinkled on its joyous face from a myriad fountains, that rose from the earth, as if by a miracle. While in the distance rose majestic mountains, their peaks lost in the morning mist.

CHAPTER XVII

MORTIMER GOT A SHOCK when the train arrived at Pasadena, where he had decided to leave it. Neither Bud Tracy, nor his wife, nor Junior Mortimer, a boy of sixteen whom he had purchased from an orphan asylum in Chicago as a baby, were there to meet him. Tracy had sent Sam Gunn, the screen writer, and Lee Donlin, his assistant. They explained that Tracy himself was unable to come, owing to being on what they called "a barefooted drunk."

"What the hell for?" said Mortimer. "He only does that when he gets sore about something. What's he sore about?"

"Don't know," said Gunn. "Guess he's sore about something."

"I see," said Mortimer.

He could tell by the attitude of Gunn and Donlin that Tracy was sore with him, Mr. Mortimer.

"Aw, never mind," he said. "Tell Bud to be at my office this afternoon at four. I'm going right out to the ranch. Hey! Sid, where's the family? "

Sid Marx, the magnate's private secretary, coughed on to

the back of his hand and drew his employer aside.

"Mrs. M. has loaded a blow-pipe for you," he whispered.

"Huh?" said the startled magnate. "God sake !"

"Yeah," said the private secretary, "she sure has. These reports in the newspapers that you had fallen for some Irish dame got her goat. She wouldn't let Junior come either."

"Aw! Never mind," said the magnate. "I'll settle that. You look after the stuff. I'm going right out to the ranch. Goddam women!"

An enormous and magnificent car, driven by a Filipino chauffeur, and guarded by a gunman, was waiting. Mortimer and Dafoe hustled the veiled Angela into this car and drove off, refusing to pose for the crowd of cameramen, who had made the trip to Pasadena in the hope of getting a photograph. Shultz's wife had come to fetch him. Carey went off with Gunn and Donlin. He was heart-sick at leaving Angela, especially as he had been unable to get a word with her since the previous night; or even to look into her eyes, since she was kept closely veiled. However, Dafoe had whispered to him to be of good cheer and that consoled him somewhat. Even so, he was in a bad mood.

"What's all this hooey about the veiled lady?" said Gunn, when they had got going. "Looks good to me, all I could see of her."

"Angela Devlin is her name," said Carey.

Both Gunn and Donlin laughed aloud.

"Thanks for the information," said Donlin. "Why, that dame's better known than the President by now."

"Terrible, terrible, terrible," said Gunn.

He put his head in his hands and shuddered. Carey was sitting in the back of the car with Gunn, while Donlin was driving, with Carey's luggage beside him. Donlin was a fat little man, with curly brown hair like a child's, a snub nose and shoulders that were almost level with his ears. He hardly ever stopped smiling, and seemed to be a very happy fellow indeed. Gunn was quite the opposite.

He was about thirty years of age and his straight black hair, very thick and glossy, suggested that he had Indian blood in him. He had a fine head, with large, sympathetic, nervous, blue eyes. His skin was tanned a deep brown. On the whole, a very handsome and intelligent face, except that it had the slightly furtive, almost mad expression of the extremely vital and nervous man. Tall above the average, of full build, he bore himself like a man of quality. His clothes were expensive, well-cut and selected with an obvious respect for good taste. Carey was fascinated by him and wondered why he had made that remark.

"What is terrible?" he said.

Gunn raised his head and smiled sadly.

"To the student of history," he said, "man appears to be, on the whole, a consistent and extremely vulgar fool, but now and again the expression of his vulgarity is akin to genius. Hollywood is a proof of that."

"He's off," shouted Donlin. "Pay no heed to him Mr. Carey. He always gets a religious fit after a night's drinking."

"Never mind, never mind," said Gunn, speaking at a feverish speed. "I'm not a painter, but I have been told there are several million points on a canvas where an artist may begin, but that only one is the correct point. In the same way, there was only one point on the world's map for the creation of Hollywood, at the foot of the Beverley Hills in Southern California. Look at it this way. On one side the dreary Pacific Ocean. On the other sides a dreary desert, with no history whatsoever. Inhabited in the past by mountain lions, snakes and

Indians, deplorable human types dying out, until we came here in search of gold and made them die quicker. Left nothing. There was nothing but what was brought here, paltry lot it was, too, by some Spanish monks and rancheros. A desert. I am told, on what authority I can't remember..."

"So we're goin' to do *The Emigrant*, Mr. Carey," said Donlin. "Should make a swell picture."

"The Sahara desert," continued Gunn, speaking still faster, "owed its origin to the Mahomedan religion, since they use goats' milk and goats devour the bark of trees. Trees die, the earth is at the mercy of the winds, the grass without shelter is swept away, until finally there is only sand and desolation. However, the more commonly accepted cause is an absence of water. Such, at least, is the case in Southern California, until man circumvented this lack by irrigation. With artificial rain he turned the Southern Californian desert into a land flowing with milk and honey."

"What a bore this fellow is!" thought Carey.

"Am I boring you?" said Gunn.

"Not at all," said Carey. "Please continue. It's awfully interesting."

"Safe from the destructive hand of God," continued Gunn, "except for an occasional earthquake, which is, of course, the work of the devil as it comes from underground, this artificial garden gave birth to incredible wealth at incredible speed, so that the city of Los Angeles grew over-night from a miserable village to a city extending fifty miles in length. Oil, fruit, vegetables were there as well, so that the inhabitants became so rich that Croesus is a beggar in comparison. But man cannot live by bread alone. He must have a God and history teaches us ..."

"What did I tell you?" shouted Donlin. "I'm a son of a gun if

112

it doesn't always take him like that. God only knows why it is."

"His gods are always representatives of the way he earns his bread," continued Gunn. "I'm telling you this, Mr. Carey, not because I'm cuckoo as Donlin thinks, but so that you may understand Hollywood from the beginning. Do you mind?"

"Go ahead," said Carey. "It's all very interesting."

"The sun, moon, stars," continued Gunn, now in a frenzy, "storms, rain, thunder, lightning, the sea, rivers, the earth, corn, cows, bulls, lions, snakes, elephants, war, peace, love and the more precious of the human organs have been deified and worshipped as gods. But man in Southern California, living in a completely artificial environment, no seasons, no natural calamities except an occasional earthquake, no poverty as it is understood, had to invent artificial gods. So he made celluloid gods by means of the camera and Hollywood is the factory in which they are made. The celluloid city."

He paused, apparently exhausted.

"So what?" said Donlin.

"I'm speaking for the benefit of Mr. Carey, not for your benefit," retorted Gunn angrily. "You're not cursed with a divine intellect, Donlin, so you escape being hurt by the horror of this life. You are happy as long as you have somebody to give you orders and money to satisfy your brute instincts. Mr. Carey, to give you an idea of Donlin's mentality, it's sufficient to say that he thinks Jack Mortimer a man of genius."

"And what do you know about that, you lousy word pedlar?" cried Donlin cheerfully. "What's the use you knocking Jack, when we all know he pays you two grand a week? Sure. And damn right you crawl for it, too."

"That's deep, very deep," said Gunn, speaking at the same terrific speed, which, in conjunction with his slightly furtive expression, gave Carey the uneasy feeling of being in the unreliable and exhausting company of a garrulous lunatic. "I'm a prostitute, I know, but that does not force me to love my keeper. Excuse me, Mr. Carey, for boring you with this rubbish. All Hollywood conversation is like that. It must appear insane to an outsider. I've been seven years here. It's like dope, this place. One visit is amusing, provided it's cut short and one doesn't come again."

"So you don't think the screen is going to become..." began Carey.

"The medium of a new form of art," interrupted Gunn, "the greatest man has yet invented. I know the formula. There is, has been and always will be only one form of art and that is the art of poetry. It cannot exist in a place like Hollywood. You can't satisfy the thirst of the human intellect with a hose pipe. It must drink from a natural spring. There is only one thing to do in Hollywood. To get as much money out of it as possible. I've got a farm in the East. One of these days..."

"Oho!" shouted Donlin. "Now, he's takin' off to his farm. You'll die here, Sam, and, take it from me, you couldn't die in a better place. Pay no attention to him, Mr. Carey. This is a swell joint. Stick around."

"Where are we now?" said Carey.

"L.A.," said Gunn. "Short for Los Angeles, fear you mightn't know. One thousand and one Californian nightmares in search of a city."

"Never you mind," said Donlin, spitting out the window. "Swellest burg in America. Born and bred here."

Gunn suddenly collapsed as if his body had been punctured. His head drooped between his shoulders. He drew his hands through his hair. His face assumed an expression of great agony. The tan on his cheeks suddenly became pale, just like an evening shadow passing over the green surface of the earth.

Then he shrugged himself, looked at Carey, smiled and said gently:

"Never mind. I like your work, Mr. Carey, very much. *The Emigrant* is a great book. We'll do *The Emigrant*. To hell with Mortimer. I must go to bed. Drinking all night with Bud. Step on it, Donlin. What's this? A funeral?"

"Okay, fellah," said Donlin.

The car was already going at the rate of sixty miles an hour, in spurts between traffic lights, but now it went seemingly twice as fast, with the phlegmatic Donlin lounging idly at the wheel. Carey felt completely bewildered. He gaped like a rustic being in a city for the first time. But was it a city? They had already gone ten miles, passing through streets that were identical, with identical houses in each street, through a maze of automobiles, which even at that early hour covered the ground like a horde of scurrying ants, screeching, rumbling. Irritated by Gunn's neurotic conversation, he felt that he was caught in a labyrinth from which he could never extricate himself and he thought the place was the most frightful place he had ever seen. It gave him the impression of having been devastated by an evil genius, who, with a gigantic comb of uneven teeth, had torn away the upper layers of the city, leaving only the jagged base, with the interiors of the houses exposed and the furniture scattered about in disgusting confusion.

"Hollywood," cried Donlin a few minutes later.

"Where?" said Carey, leaning forward excitedly and looking in all directions.

"Right here," said Donlin. "We're right in it."

"I agree with you," said Gunn. Then he laughed and added: "That's excellent. Where, indeed? It's merely an illusion. It's a point of view, not a place. A mirage. Later. Later. The thing is to relax."

Then Carey saw written on the side of a mountain to the right, in enormous letters, the word:

"HOLLYWOODLAND."

"By Jove!" he said. "Imagine that! So this is really Hollywood!"

CHAPTER XVIII

IN A WAY, BUD TRACY WAS QUITE AS BIG a shot as Mortimer, at least in so far as Shultz was concerned. After having had breakfast with his wife and his two merry children out at his delightful cottage in Laurel Canyon, Shultz decided to visit Tracy.

"We're on the up an' up, Jane," he said to his wife, as he hugged her. "With this rise we can get a little boat an' go sailin' between pictures, same as you always wanted to. Gee! This Angela Devlin is the biggest stroke o' luck since I met you, kid. Same time, mustn't forget old Bud. It's he gave me my first break. Am I right, Jane?"

Jane said he was right and Shultz set forth in his Chevrolet to visit Tracy. As he drove down Hollywood Boulevard, the main thoroughfare of the celluloid city, to use Gunn's description of it, he was just as enraptured as he had been on catching sight of the desert. And, indeed, the delight of his simple nature is to my mind preferable to the carping criticism of individuals like Carey. There are some people who always expect gates, walls, soaring towers, hanging gardens, magnificent cathedrals, palaces with uniformed lackeys and God only knows what else on entering a city. There are others, and they are the wiser people, who turn sordid reality into the palaces of the imagination. But frankly, it must be admitted that a considerable imagination was required to become enthusiastic about the street in question, which resembled somewhat closely a hand-me-down but gaudy desert settlement, or a theatrical reproduction of a great mining-camp during the gold rush period. In any case, Shultz saluted it with enthusiastic cries and then turned up a steep side street towards Tracy's house, which lay near the top of a neighbouring hill. The summit of the hill, covered with parched grass, lay immediately behind the house.

Shultz parked his car and began to run up a steep flight of stone steps that led to the door. Half-way up he came to the battered carcass of an electric gramophone.

"Gee!" said Shultz, as he stepped over the wreck. "Must have been *some* party."

"Hey, Bud," he cried, addressing the house as enthusiastically as he had addressed the desert, his wife, his children and Hollywood Boulevard. "Why'd you go an' break another goddam music box? Hey! Bud, here's old Dutchy back to see yuh."

He began to knock on the door and ring the bell. The door opened and a man said:

"Let up on it. Bud's havin' a nap."

The man was Tracy's secretary, a little, bald, round-faced, tubby person called Rummy. Shultz immediately calmed down and tip-toed into the room. Gunn and Donlin were sitting there, drinking beer from bottles. Tracy lay asleep in his clothes on a couch by the window. He had a rug around his middle. His bare feet stuck out at one end. He wore horn-rimmed glasses. One hand, hanging limply by the side of the couch, clutched a bottle of beer that had obviously spilt some of its contents on the floor, as there was a stain on the carpet. After shaking hands with Rummy, Shultz went through a curtain into another room, found a bottle of beer on a table, returned with it and sat down. Rummy had now placed a golf hall on the floor and, with a club, he was preparing to hit the ball towards a ring he had set up in a comer.

"Wake him up," said Shultz. "It's past noon."

"Not me," said Rummy. "Relax."

"How could a man relax in Hollywood?" said Gunn. "That's just a slogan. We live on slogans."

"Where's Carey?" said Shultz.

"Yeah," said Tracy, sitting up suddenly. "What's all this noise? Who said something about Carey?"

"Hello, Bud," said Shultz. "How is everything you've got?"

"Jees!" said Tracy, gathering the rug about him. "Who let in that fellah?"

"Ain't yuh glad to see me, Bud?" said Shultz in a pained tone, as he halted half-way across the floor.

Tracy muttered something under his breath. He put his glasses up on his forehead, drew his palm across his mouth, scratched his belly and swung his legs to the floor.

"Tryin' to pull a fast one, huh?" said Tracy. He got to his feet, hunched up his shoulders, spat on his palm and took a pull at his belt. He was just wearing dungaree pants and a blue, sleeveless, cotton shirt.

About fifty years of age, he was short and rather fat, powerfully built, with a bald head and slightly protruding eyes, like a surprised bird. His face was an ash-brown colour and deeply wrinkled. A powerful, dominating personality, especially now that he was angry.

"What do you mean, Bud?" said Shultz, drawing back.

"What have I done? "

"Where's Carey, Sam?" said Tracy.

"The International," said Gunn. "He's gone to bed."

"How come you didn't bring him here?" said Tracy.

"Didn't want to come," said Gunn.

"Say, listen, Bud," said Shultz, "what have I done wrong?"

"What's all this hooey about a veiled goddess?" cried Tracy. "You go over to Ireland to get a girl for *The Emigrant* and you come back like a Barnum an' Bailey circus, or a Religious Revival, with a veiled goddess. What's the game? Are you in on this? Is Carey in on it? Where is he?"

"He took the dive, Bud," said Donlin.

"In bed, huh?" said Tracy. "Come on, open up, Bummer. Who is the dame?"

"She's the greatest sensation..." began Shultz.

Gunn, Donlin and Rummy interrupted him with their laughter.

"Colossal in a sensational way," said Donlin.

"In other words, quite good," said Rummy, settling his golf ball for another putt.

"I give you your first break," said Tracy, "and then you double-cross me with the first producer that takes you for a holiday. Did you get those shots I wanted?"

"Why, sure," said Shultz. "How d'you make out I double crossed you?"

"Forget it," said Tracy, suddenly changing his attitude and becoming friendly. "You big heel, I was just trying you out. Here, have a go at that, to show there's no ill-feeling."

He stuck out his jaw towards Shultz. Shultz hit the jaw quite a powerful blow with his right palm. Then he stuck out his own jaw and Tracy treated it in a similar fashion. Then the two men, uttering cries of joy, embraced one another enthusiastically. It was several minutes before they were able to resume their conversation. Then Shultz gave a rather disjointed account of the expedition since the discovery of Angela, keeping in mind the whole time that "he had religion." As his mind was rather a crude one, his narrative was unconvincing.

"So he fired Carey," said Tracy. "What d'you know about that?"

"No wonder," said Shultz. "That guy is impossible. Too goddam stuck up."

"Nonsense," said Gunn. "He appeared all right to me."

"Well! He behaved badly towards Angela," said Shultz.

"Say, are you gone cuckoo about the dame?" said Donlin.

"Why, listen," said Shultz, miming a religious ecstasy and with his mind fixed on his doubled salary and on the sailing boat, "the first time I laid eyes on her, I was lifted up and thrown down arid changed and I ain't been the same man since. You guys know me. I ain't been a religious man, but this dame has got something that just made me believe in God. I'm a different man."

He had worked himself into a state of excitement that was akin to a religious ecstasy.

"I'm a different man," he kept repeating, as he looked from one to the other of those present. They were visibly astonished. They laughed nervously and jeered at him, after the manner of people who are inclined to believe in something miraculous, or occult, and yet are ashamed of their inclinations. He went on ranting, until finally they became serious.

"She must have something," said Tracy.

"Hasn't been as much ink spilt over any single dame since Marie Dressler died," said Donlin.

"At the same time," said Gunn, "no matter what she is, Bud, she mustn't interfere with *The Emigrant*. And we mustn't let Gentleman Jack fix her. He's like the famous producer that was out in the desert on location with a director. Parched with thirst, they found a thermos flask of ice water. The director opened it and was about to quench his thirst when the producer said…"

"You can't drink it like that," interrupted Donlin. "Wait till I fix it. Told for the five hundred and first time."

"It's true and you can't deny it," said Gunn, getting excited. "All that is beautiful and creative and real in life is fixed in Hollywood."

"She's got all you say?" said Tracy to Shultz.

"She sure has," said Shultz fervently. "She's the biggest thing the industry has seen. That's why he wants the script fixed to suit her, see?"

"What?" yelled Tracy, Gunn and Donlin in unison. "He wants to fix the script?"

"Why shout at me?" cried Shultz. "Go and ask himself."

The three men, in a fury, crowded around Shultz.

"He can't take me for a ride like that," cried Tracy. "I'll show him. Wouldn't have touched the goddam thing if I thought he was goin' to fix it. Sober up, boys. We're goin' to fight him for it. We're goin' to make the greatest picture the industry has seen. Come on, Sam. Let's get ready. We'll go an' see him. He can't fix it."

"Damn right he can't," said Gunn. "We'll see him at four o'clock."

"Stick to me, Shultz," said Tracy, "if you know what's good for you."

"Wait till you see this dame, Bud," said Shultz in an appealing tone.

CHAPTER XIX

AFTER A TURKISH BATH and a shave, Tracy and Gunn set forth to keep their four o'clock appointment with Mortimer. Smartly dressed in a white jacket and tie, a blue shirt, grey trousers and black and white shoes, Tracy looked quite a different person. Gunn was more normal. They were both in a serious mood and drove in silence. Indeed, it was a very serious matter for them, this business of fixing *The Emigrant*; and the ballyhoo about Angela Devlin.

They had both been connected with Mortimer for some time. Mortimer, Tracy and Gunn formed one of those "teams" that were fashionable at the moment in Hollywood, a combination of the same producer, director and screen writer for successive pictures. Together they had now made four pictures that had earned a profit. They were shoddy pictures, efficiently directed and with a serviceable, well-written script. But Tracy and Gunn knew that they could not go on turning out shoddy pictures and retain the attention of the public. The public always demanded something new. It had no mercy on directors and screen writers that failed to give them something new. So they had picked on *The Emigrant* as something new and different, to startle the public appetite. Furthermore, they were ambitious to attract the attention of the highbrow critics in New York and London, by turning out something that would be called "artistic"; especially as a director had been given a gold cup by a European dictator during the previous winter (there was even a rumour that the director in question was going to receive some mark of recognition from His Majesty the King, and that of course made their mouths water, as only the mouths of republicans can water).

And now Mortimer had returned from Europe with Angela Devlin, obviously with the intention of fixing *The Emigrant* to make it a suitable medium for a new star, reeking with slush, sugar and nonsense. Tracy and Gunn were very grave indeed. As they drove down the Boulevard, it was the hour when that thoroughfare is crowded by an endless procession of the most beautiful creatures imaginable, women gathered in to Hollywood from all the corners of the earth by the lure of a screen career, all dressed with a view to giving the onlooker an exact idea of their form. Many an eye tried to catch the attention of the two men, greedy female eyes that were willing to pay any price for the favour of recognition by two of the most famous and important triumvirate in the celluloid city. But the two men never smiled nor looked. The owners of the lovely eyes said to themselves as they looked:

"God! Wouldn't it be wonderful to be either Tracy or Gunn. Even to spend an evening with them."

And even then, Gunn was saying to Tracy:

"If I had enough will power left to get really angry, Bud, I'd blow up this town with a monstrous bomb."

"Good idea," said Tracy savagely, "if you blew me up with it. If it weren't for the wife an' kids, I'd do the job myself."

They swung out of the Boulevard down a side street, and after going a mile or so they parked their car on a lot opposite a large mass of buildings that were done in a dull yellow colour. These buildings were World Studios Incorporated. Outside the studio gates there was a crowd of people waiting, all dressed in costume, some as cowboys, others as Western "bad men," others as peasant women from Europe, others as harlots of the 'nineties, others as Cossacks, others as monks. They were all middle-aged and wan, with expressions of despair on their faces, rather like the expressions of old gamblers that hang around casinos, where they have no longer the ability to play, owing to their penury. When they caught sight of Tracy and Gunn, their bodies became rigid, like dogs that have sighted prey. Their lips moved in silence. Their eyes appealed. They made slight forward movements like beggars. And then, when the two men had been admitted through the gates by a uniformed gunman, they sank back once more into listless attitudes. Outcasts.

Within the gates, a harsh-faced man sat behind a desk in an ante-room. A number of young men and women stood before the desk, seeking for admission to somebody or other in the studios. As soon as the man behind the desk saw Tracy and Gunn, he pressed a button. The door leading from the ante-room to the studios went click-click. They pushed through the door. A man from among those before the desk tried to rush through the door, but the official behind the desk shouted at him to halt. The man turned back. In any case, even if he had succeeded in passing through the door, he would not have got very far. Two gunmen in uniform stood immediately beyond, with revolvers at their belts, ready to fire on intruders. The gunmen saluted Tracy and Gunn respectfully.

"Better let me do the talking," said Tracy. "We got to let

him know that we are both of one mind."

"Okay," said Gunn.

Now they seemed not so sure of themselves, as they approached the conference with the magnate. They crossed a great quadrangle, surrounded on all sides by blocks of yellow buildings, from which a great clatter of typewriters reached their ears. A number of roadways, lined by great buildings that looked like sheds, ran in all directions from this square, which was adorned with flower-beds, fountains and statues, like the main square of a city. However, unlike the square of a city, it did not seem to have any particular nationality, as the objects that adorned it must have come from nearly every corner of the globe. Crowds of people, all as exotic as the flowers and the ornaments, passed back and forth. Some were actors and actresses, dressed "in character," their faces painted a dull yellow colour, like the buildings.

"Better take it easy, Bud," said Gunn. "We'll gain nothing by going bald-headed for him."

"That's right," said Tracy.

Their revolt against Mortimer had now simmered down into a very lukewarm state indeed, as they was an enormous shed, through whose open doorway could be seen a crowd of magnificent young men, dressed as gladiators, their bodies painted a dull yellow colour, having at one another with swords, while a man on a platform cried out: "One, two, one, two, Christ sake, put some pep into it." On the opposite side of the street, a crowd of workmen were building a battleship for a scene in the Crimean War. A little further down, in another shed, there was a great tumult, as a number of actors and extras herded pairs of different animals into Noah's Ark. And in still another shed, Queen Elizabeth was on the point of having an affair with the Earl of Essex.

Gunn halted suddenly and in great excitement he seized Tracy by the arm and whispered tensely:

"For God's sake, Bud, here's our chance to make a gesture of revolt, not only against Mortimer but against the whole thing."

"What's gettin' yuh all worked up?" said Tracy gruffly. "Don't get shirty, far the lave o' Mike."

"I can't help it," said Gunn. "Don't you think it's a shame that you and I, intelligent men with some talent, should be the pot-boys of the common ruffians that run this joint, this celluloid city, human offal like Mortimer and his kind? Even they are only the pot-boys of the New York bankers that collar most of the gravy. They have dug into our brains and sucked us dry. You and I are no longer men, Bud. We're ghosts. Somebody should go to the chair for a serious crime in order to make the world realise the position of the intellectual in Hollywood. By God! I think I'll kill Mortimer with what little is left of my manhood."

The man was on the verge of hysteria. Then Tracy caught him by the nose and gave that organ a severe pull. Gunn began to howl.

"None o' that nonsense," said Tracy. "Have a stick o' chewing gum? You get two grand a week and I get three. There ain't many pot-boys earn that much dough a week in this day an' age. Huh?"

"Okay," said Gunn, with a gloomy laugh. "You're always insane, Bud. You know, though, it's occasional moments of sanity that are the curse of inmates in a lunatic asylum. It's during moments of sanity that lunatics attack warders and one another, attempt to commit suicide, go into fits of hysteria and get put in strait-jackets and locked in padded cells, until the coma of insanity again makes them harmless. I have rare spells of sanity during which I want to kill one of my keepers and go to a farm back east, to till the earth like an honest labourer. But I become insane almost at once and go on working for what you call big dough. I wish I could be always either one thing or another."

"Oh! Yeah?" said Tracy, chewing his gum. "Better turn on the insanity tap right now and let me do some talking. Okay?"

"Okay," said Gunn in a low voice. "Lies. Lies. I've been telling lies for money since I grew up, first on a newspaper and now here."

They rounded a corner and came upon a house that stood apart, between a crowded parking-space and an artificial tenement house that was being erected by a gang of workmen, near a rusty, corrugated-iron fence.

It was a beautiful little house and over its door was written in ornamental letters: JACK MORTIMER PRODUCTIONS INC. It was the exact replica of a Greek temple which Mortimer's predecessor had discovered in his travels in that country, while looking for a Greek shepherd to play the part of Bacchus in a story about the daughter of a Chicago meat packer who tried to found a classical colony on an island she had bought in Lake Superior. The film was a complete failure and the producer committed suicide as a result, but the temple remained to the greater honour and glory of Mr. Mortimer, who stepped into the suicide's shoes.

They marched up the marble steps that led to the door of the temple. They passed between two marble Doric columns and then through a swing door into an office, where a number of typists were busy at their machines, chewing gum as they worked.

"Boss in yet?" said Tracy to one of them.

"Yep," she said.

She pressed a button, took up a speaking-tube and spoke into it.

"Allrightee," she said in a cooing voice. Then she added gruffly to Tracy: "Okay. Go right in."

The door opened just as Tracy reached it.

"Pappy," gurgled Mortimer, with outstretched arms. "You old gila monster!"

CHAPTER XX

THE INTERIOR OF MR. MORTIMER'S OFFICE did justice to every one of the fifty thousand dollars that had gone to furnish it. Every single article was what is known to the antique trade as "a museum piece." Even the spittoons came from some remote place in Kentucky and had an historical value, both of them having been used in some expectoratory contest between two famous "Southern Colonels" before the Civil War. The most interesting piece of furniture, however, was a plaster replica of the famous duck "Kush Kush," with which he had first muscled in on the motion-picture racket. From newsboy, Mortimer had graduated into a vaudeville entertainer. "Kush Kush, the wonder duck," gave him his first break and the animal's popularity among small-town vaudeville audiences attracted the attention of a film producer, who invited Mortimer to Hollywood. The celluloid city was then in its infancy and its productions were a source of ridicule to all but children and village idiots; but Mortimer saw its potentialities and he stayed there with his duck, which became one of the first stars. On its death, Mortimer had it stuffed and carried it about with him everywhere. But as fortune favoured him, he thought a plaster replica more artistic and "classy." So there was a statue of "Kush Kush" on his desk.

The furniture in which his body was encased was just as expensive as that of his office. He wore a white suit, with a narrow blue stripe, a pink shirt, a black tie spotted with white, a monocle, a massive tiepin in which there was a rare jewel, four exquisite rings and a wrist-watch strap composed of small diamonds set in platinum. His body was perfumed to such an extent that Tracy put his fingers to his nose after the two men had embraced enthusiastically.

"For the love o' Mike," said Tracy, "why do you use that stuff?"

"Nerts," said Mortimer. "Do you know how much that scent cost a bottle the size of a...Howdy, Sam?...the size of a... Say, listen, Bud, I've gone an' done it. Sit down, boys, I've got the biggest news for you since I...Mix yourselves a highball. Listen..."

Myron Luther, the studio head of World Films Incorporated and Roger Kent, his second in command, were also in the office. Luther was an enormous man, corpulent, with a thick neck and a florid countenance. His expression was as deceptive as the hide of a green lizard among green foliage. Were it not for his size, he would look like a pick-pocket. He picked brains, however, instead of pockets ; a remarkably able man in his own way. His assistant, Mr. Kent, offered a striking contrast, being quite small, with a round, genial face and merry blue eyes. Luther leaned back, twiddling his thumbs on his capacious stomach and eyeing the men in the room in the remote, gloomy way that was habitual with him. Kent was sipping a highball.

"Now, listen, Jack," said Tracy, "how about *The Emigrant?*"

"Ain't I goin' to..." began Mortimer, taking a seat at his desk.

"Yes," interrupted Gunn. "Let's do the book. The whole book."

Tracy nudged Gunn in the shin with the toe of his shoe, as they stood by a little cock-tail bar in a corner of the room, getting drinks. Mortimer spread out his hands in a gesture of appeal to Luther and Kent.

"What d'you make o' those two guys?" he said. "I can tell you, Myron, it's no sinecure, this job I've got tryin' to handle that team."

Kent laughed aloud and Myron Luther grunted. Then he leaned back further, closed his eyes and muttered:

"You're tellin' me, Jack! Directors are out on their own when it comes to temperament."

"Let's get sized up, Jack," said Kent.

Tracy and Gunn sat down with their drinks.

"How's the wife an' kids, Bud?" said Mortimer.

"Honolulu," said Tracy. "How's yours?"

"Just bought a ticket to Reno, I hear," said Gunn.

While Tracy hit Gunn once more in the shin, this time more viciously, Mortimer turned round and said to him angrily:

"I want none o' your wise-cracks, Sam. I'm paying you two grand a week as a result of *Little Virgin*'s gross, but you don't get the right to make impertinent remarks, just because you wrote a swell script for that picture. If you got any kick comin', how about goin' back to Noo York to work on that rag that paid you sixty bucks a week? Huh?"

"Aw! Listen, Jack," said Tracy. "He didn't mean anything."

"I'm sorry, Jack," said Gunn. "I didn't know you'd take it like that. I only..."

"Oh! Yeah!" said Mortimer. "How about investing in a wife for yourself? Then you might understand..."

"Goddam bunch o' kids," said Luther. "Let's get on with

this conference, Jack. Let's get serious."

"I certainly had no intention to give offence," said Gunn excitedly.

"Now just keep that trap o' yours shut, Sam," said Tracy. "Come on, Jack. Let's hear all about Angela Devlin. So you brought back a star for *The Emigrant*, huh? Swell piece o' work."

"I certainly have brought back a star, pappy," said Mortimer, "but .. "

"So there's a but in it," said Tracy.

"Yeah! A big one," said Mortimer, "if you've got *The Emigrant* in mind."

"You don't say so?" said Tracy.

He and Mortimer now looked at one another with bitter hostility. Gunn sighed and tossed off his drink. He rose, went to the bar and poured out some more whiskey, which he drank neat.

"We're all just human offal," he muttered. "Human offal."

"Now listen, Bud," said Mortimer, "you an' me have been associated for a long time. We've gone places together."

"Yeah," said Tracy curtly. "Come on. Come on. Let's hear it. What's the racket."

"It's like this," said Mortimer. "I've brought a dame over here that's going to make history in the motion-picture industry. I want to sell her to the world in the most suitable manner I can. Now, on the other hand, you guys, you an' Sam, want to do a story. You think it's a swell story and that it's going to make a swell picture and I hold the contrary view. In spite of that, I didn't say no when you asked me to produce it. Did I, Bud? Did I, Sam? Did I, Roger? You know it. You know I went on my knees to get my backers in favour of the proposition. I made the journey to London and bought the book and the guy that wrote it. I promised to produce that picture and I'm not going back on my word. But not now. And here's where I want you guys to do me a favour, in exchange for the favour I'm doing you. I want you to postpone *The Emigrant* and get to work on a suitable medium for Angela Devlin right now."

"Just put *The Emigrant* on the shelf, huh?" said Tracy. "That what you want to do?"

"Only for the time being," said Mortimer.

"That means for ever," said Gunn. "Bud and I went down to Mexico and wrote a really good script. It's all ready to shoot."

"Now, for God sake," said Mortimer, "can't you see what I'm trying to do? Angela Devlin must have a medium right away and she must have a medium that will appeal not only to the highbrows, but to the lily white hands that clutch the two-bit pieces. What's the good, Sam, you gettin' sore about a script? I'm askin' you to write a script, an original script, that'll make anything you ever wrote look like an extract from a dime novel. I want an original by the greatest writer in the industry, directed by the greatest genius in motion pictures, produced by myself, for the veiled goddess of love that I have brought over from Europe. Gee! Surely, you guys must be made of wood if you can't see the glory and magnificence of that proposition. I'm only flesh and blood an' I can hardly speak when I think of the possibilities...Oh! Bud!"

He got to his feet and held out his hands towards Tracy and said:

"Pappy, are you going to let me down?"

"Forget it," said Tracy. "Put it that way, Jack, just lay *The Emigrant* aside, a little while, another proposition altogether. I thought you were, know what I mean, going to fix the script to make..."

"Fix the script!" cried Mortimer. "What put that idea into your head?"

"Shultz said something," murmured Tracy.

"He's nuts," said Mortimer.

"An original?" said Gunn, in an interested manner.

"Sure thing," said Mortimer. "*The Veiled Goddess*, a Bud Tracy direction, original story by Sam Gunn, a Jack Mortimer production. Can't you see it? Starring the veiled goddess herself. It's colossal."

"*The Veiled Goddess*," said Tracy. "What's that? The usual muck? I told you I was sick an' tired of tripe."

"I don't know, I don't know," said Gunn, excited by the idea of being asked to write an original story. Perhaps, he thought, the impossible was at last going to happen and he would be allowed to express himself the way he wanted.

"Good title," said Luther. "Written around the publicity she's getting...I recollect that phrase was used..."

"Why, sure," said Mortimer. "It was all my idea. *The Veiled Goddess*—the mystery woman. Sam, you could write a story about her..."

"*The Veiled Goddess*," said Gunn, getting excited.

"That the title?"

"Sure," said Mortimer. "I'm giving you the title and the star. Give me the script. Give me something you've put your soul into, something worthy of the most beautiful creature that ever trod this earth."

"Gee," said Tracy, "he's fallen for her. She must have something. Have you really fallen for her, Jack, or is all this hooey, like the armoured car and the veil? Tell us, Jack, on the level, I mean, hooey is all right for the world outside, but among ourselves, you know what I mean, has she..."

"I'm telling you, Bud," cried Mortimer with great enthusiasm, "that you'll see what's got me, as soon as you lay eyes on her. This ain't hooey. Aw! Listen, fellahs. Here, take this goddam outfit, Myron, throw me out on the road to starve and I'll ask only one thing of the guy that takes my place. That one thing is to give this dame the break she deserves. Something came over me, Bud, the moment I laid eyes on her. I felt myself lifted up and hit hard against the ground. I was socked into unconsciousness and by God I don't ever want to wake up. I'm ready to sacrifice everything I have and dig ditches for a living, so long as I have the pleasure of knowing that her divine beauty is getting a break."

"I'm a son of a gun," said Tracy, beginning to be impressed, "if Shultz didn't say the same thing. Didn't he, Sam?"

"Yes, he did," said Gunn. "But I don't fall for this religious revival business myself. If the girl is really beautiful, we might be able to write something worthwhile around her."

"But she's more than beautiful," said Mortimer in a voice shrill with emotion. "She's something beyond that hick word beautiful. I'd like to hire a smart guy to make a word for her, one the Greeks hadn't got."

"Say, listen," said Tracy, "where is she? Where did you find her? Can she act? Open up, for the love o'Mike. On the level, what has she got?"

"Down at the ranch, Bud," said Mortimer. "I'm taking no chances. She remains veiled and under close guard, until we're ready to shoot. She's different, see? I don't want her devoured by the vultures of Hollywood. She's as pure as a little flower growing on a hillside of her native Erin, as sweet as a wild Irish rose. I tell you, brother, she's the original bit of Heaven that the angel found in that song that sold ten million copies."

By his eloquence and the tremendous power he put into his words, he worked them into an enthusiasm almost equal to his own. Tracy and Gunn forgot their inclination to revolt, in their excitement about this mysterious woman whose very arrival in the country had caused such a commotion. Even Luther got to his feet and mixed himself a highball.

"Let's go down to the ranch," he said. "I want to see her."

"Veiled, Myron," said Mortimer. "Only veiled. I swore an oath. We all swore an oath–Dafoe, Shultz and myself..."

"How am I going to write a story around her," said Gunn, "if I can't see her?"

"That's right, Jack," said Kent. "Guy has got to get acquainted with her before he can..."

"Nerts," said Mortimer. "He can feel the mystery of her, that wonderful quality she has, something beyond this earth, something from the region, where ever it is...I mean...Sam, when you're writing this story, you've to realise that you are writing the bible of love."

"Let's take Mervin and Joe along," said Luther.

"Yes, let's go, fellahs," Tracy said.

"Okay .with me," said Mortimer. "Let's go get Mervin and Joe."

"Yes. Let's get Mervin and Joe," said Kent. "Then we can sit around down at the ranch and discuss production."

"Fine," said Gunn. "Let's get Mervin and Joe."

For fully half an hour, they stood around, now terribly excited, drinking highballs and encouraging one another to set forth in search of Mervin and Joe.

And then, finally, all slightly intoxicated, they left the Greek temple and got into their cars and drove at a furious pace out to Beverley Hills, where the rolling, parched uplands were studded with the exotic palaces of screen stars and producers. They halted at an hotel that rose to a height of fourteen stories. They entered and were whisked up in an elevator to an apartment on the tenth floor, where they found two men comfortably seated in their underwear at a table that was littered with telegrams.

One was Mervin Clapp, the sales manager of World Films, a tall, handsome man, with a slightly protruding stomach and a scar on his right cheek. The other was Joe Boloni, publicity manager for World Films, a crude-looking man, with enormous ears and nose. His face was pockmarked. He and Mervin both looked very cross.

"Some goddam fool having a game," Mervin said, as the party entered. "Was it you, Roger? Just about your line."

"What game?" said Kent.

"All from the same dame," said Mervin, pointing to the pile of telegrams. "A lot of hooey. Have to open them for fear one might be important. Every quarter of an hour."

"Yeah," said Joe. "Some smart guy…'Darling, I can't take it' …What the hell? One might be genuine, see?"

"Well!" said Tracy. "What else do you guys know?"

"Nothing," said Mervin, "only this sudden mobilisation order. Had to take the first plane out from New York, Joe an' me. Where did you locate this dame you're tryin' to sell us, Jack? What she got that makes 'em all go loco?"

"Everything, Mervin," said Mortimer, with the air of a man imparting a tremendous secret. "I'm telling you she's the exact commodity this industry has been aching to buy…"

"Say, Mervin," said Joe gloomily, "how many of 'em have we seen go like that?"

"It gets them all," said Mervin in an equally gloomy tone. "But we got to pay the penalty trying to sell the … "

"You guys think I'm cuckoo?" cried Mortimer.

"Why not read the … ?"

"For two hundred grand you can buy enough publicity," said Joe, "to make the public believe a Hottentot broad is Lady Godiva."

"Stop grousin', you guys," said Luther. "We got to talk

business."

"Swell business you're goin' to get outa *The Emigrant*," said Joe savagely. "It won't gross fifty grand."

"Forget it," said Mortimer. "*The Emigrant* is on the shelf. We're right up another street."

"Thank God for that," said Mervin and Joe together.

"Let's have a drink," said Kent, "before we go out to the ranch."

"What ranch?" said Mervin. "I'm goin' on no party, I want to take a nap after that air trip."

"This is no party," said Mortimer. "We're going to see Angela Devlin." Neither Mervin nor Joe showed any enthusiasm.

"She might do something with Jerome Broadbent," Mervin said. "Co-starred with Broadbent she might get across. We're lapping up the gravy right now on his new picture. He gets the dames, that guy."

There was a knock at the door and Mervin said:

"Guess that's Annie. Step right in."

A beautiful girl with platinum blonde hair entered the room. She glanced around the room with a most charming smile and then crossed over to Mervin, who went on opening telegrams without rising. He merely reached out his hand towards her and drawled :

"Things breaking right for you, Annie?"

"Uh-uh," the girl said.

"Just step into my room, got to finish opening these ... " Mervin said. "Just be with yuh in a minute."

"Uh-uh," the girl said.

She moved gracefully towards a door that led into another room. She wore an exquisite white dress and her carriage was that of a well-bred woman. Her manner was delightfully polite and pleasant. But she seemed to be completely devoid of personality and of facial expression. Just as if she had been made in a factory, to measure. None of the other men took any notice whatsoever of her.

"Let's get going," Gunn said. "Let's go out to the ranch."

"Come on, Mervin," Kent said. "Get dressed. Let's get going, Joe."

"Come on," said Tracy. "Let's go to the ranch."

"Can't you see it?" said Mortimer. "With Broadbent playing up to her, it's a knock out, no matter how you look at it. That guy is smooth. It's a ten million dollar combination."

"What's it called?" Joe said, getting to his feet and stretching himself. "Guess that's the lot, Mervin. What's the new picture called?"

"*The Veiled Goddess*," Mortimer said. "Come, let's get going."

Gunn sat down, stared into his highball and muttered: "Seven years. I can hardly remember when I was alive. I can't stand being sane any longer. Get drunk. Only thing to do."

He emptied his glass and went to get another drink.

CHAPTER XXI

B Y THE TIME THE SEVEN MEN WERE ready to set forth, they were all more than slightly intoxicated. Mortimer had drunk very little and he was merely intoxicated by his own enthusiasm. But he saw to it that the others all drank a good deal. It was vital to his plans that these six men should "be lifted up, hit hard against the ground and socked into unconsciousness" when they met Angela. A state of slight intoxication, even more than two hundred thousand dollars' worth of publicity, can turn a Hottentot lady into a Lady Godiva.

Gunn was the only man that made him nervous. And Gunn, who was to write the script for *The Veiled Goddess* was, for the moment, important to his plans. After a sleepless night, what he had drunk during the afternoon affected Gunn to such an extent that he fell asleep in the car on the way to the ranch. Mortimer, who was sitting beside him, thought:

"Better wake him up and keep him awake."

He roused Gunn, who opened his eyes and said wildly:

"It's impossible for me to give you an opinion on the screen possibilities of Hamlet by reading a synopsis of the play. The book is the thing. You must read the book and see for yourself …"

"How do you feel?" said Mortimer. "Sit up and let the fresh air…"

"I feel ill," said Gunn. "Was I asleep? I was apparently dreaming about a story conference. Somebody wanted to adapt Hamlet for the screen and had a synopsis made."

"Sorry for waking you up," said Mortimer, "but I want to talk to you about your new story."

"What story? " said Gunn.

"*The Veiled Goddess*," said Mortimer. "It's like this. This is the slant you must get."

"The greatest punishment in Hell must be satiety," said Gunn irrelevantly. "Christian saints imagined they were punishing themselves by denying satisfaction to their passions, by fasting and masochism, but the opposite is really the truth. If they really wanted to punish themselves, they would have given free reign to their passions. Money, luxury and poverty of spirit are far more painful than hair shirts and fasting. We are poor in spirit. What veiled goddess are you talking about? There can be no such thing. You and I have torn aside every veil."

"Now, listen," said Mortimer, paying no attention to this outburst, "the idea of the veil is this … "

"It's slogan," said Gunn. "We live on slogans. Why bother to tell me? I know the whole formula. I could write *The Veiled Goddess* without pausing to think. There is only one formula. The boy gets the girl."

"But listen … " said Mortimer.

"Oh! All right," said Gunn. "I'm listening. You mean you have a variation on the theme. A new slant?"

He laughed mockingly. Mortimer's sloe-black eyes got vicious for a moment. Then he leaned back, sighed and said gently:

"Well! I guess I've got to get another writer, that's all. Maybe you've been too long in Hollywood, Sam."

Gunn's manner immediately changed.

"I'm sorry, Jack. I've been up all night. My nerves are on edge. I worked very hard on the script of *The Emigrant*. I just need a night's sleep and then I can tackle *The Veiled Goddess*. It's a good title. A really good, fetching title."

"I know how to make them all toe the line," said Mortimer to himself with pleasure.

"This is something altogether different, son," he whispered. "This industry has gone stale and it needs something new, something vital that we're going to give it now, a blood transfusion that's going to give it back its youth. You have a mission to humanity, when you start in on this script, Sam, and I'm going to tell you what it is. The whole world is sick right now. Men, women and children are starving in the midst of plenty..."

Gunn closed his eyes and shuddered, as Mortimer continued to disclose "his slant." In the meantime, the car had reached the summit of a mountain and the Pacific Ocean came into view, stretching away to the western horizon. The shores of the ocean were lined with automobiles as far as the eye could reach. Hot-dog stands, advertisements, oil-well pumps and beach houses appeared here and there among the automobiles. The whole scene was painted by the glory of the Californian sunset.

"Right now," said Mortimer, "over the whole world, the main question that occupies the mind of humanity is the industrial depression and how to escape from it. Politics, economics and war have been tried as a means of escape from it, and they have all failed. Now we offer the world a means of escape through the gospel of love."

With his eyes closed, Gunn gritted his teeth and muttered to himself:

"My God! My God! Why hast Thou forsaken me?"

The car suddenly turned aside from the main road and rushed into a valley, which contained a polo field and Mr. Mortimer's ranch, as the magnate continued:

"We are going to offer the world, through the medium of Angela Devlin, a conception of love that has been forgotten in the rush to make money; the pure love that moves mountains and softens the heart of avarice and turns the sword into a ploughshare, that's going to make possible the Christian doctrine to love thy neighbour as thyself, that's going to make capital and labour end their historic quarrel and join hands in peace and goodwill. Here's how it's going to be done."

"I know, I know," said Gunn cynically. "Jerome Broadbent plays the part either of a dictator or the head of a giant corporation and he's on the point of..."

"That's the idea," said Mortimer. "You snapped right into it, just as I thought you would. Swell!"

At that moment they drew up before the ranch gates.

CHAPTER XXII

RANCH IS DERIVED FROM THE SPANISH WORD *rancho*, which means farm in our language. In Hollywood, however, it has no such meaning, although, as in the case of Mr. Mortimer's ranch, a charming attempt is sometimes made to introduce farming symbols into the furnishing of such suburban villas as are called ranches. In the case of Mr. Mortimer's villa, that effect was achieved by an artificial cow, which stood within the gates.

The artificial cow was a plaster replica of the famous animal called "Colorado Nellie," which played one of the chief roles in the great film of the pioneer days, a production called *Let 'Em All Come, Buddy*. It grossed two and a half millions, which was a record for those early days. Colorado Nellie became a national figure as the result of its success. When she died, a short time afterwards, of a surfeit of pop-corn curiously enough, her corpse received what would have been called divine honours in Ancient Roman days. It was eaten at a public banquet, which was attended by all the most important people at that moment in the motion-picture industry, including the famous dog "Pit-

Pat-Pit," who drew the greatest laugh of the evening by growling out the opening bar of "Way Down upon the Swannee River," while gnawing Colorado Nellie's hip bone. It was at this banquet that the plaster replica of Colorado Nellie was auctioned in aid of the dead cow's human dependants. Mortimer purchased it for the sum of ten thousand dollars. Now it stood to the right of the entrance gates, holding out its mouth towards a bag of pop-corn that was being offered to it by a figure in the uniform of a cowboy. Both the pop-corn and the cowboy were also cast in plaster.

In front of the gates there was a trap door and when the first car passed over this door an electric bell began to ring with a terrific clatter. The gates swung open, as if in answer to this bell, and as it did, four mastiffs, housed in kennels to the left of the drive, rushed forward to the ends of their chains. They were, however, only allowed to reach the border of the drive, where they bayed savagely, hauling at their chains. They had been trained back to their original savagery, by a Hindoo expert, from the comatose idiocy with which we associate them in western Europe.

The grounds were considerable and some attempt had been made to model them on the Alcazar Gardens in Seville. The house itself was surrounded by a high wall and there was still another gate, through ,which they passed, between two uniformed and scowling giants, each of them armed with a Thompson sub-machine-gun.

"Like a goddam fortress," said Gunn.

"Brother," said Mortimer, "while I have a ten million dollar property in Angela on these premises, I'm taking no chances with kidnappers."

Immediately within these gates, in the courtyard of the ranch-house, there was a cock-tail bar, made like a Chinese pagoda, where visitors could relax and get into a good humour on entering. The pagoda was reminiscent of one of Mortimer's great successes, a thriller called *The Sword of Chang Li*. The whole party dismounted from their cars by this pagoda. The cars were seized by lackeys, dressed in the uniform of Swiss Guards, and whisked away to a garage on the right. The garage was concealed within a grove of English hawthorn bushes, grown to an enormous size in the artificial Californian soil. They had been imported and kept continually in flower, at enormous expense, by an expert Scottish horticulturalist.

"Goddam lot o' nonsense," said Tracy, as they stood by the circular bar of the pagoda, drinking old-fashioned cock-tails. "Wasting his money on this truck. Whenever I come into this dump I get a headache. Why can't the guy be natural?"

Mortimer had left them at the bar and he had run ahead along the bank of a beautiful swimming-pool, which occupied most of the courtyard. Now he waved to them from the terrace on the opposite side of the pool. The main part of the farm-house was on that side. It was a two-storied edifice, done partly in the adobe of Indian pueblos and partly in the English Tudor style, with mahogany beams that had come from the southern part of Mexico. The terrace, however, was copied from a house built in Jamaica by an Italian that had married an English planter.

"Soon as you're ready," Mortimer called to them.

"Yeah," Luther said, "he's cuckoo, wasting all that money on a love nest."

"Parks out here with his dames?" Mervin asked. "What's his wife say?"

"She doesn't care," said Kent, "long as she gets her dough."

"What's real estate worth around here?" said Joe.

"It's horrible to think," said Gunn, "that even human vulgarity is degenerating. When one considers what a Roman villa must have been like on the African coast during the period of the Pax Longa, compared to this monstrosity."

"Aw!" said Tracy. "Forget you were born in Boston."

"I dare say," said Gunn, "that the Romans were just as boringly vulgar as the modern bourgeois."

"I don't suppose this whole outfit," said Joe, "would collect more than a hundred grand if it was thrown on the market right now and it musta cost anything up to a million. That's the worst o' these curios. They ain't good investments."

"Drink up, lads," said Tracy. "I'm dyin' to see this dame."

"Come on, fellahs," said Mortimer excitedly from the terrace.

They walked around the pool and then followed Mortimer on to the terrace. Then they went through a Roman arch into a vast drawing-room, which was astonishingly furnished in the Persian manner. At least, the furniture had been sold to Mortimer as the property of the Emir of Bokhara, who disposed of it after being overthrown and expelled from his palace by the Bolsheviks. At the far end of the drawing-room there was an alcove containing a divan, supposed to be that of the deposed Emir. Angela was seated on this divan, surrounded by three men, one of whom was Dafoe. She was wearing a Persian dress stiff with gold, and appeared to be quite dazed; in fact, in a stupor.

"I'll be goddamned," said Tracy. "He's gone an' done it, just as I thought he would."

"Now what?" said Mortimer nervously. "What's wrong now, pappy?"

"You went over to Ireland," said Tracy angrily, "to get something fresh and unspoilt and then you start in at once to

148

fix her up as a lifeless doll, after the Hollywood model."

"Sure thing," said Gunn. "He's fixed her. My God! What a sacrilege! She's as beautiful as a Shakespeare sonnet."

"Who are those guys?" said Tracy, pointing to the two strangers.

Dafoe signed to the two strange men and they slipped out of the alcove, through a small door at the side.

"They are helping Larry," said Mortimer.

"What at?" said Tracy, becoming more and more angry. "Destroying the girl?"

"Take it easy, Bud," said Luther. "She looks swell to me."

"She's got something all right," Mervin said.

"Yeah," whispered Joe. "She's got the whole works."

"This goddam Persian costume," Tracy grumbled. "I expected to see an innocent Irish girl."

"Ha, ha, ha," cackled Dafoe. "Bud can only see life through a heap of sackcloth and ashes."

"Oh! Yeah?" said Tracy. "I'll take no wisecracks from you."

"Aw! Come on, fellahs," said Mortimer appealingly. "What's Angela goin' to think? Can't you guys keep quiet an' step right up and get acquainted with her? Is that the way to behave?"

It was all very strange, the way they had stood at a distance from the divan, staring at Angela and passing remarks about her in loud voices, in her hearing, just as if she were a slave in a market-place. Nor did she seem to take any notice of them. There was something extraordinary the matter with her. It was not her exotic costume, nor the studio paint with which her face was coated (instead of a veil and much more concealing than a veil), but something in her attitude and expression that was extraordinary and even terrifying. In her strange costume, she looked even more beautiful than before, but her eyes were unnaturally bright and she seemed to be in a trance. It was something that Dafoe had given her. Now when the men approached her and shook hands, one by one, she just smiled on them, apparently without comprehension of who they were and why they had come to see her. At the same time, the magnetism of her personality had definitely increased, for they were all overwhelmed by contact with her. Strangely enough, Gunn was affected most of all, perhaps because he was the most sensitive and neurotic among them.

"Well!" said Mortimer, delighted by the effect she had produced. He had been really nervous about how they were going to receive her. "What do you think, Bud? Ain't she wonderful?"

"I'll say she is," muttered Tracy. "Only I don't see...I mean these Persian rags and this perfume...why, this room is like a perfumery or a dope den."

"Tell these guys, Larry," said Mortimer, "what we are trying to do. Larry has a new slant, see? Me an' him are tryin' out a new technique for getting a star ready for the screen."

"It's the crystallisation of creative energy," said Dafoe with a mysterious smile. "I figure it this way. Many girls have appeared in Hollywood with natural acting ability, but none of them have been able to change completely, in response to the character they are called on to play, in the way that Angela does. Just now she is a Persian princess, simply because she is wearing those clothes. That, however, does not mean that she is what Tracy calls fixed. To fix is to change from the natural to something artificial. If you wish, I'm going to show her to you as an Irish street singer."

"Go ahead," said Tracy. "That's how I want to see her."

Dafoe, smiling in a manner that suggested he was having a game with these slightly drunken men, gave Angela his arm and marched out of the room with her, through the same door as the two strangers.

"Well!" said Mortimer. "We've got it in the bag, boys. Can't you guys see now why she has caused this sensation? Sam, if you don't write a knock-out around her, you're a moron."

"She's wonderful," said Gunn. "She's really wonderful!"

A Filipino servant brought them a tray of drinks, while another wheeled into the room a table that was while they shouted at one another excitedly about Angela, using adjectives that have not yet appeared in any known dictionary. Even Tracy was now as excited as the rest. And then Dafoe appeared, leading Angela by the hand. Silence fell at once on the gathering, except for some whispered exclamations of awe. Mortimer himself stared at her with open mouth, hardly able to believe that this exquisite creature was the same person he had seen sporting on the grass in a wood near Ballymorguttery.

"That man is an artist and no doubt about it," he said to himself. "He thinks of everything. I'm sittin' pretty, as long as he plays ball with me."

Angela was dressed as an Irish peasant girl, but in clothes of a quality that no Irish girl ever wore except on the stage. Her shawl, that covered her whole body except her face and her bare legs, was an exquisite creation, bought by Dafoe in London. Her face was "done up" differently from what it was when she was dressed as a Persian princess. Now it gave her the correct Irish expression of excruciating sadness and innocent wonder. Her cheeks looked pinched, as if from hunger. Her lips drooped slightly, as in fear of an imminent catastrophe. Her attitude was one of submission, humility, modesty and gentleness. And yet she retained her power of exciting whoever looked upon her.

"Sing for the gentlemen," said Dafoe.

"Give us 'Bantry Bay'," said Tracy, with tears flowing down

his cheeks.

When intoxicated, he recovered the sentimentality of his Irish ancestors. Angela obediently threw back her shawl from the crown of her head, disclosing her magnificent red-gold hair. She began to sing in a voice of exquisite quality. The whole company was in tears almost at once. And when she had finished, Dafoe led her at once out of the room, through the side door.

"What d'you think?" whispered Mortimer. "Was I right, Bud?"

Tracy could not speak, but he went over to Mortimer and kissed him fervently on both cheeks.

"*The Veiled Goddess*," Luther said. "It's a knockout. We're behind it to the last dollar."

"That goes for me," Mervin said. "This is something that is going to take the industry by the snout and put it permanently on the hook."

"Say, give me a free hand," Gunn said, "and I'll write a script..."

"My God, you'd better," Kent said, "or I'll murder you. This is the biggest opportunity..."

"It's a landmark in human history," Mortimer said in a shrill voice. "We're going to hand out the gospel of human salvation. The goddess of love and of purity, giving voice to the solution of the world's economic troubles. Let's sit around, boys, and straighten this thing out while we're hot for it. Sit around."

They sat around the table and began to draw up plans for the scenario of *The Veiled Goddess*, starring Angela Devlin.

CHAPTER XXIII

O N ARRIVING AT THE INTERNATIONAL HOTEL, Carey had gone to bed. He slept until late in the afternoon. He was awakened by the ringing of the telephone at his bedside. When he picked up the telephone, a man's voice said:

"That Mr. Brian Carey?"

"Speaking."

"This is Puff Green of the Pacific Eagle. Could I come up to see you?" .

"Well! As a matter of fact..." began Carey.

"Okay," said the voice. "I'll be right up."

Carey barely had time to get out of bed and in to his dressing-gown, when Mr. Puff Green arrived at his apartment. He was a tall, very thin man, with a most gloomy and cynical expression, exactly the opposite of Mr. Cooney. Judging from the way he saluted Carey and the limp way he offered his hand, it seemed that meeting the writer was a catastrophe of major importance for him. Indeed, he appeared to be a man of no ability, or personality whatsoever. But one must never take the book by the cover, and in Mr. Green's case it would be a very grave mistake indeed.

In his early manhood, he had been a member of a gang of robbers, operating in a Middle Western city, under the protection of the municipal administration. The city's government suffered a change and Mr. Green's gang had to suspend operations, as the new administration demanded such an exorbitant sum from the gang for protection as would leave only a very small margin of profit on its criminal undertakings. Then Mr. Green came to Hollywood, where he found employment as the bodyguard for one of the most prominent male stars. The star died suddenly from a surfeit of wood alcohol and Mr. Green was left again without employment. In the meantime, however, the unscrupulous Green had learned a great deal about the private life of prominent film people, material that he embodied in a scandalous book called *I Strip the Stars*. It delighted Hollywood, instead of infuriating as might be supposed, and it gave Puff Green a new profession as sort of official detractor in the celluloid city. He was now earning a large salary on the staff of the *Pacific Eagle*, while he now and again contributed to fan magazines and ghosted for magnates, who wished to get publicity by attacking something or other.

"Gee!" said this gloomy man, after he had shaken hands with Carey. "I'm sorry to see you here."

"Why?" said Carey.

Green dropped into a chair, crossed his long, thin legs and shot a cigarette from a packet with a nick of his second finger and thumb.

"You've been taken for a ride, kid," said Mr. Green.

"How do you mean?" said Carey nervously.

"You came out here with Jack Mortimer and this new star Angela Devlin?" said Green. "Am I right? Okay! They brought you over here in connection with your book *The Emigrant*, which was to be Miss Devlin's first medium? That right?"

"Yes," said Carey. "That's right."

Green casually cracked a match against his thumb nail and said:

"Well! It's on the shelf."

Then he coolly lit his cigarette and blew out a column of smoke.

"It's on the shelf right now, kid," he added.

"You mean..." began Carey.

"Why, sure," said Green. "That's exactly what I mean. Mortimer handed a statement to the Press this afternoon saying that something called *The Veiled Goddess* was going to be Miss Devlin's first picture."

"The what?" cried Carey. "He's not going to do *The Emigrant*? But I'm under contract to..."

"Take it easy, kid," said Green. "Gee! I'm sorry to see them take a man like you for a ride. That's Hollywood all over. They brought you out here as a kind of an advertisement for this new star. Now that they've got her before the public they have no further use for you. However, I've got a proposition to make to you. I know a way you can get even with them. Listen, kid. Get dressed and we'll take a little walk."

"Oh!" said Carey. "I see it all now."

What exactly there was to see was not at all apparent to his mind, but he felt that he had been gravely injured and insulted in some way. A murderous hatred of Mortimer, as the man who had insulted and injured him, resulted from this conviction. As he dressed hurriedly, he swore vengeance, not only on Mortimer, but also on Dafoe, by whom he felt that he had also been tricked.

"By God! I'll kill them both," he said to himself.

However, when he had finished dressing, he suddenly

thought:

"Better be careful. Suppose this fellow is tricking me, too."

This he found a good excuse for postponing the murder of his two enemies. Curiously enough, not a thought of Angela entered his mind at this moment. But is it curious? The love instinct in the intellectual is always subservient to that stronger form of egoism which is called the creative instinct. After all, it is far harder to write a book than to make a child.

"Well! Let's go," said Green, when Carey appeared.

"We'll take a little walk and discuss this business."

The man's calm, cynical tone irritated Carey and made him still more suspicious.

"Can't we discuss it here?" he said.

"I hate this dump," said Green. "I know a little place where we can be quiet."

Realising that he was not alone in his peculiar profession he wanted to get Carey out of the hotel before his rivals began to come after their prey.

"Very well," said Carey.

"I'll hear what he has to say, in any case," he thought.

They left the hotel, got into Green's car and drove down to a tavern on the Sunset Boulevard. On the way, Green said:

"Publicity is the life and soul of this industry right now, if you play your cards properly, you can get into the news in a big way and, by so doing, you automatically get the opportunity of collecting some big dough. Then you can sail back to Europe with your head in the air."

"Really?" said Carey.

"Why, sure," said Green. "This place is lousy with dough and if a guy is clever, especially with a reputation like you've got, it's dead easy picking it up. What salary did Mortimer pay you?"

"But I'm still under contract to him," said Carey. "Why do you say did?"

"Looks to me," said Green, "as if you're no longer under contract. However, I'm not trying to rush you into anything. You can find that out to-morrow. I'm merely trying to tell you what to do, in case you find yourself without a job to-morrow. And I'll tell the world that you're sittin' pretty if you follow my advice. Boy! And how!"

He parked the car and they walked to a tavern called Zum Brauhaus. It was anything but the quiet place which Green had claimed it to be. Indeed, it was infernally noisy, but entirely in keeping with the character of that strange city. A gregarious person, finding himself in a strange town or village, naturally goes to a café, or bar of some sort, a tavern, hostelry, dram-shop, inn, pot-house, or what not; in a word, he seeks out the idlers of the place, those who are taking their ease with their friends, or taking their ease while on the look-out for a new acquaintance with whom they may engage in conversation. The more civilised the country, at least from our point of view, the more easily does the stranger accommodate himself, since the chief objective of civilisation is to enable the citizen to take his ease. In fact, France, which is the paradise of the civilised person, arranges its life around the café; so that the stranger in France, unless he be a very rude fellow indeed, feels himself immediately at his ease, as soon as he seats himself at table in a *débit*, no matter how humble, and calls for a glass of one of the country's multitudinous vintages. He is immediately brought into polite contact with the good woman or the good man who waits on him, and the life of the neighbourhood gently insinuates itself into the scope of his consciousness and he becomes at one with the wisdom and subtlety of that delightful country. "Ah!" he says to himself. "How good it is to be here!

How restful! How sane! How well ordered!" To such a café, *débit*, dram-shop, tavern, or inn, this hostelry called Zum Brauhaus offered a horrible contrast.

An artificial vine-tree of enormous proportions (it was really made of camouflaged ferro-concrete) formed the front of the building, and among the clusters of artificial grapes that hung from its boughs, there were cardboard figures, representing artificial waiters offering steins of artificial beer. They passed through a doorway, situated in the trunk of this artificial tree, into a hall that was partly in darkness and resembled a clearing in a wood from which the light of day has been almost shut out by the interlacing foliage overhead. Artificial trees grew thickly about this hall, not only vine-trees, but fig-trees, oaks, firs, and palms. Having groped their way to a table under a palm-tree, they sat down. A waiter approached them from around the corner of an oak-tree. He wore Bavarian costume, but he was undoubtedly a Jew with a dash of Negro blood.

"Two steins of Pilsner," Mr. Green said.

The waiter immediately began to sing. He sang his way out of the room and then he sang his way back again. Having delivered the beer, he climbed a little way into the oak-tree, where he perched on a branch and continued to sing.

"What's the idea?" said Carey. "Why does he go on bawling like that?"

"He's a singing waiter," said Mr. Green.

"Can't we persuade him to stop?" said Carey.

"He'd get sore," said Green. "This place is famous for its singing waiters."

"Thought you said this was a quiet place," grumbled Carey.

"The more noise there is," said Mr. Green, "the less likelihood there is of my being overheard. See? Hollywood is the goddamnedest place. There are thirty-five thousand people employed in this industry and the majority of them are pretty smart. They've got everything but new ideas. That's why, if a guy gets a new idea, he puts his mouth under lock and key until he's sold it. And I'll tell the world, I don't want anybody listening in on my big idea until I've sold it. It's like this. This dame, Angela Devlin, is ... "

"I beg your pardon," said Carey angrily.

"Now what?" said Green.

"She's not a dame," said Carey insolently. "At least, I dislike that word."

"Sorry," said Green, with a smile. "I forgot you're in love with her."

"Who told you?" said Carey, getting still more angry.

"Christ sake," said Green, "don't get shirty. It's in all the papers. Ain't that why Mortimer was able to persuade you to quit London and come to Hollywood?"

"Nonsense," said Carey. "I left London to come to Hollywood, to work on the scenario of my book *The Emigrant*."

"Then where does Angela Devlin come into the story?" said Green, pretending to be mystified.

"I'm not a gossip-monger," said Carey, "and, in any case, I don't like your attitude."

"Aw! Forget it," said Green.

"I don't like this place," said Carey, getting to his feet, "and I don't like you."

"Aw! Come on," said Green, also rising. "You're just in a state of nerves. Listen."

He threw some money on the table and followed Carey out of the tavern. He caught him by the arm on the pavement and said earnestly:

"Can't you listen and have sense. I'm just trying to help you and you fly at me for no reason at all. Are you let those guys make a sucker out of you? What have you got to hide?"

"I've got nothing to hide," shouted Carey.

"I'm glad of that," said Green. "A man needn't be ashamed of being in love with a beautiful girl."

"Who said I was ashamed of it?" said Carey. "I'm ashamed of nothing."

"I'm trying to help her as well as you," said Green. "Can't you have sense and listen to what I'm going to tell you. I have a proposition that can put thousands of bucks in your pocket, just as simple as falling off a log. Thousands of dollars for nothing. Good God, man, don't be a fool."

"Thousands of dollars," said Carey. "How?"

"Let's go and eat," said Green. "A man can think better with a good feed under his belt."

They got into his car once more and drove to a restaurant, where they sat in an alcove and ordered dinner. Green insisted on being the host and ordered champagne, together with the most expensive food that the place offered. It was, at the moment, one of the most fashionable restaurants in Hollywood and it was crowded with celebrities. Carey was awed, in spite of himself, by his environment and he began to be awed by Green, because the latter was by no means awed. In fact, during the meal, he suddenly changed his tactics and avoided discussing the important proposition, which he had been so eager to put forward in Zum Brauhaus. He kept up a running commentary on the other diners instead. In this way, of course, he excited Carey's interest in his mysterious proposition.

"See that guy over there?" he would say. He mentioned the name of a prominent male star and added:

"That simple-minded little bastard gets four grand a week, and just think of it, two years ago he was slingin' hash. Doesn't it make you sore? See the little dame two tables down from us?

The platinum blonde. Her legs are insured for two hundred grand. Lucky break for her she's got those legs. From the neck up she's not worth a dime. There's Jerome Broadbent. He's going to play opposite Angela Devlin in…"

"Where?" said Carey excitedly. "Which is Broadbent?"

Green indicated a dapper little man, with an anæmic face and a charming smile. He was twirling a flower between his fingers and whispering to a beautiful, dark-haired girl, who looked up at him in an adoring fashion. Carey got furiously jealous of the man and turned to Green.

"What was the proposition you were talking about?" he said.

Already he could see Angela in the dapper little fellow's arms and he was eager to do anything in his power in order to prevent that happening.

"Not now," whispered Green. "We'll go somewhere else and talk as soon as we finish dinner. There's plenty of time. This is no place to talk about anything private. In Hollywood you can't be too careful. These guys stop at nothing."

"I don't give a damn about them," said Carey.

After several glasses of champagne he felt contemptuous of anything "these guys" could do to him.

He had in his pocket about twelve hundred dollars, all that remained of his fee for the screen rights of The Emigrant and of the salary he had hitherto received. The possession of this money, added to the champagne, gave him a false optimism and vicious desire to have revenge. On whom? He did not exactly know. Green, however, seemed to be getting more and more cautious. He absolutely refused to utter a word about his proposition, until they had left the restaurant and drove to a night-club in Beverley Hills.

"That guy Broadbent," he said, "gives me a pain in the

neck, trying to come that retired English colonel stuff. Goddam easy here in Hollywood, where you get every crook from Europe calling himself count, duke, lord and God knows what else. He can't put anything over on me, though. No, sirree. I know he was a stable boy back home in England. That's the guy that's going to play opposite to Angela Devlin. She must be a swell kid and I'm sorry to see her get into the clutches of that guy Broadbent. He treats them badly. She'll last no more than a year and then she'll take the K.O. like the rest. I've seen 'em all come and go. Hollywood just sucks them dry. Writers, actors, actresses, they're all sucked dry and thrown in the ash-can. Guys like Mortimer are the only wise birds here."

"Let's drive out to this ranch of Mortimer's," said Carey, in a frenzy of rage. "I want to talk to Angela."

"Nope" said Green. "Christ sake, that joint is a fortress. You couldn't get within rifle range of it, not if I know anything. Keep your shirt on and listen to what I have to say. There's only one way to fight these birds. If you want to get the girl out of his clutches, you got to be as cute as he is ."

"I'm not afraid of him," said Carey.

They entered "The Golden Unicorn," a large nightclub, with a bar, a restaurant and a gambling-room. It was just as crowded as the restaurant by all manner of celebrity. At the bar, Carey continued to drink heavily. Then he paid a visit to the gambling-room and lost all his twelve hundred dollars in a short while. Then he sat down at a table in the restaurant, maudlinly drunk and despondent over the loss of his money, and began to tell Green about his love for Angela.

"That's all right, kid," said Green. "You'll be all right. I'll see that you get a break. Will you do what I tell you?"

"I'll do anything you say," said Carey.

"Okay," said Green. "I'll see that you get a break. You leave it to me. You and I, we're going to put the skids under that guy with the monocle. Take it from me, we're going to deliver a broadside that'll rock that guy to his heels. You come along and stay at my apartment. Don't you worry about anything. I know this town."

CHAPTER XXIV

AT TWO O'CLOCK IN THE MORNING, Angela suddenly awoke and began to scream. She had been having a nightmare, during which she had seen Dafoe, smiling in an evil way, approaching her with a glass that contained poison. Now that she was awake, she felt terribly sick and afraid. Her tongue was parched. She had a headache and a horrible feeling in her stomach. She turned on the light over her bed and looked around the room. Then she continued to scream. She remembered how Dafoe had given her something to drink that afternoon, when she had got lonely and begun to cry. She could not remember anything since then.

The door opened and Dafoe came into the room, followed by Mortimer.

"Don't come near me," screamed Angela.

Then she hid under the bedclothes and shivered, holding her breath.

"What's the matter, kid?" said Mortimer, approaching the bed. "Got a pain?"

Angela removed the clothes and cried:

"Send him away. I don't want him to come near me."

"Send who away?" said Mortimer.

"Him," said Angela, pointing at Dafoe. "I'm afraid of him."

Mortimer turned on Dafoe angrily and said:

"What've you been up to? Huh?"

"He poisoned me," screamed Angela.

"I just gave her a sleeping-draught," said Dafoe. "She felt lonely and couldn't go to sleep, so I gave her a sleeping-draught this afternoon."

"It was poison," wailed Angela.

"Don't worry, kid," said Mortimer.

"Let me out of here," said Angela hysterically. "I don't want to stay here. I want to go home. Where is Brian? I want to see him."

Mortimer looked at Dafoe and pursed up his lips.

"Now, can you beat that?" he said. He turned to Angela and said soothingly: "What do you want to see him for? Ain't I treating you right?"

"I want to go home," wailed Angela, becoming more and more hysterical, so that her voice became almost a whisper. "I'm afraid here. You're keeping me here against my will. I'll take the law of you. Oh! I'm sick. I want a doctor."

Mortimer tried to put his arms around her to soothe her, but she clawed at him and hid herself once more under the clothes.

"Gee!" said Mortimer. "What are we going to do now?"

"Send her a doctor," said Dafoe.

"What's that?" said Mortimer.

"Just a moment," said Dafoe.

He beckoned to Mortimer and they whispered together outside the bedroom door.

"I don't like it," said Mortimer. "Gee! I'm in a nice fix if she..."

"Please yourself," said Dafoe. "It's just nerves. How is she to know? Let me handle it."

"Okay!" said Mortimer still more nervously. "You handle it, but for the love o' Mike be careful. Just when I'm all set for the biggest sensation of my career, I don't want to have the whole thing ruined by any…"

"Leave it to me," said Dafoe.

"I think I'm leaving too much to you," said Mortimer.

"Very well, then," said Dafoe casually. "I step out of it."

"What was that sleeping-draught you gave her?" said Mortimer still more suspiciously. "What dirty work are you up to? Are you double-crossing me? If I thought you were I'd…"

"One thing at a time," said Dafoe. "We must calm her down first and then you can say what you want, or do anything you please, but you must listen to my side of the argument."

The two men stared at one another and then Mortimer said:

"I'd hate to see inside your soul, Larry, if you've got one."

"Ha, ha, ha," cackled Dafoe. "At a late hour, you are always inclined to become melodramatic."

"None o' that," said Mortimer. "I'll be waiting for you in my room. I'm expecting a call."

He went into his own bedroom and threw himself down on his bed, with his hands clasped under his head. His brain was in a ferment. All his life, since he first began to sell newspapers on the streets of New York, he had gambled recklessly with fortune, but never before had he taken such a chance as this, to pick up an unknown girl in an Irish village and try to force the world into accepting her as the queen of screen stars ; indeed, as something more than a screen star, as a goddess of love, with a message for mankind, something divine. So far his bluff had worked, to an extent that now terrified him. What if fortune had been playing him a trick, drawing him on to these heights, so that his fall would be all the more terrible? Suppose this girl whom he had picked up should prove to be an utter failure, interesting enough as a simple country girl, physically exciting, but utterly devoid of the capacity for "standing the racket" of the screen. That would be ruin, suicide, annihilation. He was almost in tears, and beads of sweat stood out on his forehead. Then the telephone rang at his bedside. He picked up the instrument.

"This is Puff," said the voice.

"Well?" said Mortimer, making a great effort to speak in his usual manner of addressing an inferior on business.

"I gave him the works all right," said Mr. Green's voice. "He's down at my apartment right now and I'm confident he'll sign his name to anything I get written for him. He'll ring you at your office eleven o'clock in the morning. You fire him and he'll be crazy enough for anything. The guy is easy. So long."

"So long," said Mortimer. "Good work, Puff. I'll be seein' yuh. So long."

He put down the instrument and put his hands through what remained of his hair.

"Gee!" he said aloud. "What am I doin'? Am I going crazy? Larry'll send me to the chair before he finishes. Why do I let that guy...?"

He was interrupted by a knock at the door. Dafoe entered.

"She's quite hopeless, I'm afraid," he said.

"What do you mean?" gasped Mortimer, sitting up.

"I sent Zog in to her," said Dafoe. "He'll give her some more of that sleeping-draught. She'll take it from him. He was a doctor in any case, an official one, back in Europe, so he knows the patter. But you have to make up your mind, here and now, to drop the idea of using her."

"What are you trying to tell me?" gasped Mortimer, almost

inarticulate. "Are you asking me to quit now, after getting the whole bunch so het up about her that they are going to gamble to the extent of... ?"

"I'm suggesting nothing of the kind," said Dafoe. "You know very well what I'm suggesting and there's no other way out. The girl is quite hopeless. Why, you don't even know whether she photographs well."

"God!" said Mortimer. "What a fool I've been! It was a hunch. I worked on my hunch."

"Your hunch is all right," said Dafoe, "if you do what I suggest. Superb acting ability, the figure, the appearance, everything. It's a coincidence that borders on the miraculous. I thought of it the very first time I caught sight of her at the Shelbourne Hotel in Dublin."

"But supposing we were caught napping?" said Mortimer, trembling with nervousness.

"Ridiculous," said Dafoe. "How is that going to happen? I thought you had more courage than that. You are not a man to funk taking a chance, especially as there is no other way out. Unless, of course, Angela were to die and you could say, 'So sorry, but it can't be helped.' "

"None o' that now," said Mortimer. "I won't have you say anything like that. I'm going through with this. Okay. If she is a flap, we have to try out your scheme. In the meantime..."

"In the meantime," said Dafoe merrily, "until you're ready to show the realisation of that figment of your imagination, known as Angela Devlin, to the public, Miss Bridget Murphy is going to go on taking sleeping-draughts."

"This suspense is going to kill me," Mortimer said.

CHAPTER XXV

A LITTLE BEFORE ELEVEN O'CLOCK ON THE following morning, Carey was awakened by Mr. Green.

"How the devil did I get here?" he said, looking round the room.

"Don't you remember?" said Green, with a laugh.

"You had a skinful all right. You'd better ring up Mortimer. He's been on the wire wanting to talk to you. Maybe he wants to do *The Emigrant* after all. You can never tell with these birds. They change their minds from one minute to another. Want me to get the number for you?"

"Oh! God!" said Carey, putting his head between his hands. "I feel really awful. Where were we last night?"

"Goddam costly night it was for you," said Green. "You must have lost over a thousand dollars. I tried to stop you but I couldn't."

This was, of course, untrue, as Green had encouraged him to play instead of trying to prevent him losing his money. In fact he deliberately directed Carey towards the Black Jack table, at which it was impossible to win, unless the dealer wished to encourage a sucker.

"All my money gone," said Carey with a shudder. Then he clutched at the straw of Mortimer having rung up. "Do you think he may have changed his mind about the film? In any case he has to pay me another week's salary. That's three thousand dollars. I can get home on that. I'm leaving this madhouse at once. Ugh! What a head!"

"What about Angela?" said Green, a trifle worried about Carey's desire to leave the town.

"To hell with Angela," said Carey. "I never again want to hear anything about her. She has got me into this mess. I would have remained friends with Mortimer and he would have done my film were it not for her."

"Slip on your dressing-gown and I'll fix you up something," said Green. "You'll feel better when you've had something. You'd better pull yourself together before you ring up Mortimer."

Carey got out of bed, put on his dressing-gown and followed Green into a beautiful sitting-room, through whose windows he caught sight of a beautiful garden in which, among semi-tropical plants of many different kinds, he saw a swimming-pool and a tennis-court. Evidently, the profession of official detractor paid Mr. Green very well. The sitting-room was quaintly furnished in a super modernistic style. In a deep armchair, to one arm of which there was a wooden attachment made to serve as a cocktail-bar, Carey saw a young woman. She had a glass in her hand and she was smoking a cigarette.

"Meet my secretary—Miss Smith," said Green.

"How do, Mr. Carey," said Miss Smith pleasantly. "Call me Jean, short for Jeannette."

She was a dark-haired girl, with a laughing face and very blue eyes. Her manner was charming and her voice was thrilling, the throaty sort.

"Throw this back," said Green, handing Carey a glass. "A prairie oyster. Can't beat it."

Carey swallowed the raw egg and Worcester sauce.

Then Green poured some dark liquid from a jug into a tumbler.

"What's that?" said Carey, feeling a little livelier after the prairie oyster.

"It's Black Velvet. Guinness and champagne," said Green. "It's a good eye-opener."

Carey swallowed the contents of the tumbler in a few gulps. It had the effect of making him at once quite as drunk as he had been the night before, but in a different way. He felt that the world was an excellent place, but that he did not know exactly what was going on in it. He began to laugh. Green was dialling the studio number on the telephone.

"You're awfully pretty," Carey said to the girl. "You don't look at all like a Hollywood girl."

"What does a Hollywood girl look like?" she said.

"They have faces like masks and bodies that seem to have been made in a factory. At least all of them I have seen."

She leaned back, put a hand on her hip and laughed deep down in her throat. It was very thrilling.

"Why do you laugh?" said Carey, pouring some more Black Velvet into his tumbler.

"I think you're damn silly," said Jean.

"Why?" said Carey.

"This is a factory town employing thirty-five thousand people," said Jean, "turning out motion pictures. Every known type of human being is required for that purpose, not alone the would-be blonde stars you see promenading on the boulevards and in the cafés and night-clubs. The real people that run the show, why, most of 'em stay at home."

"I'm glad to hear it," said Carey. "Splendid people, I mean the real ones. Excellent."

"Mr. Mortimer?" said Green. "Right. Mr. Carey wants to speak to you. Just a moment."

He handed Carey the instrument.

"Hello!" said Carey. "Is that Mortimer?"

"This is Mr. Mortimer's secretary," answered a drawling voice. "Is that Mr. Carey?"

"Yes," said Carey gruffly, "I want to speak to Mortimer."

"He's busy," said the voice, "but he wished me to tell you that your services are no longer required by him and would you call at the office any time at your convenience for the remainder of your salary? The cheque will be waiting for you. Good-bye, Mr. Carey."

"I say..." began Carey.

But the instrument went dead and he hurled it down on the table in a fury.

"By God!" he shouted. "This is the limit! My services are no longer required."

Again Jean leaned back, put her hands on her hips and burst into a merry peal of laughter, deep down in her throat. Carey looked at her angrily and then could not help joining her. In any case, under the influence of the Black Velvet it was difficult to realise the meaning of anything.

"There you are," said Green. "You wouldn't believe me last night."

"Never mind," said Carey. "I'm to get six weeks' salary. That's three thousand dollars. A lot of money. Six hundred pounds. Can have a roaring time on that for a year in Mexico. I'm going to wipe the dust of this town off my feet at once."

"Have another drink," said Green. "You'd be crazy to leave

town now. Why not turn that three thousand into six. It wouldn't take you more than a couple of days, if that long."

"Three thousand dollars," said Carey. "How could I earn three thousand dollars in a few days? You mean honestly?"

He laughed and swallowed some more of the Black Velvet. He got dizzy and extremely happy.

"Of course, it's in an honest way," said Green.

"You didn't think I wanted you to do a hold-up?"

"No," said Carey, suddenly devoured by the urge to get out of Hollywood at once. "I can't wait. I'm going to collect my money and clear out at once."

Jean got to her feet, stood in front of Carey and said:

"Want to know what I think of you? I think you're yellow. You're running away because Hollywood didn't fall on its knees and worship you when you arrived here? You are mad because you, a writer that has published books and can read as well as write, in other words a literate person, are of less consequence here than actors and actresses and producers and truck like that. Huh? So you want to run away rather than try to fight for your rights. My God! I'm only a girl, but I have more guts than you. You should be ashamed of yourself."

"Oh! Shut up," said Carey pettishly. "What's all this about in any case? What do you want me to do?"

"You're a swell lover," said the girl. "Running away and leaving that girl there, imprisoned in that fortress."

"What fortress?" said Carey, getting angry. "I don't know what you're talking about. I think you're all mad, the whole lot of you."

"Okay," said Green. "Let him have it what way he likes, Jean. Leave him alone. The guy is nuts. That article in *Proletarian Power* was probably true. You're one of these lick-spittle guys that are afraid to say boo to a goose, provided it's dressed up as

173

a capitalist."

"I won't have you say things like that to me," cried Carey. "I don't like your tone, Green."

"Oh! Yeah!" said Green offensively. "Have a look at this."

He went to a table and fetched a copy of the newspaper that contained the article already quoted in this narrative, under the heading of "Hollywood Cemetery."

When Carey had finished reading the article, he put his head in his hands and kept muttering:

"My God! Have I come to this? Is this really true? The only thing to do is to go away and hide somewhere and never be seen again."

"Have another drink," said Green, "and then we'll talk business. I know you'll want to reply to that scurrilous attack and clear yourself. It's up to you to clear your reputation."

Carey shuddered. Then he looked up and said in a solemn tone:

"I know you want me to do something disgraceful, but it seems there is no escape from it. I wouldn't be here, if my life hadn't recently been a sin against truth. I have come to this pit, so I may as well wallow in it. If there is an escape, then perhaps it's through this confession, for I know that's what you want me to do. Escape is not through silence, or through hiding one's head in the sand like an ostrich. This Hollywood is but a manifestation of the modern hatred of the human intellect. Man, tired of the struggle for the perfection of his divine intellect, has created this factory, as this girl called it, for the destruction of all that is beautiful, in body or mind, of its species, by using the beautiful as raw material for the manufacture of Black Masses, at which lust and ignorance are worshipped. Very well, then. Angela and myself are fitting mates. Let us be crucified."

CHAPTER XXVI

A S A RESULT OF THE IMPRESSION MADE, by their meeting with Angela, on the executives of World Films Inc., a publicity campaign, the like of which Hollywood had never seen before, was started in favour of *The Veiled Goddess*. Added to the furore caused by her arrival in New York, this new campaign definitely put her in the front rank of that choice group known as *These People Make News*. The only difference was, of course, that the others among that group were really known, seen, heard and touched, while Angela remained a myth like *The Loch Ness Monster*, or *The South Sea Bubble*. Excuse me. There was one exception, an individual known as *The Man With The Hare Lip*, who was quite as mysterious as Angela. He had gained national prominence by committing various offences against morals in a wood near a small New England town. And nothing was known of him except that he had a distorted upper lip.

Professor Bumpus, the famous anthropologist of Dravrah University, listed this man at the head of those who excited most interest among the inhabitants of the United States. He placed Angela second.

"The element of mystery," said the professor, in a brilliant analysis of his own list, "is largely responsible for the interest caused by *The Man With The Hare Lip and by Miss Devlin*. The public rests under the impression that they both have got something which borders on the abnormal, if it does not come within the scope of miraculous. In the case of *The Man With The Hare Lip*, the public mind is shocked by the suggestion that among the kindly population of New England there could be found a criminal so un-American in his activities. Until the perpetrator of the S—— outrages is proved to be a foreigner, there is no reason why public interest in him, especially among our women folk, should not remain as high as it is now. In the case of Angela Devlin, whom her employers claim to be the modern goddess of love, public interest will undoubtedly not flag; on the contrary, it is likely to increase, until her performance in *The Veiled Goddess*, which is going to be the first vehicle for the expression of her genius, enables the nation to come to a decision on her merits."

The mention of *The Veiled Goddess* by Professor Bumpus resulted in the eminent professor being attacked as a degraded humbug by *Proletarian Power*.

"The bogus scientist of Dravrah," said the Red organ, "when not making attacks on the working class and apologising for Nazi outrages, spends his time publishing nonsensical lists of current notabilities. That this pastime is a lucrative one there can be no doubt after his latest outburst, when he puts in a plug for *The Veiled Goddess*, thereby showing the world that the degraded humbug is in the pay of Gentleman Jack Mortimer, Hollywood's Flesh-Peddling King."

The professor retaliated by bringing a libel action against *Proletarian Power*. On the following day, *The Man With The Hare Lip* was caught in a lodging-house at Bridgeport and discovered to be a Portuguese consumptive and therefore of no further "mystery value." A result of the libel action and the capture of the Portuguese, Angela headed all the lists of *These People Make News*, for which a craze spread like wild fire over the whole country.

"Veils, reminiscent of the balmy Victorian days," said a fashion writer in a New York paper, "are going to be in fashion this summer, but not as thick as the veil behind which Miss Devlin hides her exquisite features from the prying gaze of the curious."

Numbers of people wrote to the papers and to World Films, claiming to be related to Angela, one man going so far as to say that he was her husband, having married her while they were both playing in a touring company in northern England. It was all very astounding and most amusing, especially the efforts of the other Hollywood stars to put Angela in the shade by their conduct. Lily Valentine, who had just been three months married to Count Krasnov, suddenly decided to divorce the prince and flew to Reno, where she gave an extraordinary party. Under normal circumstances, her manager reckoned that it would have netted her one hundred thousand dollars' worth of world-wide publicity. In fact the party cost almost half that sum. The banqueting-room was entirely in darkness, except for the light given by the eyes of two hundred and forty live owls, perched like electric bulbs along the walls. Lily herself appeared in the room after all the guests were seated, dressed solely in a coat of luminous grease-paint. Yet, in spite of her efforts, the party attracted no attention whatsoever and the poor girl got a nervous breakdown, from which she did not recover for three months. A male star had his yacht set on fire one hundred miles off the island of Santa Cruz and then had himself rescued, after spending an hour on a raft, by a sea-plane which came in answer to his S.O.S. Another star flew down to the capital of a Central American republic, where a president was being inaugurated, and from the balcony of his hotel emptied a pail of offensive liquid on to the head of the newly elected president, as he was motoring past. Yet none of these acts served any other purpose than to bring ridicule on their perpetrators.

Indeed, the whole technique of publicity had been revolutionised by Mortimer. At a dinner given in honour of the visit to Hollywood of "The Motion Picture Theatre Operators of America," the monocled magnate referred to this revolution in a speech that was described as "the most brilliant talk of the year and a welcome indication that one of our major industries has cast aside the swaddling clothes of vulgarity in favour of the modest garments of self-respect."

"Gentlemen," Mortimer had said, "this industry had reached a crisis, owing to the manner in which it had shirked its responsibilities as one of the most powerful weapons for moulding public opinion. While mankind stood face to face with economic ruin and the spectre of famine was abroad in all lands, far and near, we in Hollywood dallied in the bed-chamber of faked romance. Then I decided to go out into the highways and the byways in search of a message for humanity, a message of regeneration and salvation. I found that message by the grace of Divine Providence, and a medium for giving it to the world in the person of Angela Devlin."

In the meantime, Tracy and Gunn, assisted by ten of the best writers in the studio, worked night and day at the script of *The Veiled Goddess*, under the direction of Mortimer, who hardly slept a wink. The man was almost mad with worry. Indeed, the more his plans appeared to be on the road to a phenomenal success, the more he worried. Every night, out at the ranch, it required all Dafoe's subtlety to keep the magnate from becoming hysterical, and he had, in fact, to be given small doses of the "sleeping-draught" that was keeping Angela in a state of coma while her personality was being projected into her other self.

And then, on the sixth day after Angela's arrival in Hollywood, a notice appeared in the *Pacific Eagle*, creating almost as great a sensation as her arrival in New York. In large letters across the top of the front page was printed:

"BRIAN CAREY CONFESSES IN SENSATIONAL STORY TO BEGIN PUBLICATION TO-MORROW. FAMOUS BRITISH AUTHOR CRACKS DOWN ON MONOCLED MOVIE MAGNATE'S TREATMENT OF ANGELA DEVLIN. HIBERNIAN STAR IMPRISONED IN SANTA MONICA MEDIEVAL FORTRESS."

Beneath this formidable announcement, there was single column in small type which read:

"Since his arrival in Hollywood, Mr. Brian Carey has been inaccessible to the Press. He disappeared almost immediately after his arrival, to write for Universal Publications a document which we believe is going to have an importance above and beyond the nation-wide interest manifested at the moment in Angela Devlin, the mystery woman of the screen. Here at last we have the naked truth about a personality that has intrigued the public mind as no other person has done in years, from the pen of a writer whose novel *The Emigrant* proves that he does not mince his words.

"Having concluded his amazing story, Mr. Carey is going to be the guest of honour to-morrow evening at a dinner given by Mr. Claude Bryant, prominent socialite and patron of the arts. Those slated to attend include many of the most prominent people in the motion-picture colony."

CHAPTER XXVII

"WELL! THAT'S THAT," SAID CAREY. "And what a shocking document it is! Funny thing, though, now that it's done I don't feel as badly about it as I thought I would."

"How do you mean?" said Jean. "I think it's marvellous."

"You do, really?" said Carey.

So, it's finished at last," said Green. "Is this the lot?"

"Yeah," said Jean, "that's the lot. How about our dough?"

"Okay," said Green, pulling two bundles of notes from his pocket. Three grand for you, Carey. One for you, Nellie. Fast work in five days. I'll be running along with the manuscript. You going back to your hotel, Carey? Don't forget that dinner to-morrow night. So long, you two."

He picked up the manuscript and dashed off with it.

Carey picked up the bundle of notes and crinkled them between his fingers. He laughed.

"By Jove!" he said. "You do things pretty smart in Hollywood. Rather pleasant, I must say, on the whole. Six thousand dollars. There's nothing like money to ease the pangs of conscience. You know, I never thought I could write for money, certainly not a disgusting thing like that document. What a title!"

Jean stretched her arms above her head and yawned. She was utterly exhausted.

"I think it's a swell title," she said. " 'I love Angela Devlin.' I think it's a knock-out. Lucky you. See what it is to have a name. I've done most of the work. But I only get one grand to your three and darn lucky I count myself. Usually I only get a century for a job like this."

"A century?" said Carey.

"Yeah," she said. "A hundred iron men."

"You mean a hundred dollars? You mean you often do things like this?"

"It's my job. I do a lot of work for Puff. He can't write himself."

"But he has written a book, hasn't he? He works on a newspaper, or doesn't he?"

"Why, sure, he does and he's written a book, but it was I wrote it for him, me an' two other girls, that thing called *I Strip the Stars*. One of these days I'll write a book myself under my own name. Gee! That would be swell. I get sick an' tired of seein' other people's names to things I write."

"I wish your name was to this," said Carey, picking up the rough draft of the manuscript. "I'd feel better about it. You know I hated Mortimer until I had written this, or rather until you had written it, whereas now I merely pity him. Funny thing, too, I don't feel a bit irritated about Hollywood either, not after this."

"Don't see why anybody should be irritated about it," said Jean. "I think it's the most wonderful place in the world."

Carey was so tired that he did not feel like arguing with her. In the intervals between writing the manuscript, he and Jean had gone to one party after another during the past five days and nights. Everything he had seen had convinced him that the inhabitants of the celluloid city were both mad and pitiable and to live such a life appeared to him quite horrible. But why argue about it? There were other places and environments on this mad earth equally mad and pitiable. In fact, at the moment, man appeared to him to be, fundamentally, the mad and pitiable creation of a cynical Providence, but a creation from whom he had the chance of a temporary escape by the possession of six thousand dollars. Mexico? Yes, definitely Mexico.

"I love it here," said Jean, mixing herself a strong dose of rye whiskey and White Rock. "When I came here first, I couldn't get a break, not knowing anybody, but in southern California, it's practically impossible for anybody to starve. You have to be blind, dumb, and paralysed to starve here. You can buy for ten cents enough fruit and vegetables to do you for a week. In an hour or two you can fix up a hut to shelter you against what weather there is. Go down to the shore and catch enough fish. Just pick oranges off the trees. Why, there's thousands of gallons of milk poured down the drains of Los Angeles every day. Do you know the first job I got?"

"What was it?" said Carey, getting himself some rye and White Rock.

"I want to tell you about myself," said Jean.

"Please do," said Carey, "it's always nice to know about people one likes."

"Glad you like me," said Jean, "because I'm just nuts about you. I wish you an' I could always work together. We'd have this industry on a hook in no time. Well! I come from a small town in Illinois. Was two years at the University in Chicago and then I ran away with a guy I was nuts about. He wasn't on the level,

182

though. Got as far as Denver, Colorado, where he was runnin' a gamblin' joint. I saw he just wanted a good-looking kid to attract suckers, so I hitch-hiked to San Francisco and fell in with a French guy ; my mother was French so I talk the language, an' he brought me to L. A., where he was running a gang of French cuties. They were a gold-mine right then. But I wasn't crazy about that kind of work, so I skipped him an' had a rough time for a while until I fell in with a guy who got me a job in a studio as the young French kid with the laugh in her throat."

"Curious job," said Carey.

"Held down that job for two years," said Jean, "until I ran into a guy that employs a lot of girls to write scenarios. See? He's got a big name as a writer, so he can sell stories to all the studios. He doesn't have to write them, just sits down and thinks up titles and ideas and the girls write them for him, at fifty bucks a week apiece."

"Sort of factory?" said Carey. "How much does he get?"

"Anything from seven thousand to twenty thousand dollars a story," said Jean. "Why, it's the best paying racket in this town. You and I could do it. That's what I'd like to do, you an' I go in together. With the publicity you'll get out of this story and the books you've published, you could collar as much business as..."

She mentioned the name of the gentleman who operated the script-writing factory.

"You don't mean to say that he does that?" said Carey in surprise.

"Why, certainly he does," said Jean. "He's made anything up to three million dollars in the last four years. It's yours for the taking. You leave it to me. I know the ropes. I know what the studios want. It's like taking milk from a child."

Carey swallowed his drink and then shook his head.

"No, Jean," he said. "I don't want three million dollars, not like that."

"No ?" she said. "Why not? You're crazy. All's fair in this racket."

"Let's have another drink," said Carey. "You see, I may be wrong, but to me life is not a racket. It's the most beautiful thing I possess, and you too, the fact of being alive and able to feel. Especially being able to appreciate beauty."

"Beauty is all bolony," said Jean, "unless it's a valid signature to a cheque."

Carey clinked glasses with her and swallowed his drink once more.

"Funny thing," he said, "that even though one doesn't believe in God, I mean the God of organised religion, one still has a horror of sinning against the Holy Ghost. The sin against truth. It is like one's objection to those cunning women of Paris, who dress themselves in the uniforms of nursemaids and parade the parks, in order to entice old men. Now, when you offer me three million dollars to commit the sin against the Holy Ghost I feel the same kind of horror. And I also feel once more that I love Angela, really love her and not in the way my love for her is written about in that horrible manuscript. The prelude to love is not lust, but a gentle pity and forgiveness, the kind of feeling I now have for her."

He raised, his hands above his head and whispered:

"I feel strong once more within myself. I am wise and far-seeing. I am one and need no servants. The inner places are thrown open. The waters of the seas and rivers that had stood still are flowing again."

Jean stared at him in horror as he waved good-bye to her and rushed from the room.

CHAPTER XXVIII

ON THE FOLLOWING MORNING, the first instalment of *I Love Angela Devlin* appeared in the *Pacific Eagle*. It was a most damning indictment of Gentleman Jack Mortimer and caused a tremendous sensation. While subtly avoiding the law of libel, as it is known in the celluloid city, Mortimer was painted as an abandoned scoundrel, who trafficked in human souls, in order to pander to the tastes of the most base among the public, while he denied the public a fair bargain for their investments. It gave the true history of Angela's discovery, dealt at great length on the immorality of her purchase from her aunt and suggested that a transaction of a similar kind in Abyssinia would result in creating a warlike situation at the League of Nations Assembly in Geneva.

"Was not a bloody Civil War fought in America," it cried with some effect, "to abolish this traffic in human flesh?"

In a most gushing manner, it went on to show how the possession of a common racial heritage brought Carey and Angela together on board the ship.

"We realised that there was more between us than this

sacred bond of race, that we were twin souls caught in the net of an implacable demon, who was determined to drag us down into the deepest pit of Hell. It was this realisation that awakened in our hearts the most noble and most pure of all loves, the love of those who have sinned through ignorance, but have been led through suffering to see the light of salvation and to struggle towards it at all costs. Alas! It was not to be."

Again they were thrust apart through the machinations of Mortimer and his satellites, until finally, on their arrival in Hollywood, Angela was imprisoned in a fortress, "as unapproachable as the dungeon in the *Count of Monte Cristo*, where she rests at the mercy of her jailors." An elaborate description of the fortress and the precautions for protecting the prisoner from the possibility of escape ended the first instalment. Curiously enough, in the same issue of the *Pacific Eagle*, there was the following announcement:

IMPORTANT ARRIVALS

At *The Hollywood Plaza*: Major-General Sir Henry Simpkins, British authority on Indo-China, here on a visit with Lady Simpkins and daughter.

At the *Beverley Wiltshire*: Mr. Bruce Brownley, Australian millionaire sheep-farmer, "just having a look round."

At the *International*: Mr. Brian Carey, British author, here in connection with production of *The Veiled Goddess*.

At ten o'clock in the morning, Mortimer, accompanied by Dafoe and several newspaper reporters, photographers and gossip writers, arrived at the International Hotel and asked to see Mr. Carey. The man at the desk politely shook his head and said that he had orders not to disturb Mr. Carey. In spite of the offer of a very large sum of money as a bribe, the official politely kept shaking his head, while the photographers shot the scene and the reporters made ample notes of everything that was said.

"Okay," Mortimer said, when enough business had been transacted for publicity, "we'll see what the law has got to say about this."

Accompanied by the photographers and the newspaper reporters and by Dafoe, he drove helter-skelter to his office, using his siren as honorary fire chief. Arrived at his Greek temple, he set in motion the machinery of the law, for the purpose of getting an injunction against Universal Publications, to restrain them from printing any more of the story entitled *I Love Angela Devlin*. Then he proceeded to give an interview to the newspaper men.

"Take a load of this, boys," he said. "Jack Mortimer speaking. Okay. Owing to the scurrilous attack made on his character and business methods in current issues of the publications owned by a certain news syndicate; whose proprietor, being himself the principal stockholder in a motion-picture enterprise at war with World Films, cannot escape the charge of having betrayed for reasons of personal gain the glorious traditions of impartial truth which are the heritage of American journalism, Gentleman Jack Mortimer, internationally known executive of World Films, has changed his plans in relation to his newest discovery, the Hibernian star Angela Devlin. Got that, boys?"

Mortimer paused, fixed his monocle to his eye and looked in triumph at his audience of newspapermen, who watched him in open-mouthed admiration. It was a situation which impressed even them. Dafoe had an expression of cynical amusement on his strange countenance. Mortimer coughed and continued:

"In conformity with his theory that the motion picture public was not receiving a square deal at the hands of motion-picture executives, owing to the manner in which the personalities of the stars were being exploited by means of vulgar publicity, to the detriment both of their acting ability and the quality of the pictures offered to the public, Mr. Mortimer had originally intended to keep Angela Devlin veiled and hidden from the public view, until she flashed into the firmament of the human consciousness. Such has been, and is now more than ever, his confidence in her genius and his determination to give the knockout blow to the accusations of pandering to the baser passions that have been hurled in the face of Hollywood, that he chose for the first expression of her genius a sombre story called *The Emigrant*, by a writer called Brian Carey, a crudely written and violent story, having, however, an idea behind it, which, handled by a competent screen writer like Sam Gunn, might be turned into suitable screen material. But Mr. Mortimer realised that he had a duty to humanity above and beyond his duty to the motion-picture industry and that he should not waste the genius of Miss Devlin on material that could only pander to the sensation-loving public. For that reason he put aside the idea of using *The Emigrant* and determined, come what may, to use Miss Devlin's genius in the only way it should be used, for the purpose of giving a message to humanity that would lead it out of the desert of insecurity into the promised land of prosperity. He determined to unfold the sign manual and cure-all of the world's ills, in the shape of *The Veiled Goddess*, a masterpiece of all times, written by Sam Gunn, whose handling of *Little Virgin* placed him on a pedestal as the Big Chief of scenarists, directed by Bud Tracy, whose name is a household word among screen lovers, and produced by himself. Everything was set for offering this masterpiece to the world, the production of a galaxy of genius, unparalleled in human history, either ancient or modem. Then came this stab in the back."

Mr. Mortimer paused to wipe his brow. There was a murmur of applause among the newspapermen. Dafoe cackled mirthlessly. Then the magnate continued:

"At this point, tears came into Mr. Mortimer's eyes and in a voice that was broken with emotion, he cried out to our representative—now be careful, boys, this is important. You got to work up feeling—Mr. Mortimer cried out:

" 'And to think that it is a man whom I rescued from destitution at the urgent request of my friend, Bud Tracy, who has done this! A man whom I took into my employment in spite of the fact that his work has received the attention both of our own and his country's police; a man whose reputation would have warned off everybody but a sentimental fool like myself. However ... '

"Got that, boys? Okay. Here the monocled magnate jumped to his feet and, striking his chest with his clenched fists, in a gesture of outraged pride, cried out:

" 'They have stabbed me in the back with the poisoned dagger of ingratitude, but, like a true Christian, I am going to turn around and offer them in return the voice of the angel of love.' "

As he spoke these last words, he had jumped to his feet and struck his bosom with his clenched fists and his voice had really expressed outraged pride. Then he sat down suddenly and said in a sharp tone:

"Got all that? Okay. Now listen. Here's the pay off. I'm going to put Angela Devlin on the air, over an international hook-up, at the Hollywood Bowl to-morrow evening at nine o'clock, in order to silence these accusations of keeping her imprisoned. She is going to sing a selection of Irish songs. Okay?"

The newspapermen and the photographers, who again took pictures of the magnate at his desk, fled excitedly at the termination of the interview. Mortimer, left alone with Dafoe, did not look at all as sure of himself as he had been, talking to the reporters.

"Good God!" he said. "Larry, this is more than I can bear."

"What's the matter now?" said Dafoe.

"But can he go on the air?" said Mortimer.

"Has he got anything on the air?"

"You mean she," said Dafoe. "Of course she's got something on the air. One of the best voices living. For God's sake, keep your hair on."

"We'll be three hundred grand in the red with this injunction business," said Mortimer. "These goddam judges are expensive, especially when they know it's a put-up job."

"That's nonsense," said Dafoe. "You know you can get three hundred grand from Happiness Incorporated for Angela's broadcast. They voted two million and a half for advertising at their general meeting last week."

"Can he go on the air, though?" said Mortimer, trembling. "Has he got anything on the air."

"She's got everything on the air," said Dafoe.

"But what about Biddy?" said Mortimer. "Jees! You'll kill me, Larry."

"Ha, ha, ha," said Dafoe. "I'm going to see about that now. I think, in spite of everything, that in future we should go fifty-fifty. What do you say? "

"I agree to everything," said Mortimer. "Fifty–fifty or whatever you like. I'm up against it. I've gobbled up more than I can chew."

"Okay," said Dafoe. "I'm going to draw up a little agreement to that effect. And now I'll see to Biddy and your wife."

"My wife!" said Mortimer. "My God! Whoever heard of such a business? My God! You're the devil himself."

CHAPTER XXIX

JUST AS IF THE CITY HAD BEEN HURLED IN to the abyss of war, editions of the newspapers were issued every few minutes, giving details in glaring headlines of the latest developments in the struggle between the two factions, Mortimer against Universal Publications Incorporated. The laughter that had greeted the appearance of the first instalment of *I Love Angela Devlin*, had by the afternoon changed into a serious discussion of the justice on either side; for the reason that the affair had ceased to be personal, since it involved millions of money and became internationally known. Indeed, the newspaper bulletins were issued in London Paris and Berlin almost as frequently as they were issued in Los Angeles and New York. The power of the screen is world-wide.

For the moment at least, Carey had become almost as important a figure as Angela Devlin herself. A crowd of reporters and photographers hung around the desk of the International Hotel, trying to get to his apartment. Carey was in bed at two o'clock, after a late night, when he was suddenly roused by the appearance of a strange man in his bedroom.

"How the hell did you get here?" he said.

The intruder was a man of forty or thereabouts with a very florid countenance, bulging, bloodshot eyes and a thick neck that overflowed the collar of his coat. He wore a slouch hat that came down over his forehead. He was fat around the body. His clothes were tightfitting, so that he walked as if he were in a strait-jacket, or wearing a corset.

"Josh Donovan is the name," said the intruder.

"Mr. Carey, I take it."

"What the devil does this mean? " said Carey.

"Hop out of bed," said Mr. Donovan truculently. "I want to have a talk to you."

He had his right hand in his pocket and his pocket bulged, giving the wretched Carey to understand that there was a revolver or automatic pistol concealed in it.

"All right," he said, slipping out of bed. "Needs must when the devil drives."

When they were seated in the sitting-room, Josh Donovan pulled up his trouser leg and said, through the side of his mouth, in the traditional manner of the screen villain:

"It's like this. I've come here from Chicago, where I belong, to have a little talk to you and Miss Devlin. Ever hear of an organisation called the I.A.B.?"

"Can't say that I have," said Carey.

"It's the 'Irish-American Brotherhood,' " said Donovan, "and I happen to be connected with it in an official capacity. We consider, as an organisation bound by oath to observe certain rules and agreements, that it is our duty to see that all individuals of Irish blood get the right break in this country. On the other hand, we make it our business to see that no individual of Irish blood takes a hand in lowering the prestige of the Irish race."

He coughed, looked fiercely at Carey and said:

"Got that straight?"

"I have no idea what you are driving at," said Carey.

"No?" said Mr. Donovan in a very scornful tone.

"Certainly not," said Carey.

He was, however, rather in a funk, owing to the menacing appearance of his visitor and the bulging weapon on which Mr. Donovan religiously kept his hand.

"Okay," said Donovan. "Here it is in black and white. In the opinion of the 'Irish-American Brotherhood' you have been, Mr. Carey, both by your conduct since you arrived in this country and by your writings previous to that event, acting in a manner detrimental to the reputation of our race. An article appeared in a newspaper in which you are cited as saying that you are a prostitute. Is that right?"

"There was such an article," said Carey." But..."

"According to article sixteen of the constitution of the 'Irish-American Brotherhood' " interrupted Mr. Donovan, "no Irish man or woman can be a prostitute, nor can they be allowed to make any such accusation against themselves, since chastity is the *sine qua non* of our existence as a race. Furthermore, you are cited in the public Press as stating that you love Angela Devlin, for whom a claim is made by her managers that she is the modern goddess of love. Both these claims, in the opinion of the 'Irish-American Brotherhood,' are inconsistent with a proper respect for our Holy Faith, together with being immodest. On that account, my organisation has decided to remove both you and Miss Devlin from this country, in the best interests of our race."

Carey cried out in amazement:

"You what?"

"You are expelled from United States territory," said Josh

Donovan.

"But I'm going of my own accord, you silly ass," said Carey. "Are you crazy? How the devil did you get in here ?"

"Not so fast," said Josh Donovan, pulling his right hand from his pocket.

Carey calmed down, seeing that the right hand held an automatic pistol of the Colt pattern.

"So you mean to be tough, do you?" said Mr. Donovan.

"Not at all," said Carey. "I'm just telling you that. I'm leaving Hollywood to-morrow."

"You're leaving Hollywood to-night," said Mr. Donovan, "in company with Miss Devlin."

"With Angela? " cried Carey. "You mean that I…?"

"You are now, until informed to the contrary, " said Mr. Donovan, "acting under the orders of the 'Irish American Brotherhood.' Here are your orders and I warn you that the slightest divergence on your part from carrying out these orders to the letter means instant death."

"Very well," said Carey, beginning to tremble.

"What are they?"

Mr. Donovan proceeded to give his orders.

CHAPTER XXX

A T THREE O'CLOCK THAT AFTERNOON, Mrs. Mortimer fired the blow-pipe which she had loaded for her husband. It was at that hour that the time limit set for her ultimatum to her husband expired. She had demanded either restoration of marital rights, or to have her allowance of one hundred thousand dollars a year doubled. At five minutes to three, Dafoe informed her over the telephone that Mr. Mortimer refused point blank to discuss either one or the other of her suggestions.

"Okay, boys," said Mrs. Mortimer. "Let's shoot. We'll give him the works."

Seated in the luxurious drawing-room of her Pasadena home, at the far end of which there was a merry party of young people squatted on the carpet and drinking happily while they listened to the crooning and the ukulele music of Sam Belladonna, the Hawaiian Adonis, Mrs. Mortimer cut an impressive figure, as she prepared to open her attack on the monocled magnate.

Although well over forty, she had not altogether lost the

fulsome beauty which won the heart of Mortimer when he first came to Hollywood with his duck. But she had definitely got extremely fat about the gills and about that portion of the body which her eloquent husband described as "the mid-section." Her hair was a fiery red colour and so were her cheeks. Dye was responsible for the colour of her hair and gin for that of her cheeks. She was dressed in fantastic beach pyjamas and she wore around her neck a Hawaiian *lei*, a symbol of her love for Sam Belladonna. Her adopted child, a horrible-looking, pasty-faced boy of sixteen, slouched, with his hands in the pockets of his flannel pants, at the back of her chair, chewing gum and sipping an old-fashioned cocktail.

Two representatives of International Publications, a syndicate that operated newspapers and periodicals all over the North American continent, faced Mrs. Mortimer, ready to take down the statement for which they were paying her forty thousand dollars. Two photographers waited in the background.

"Begin with early struggles." said Mrs. Mortimer, "and make it hot, because I want to make that guy ashamed of the day he was born. Don't we, Junior!"

"We sure do, mom," said Junior savagely .

"Say how I nobly shared his poverty," continued Mrs. Mortimer, "and how his love for me knew no bounds while we were poor and downtrodden, and how he promised never to forget my self-sacrificing devotion. See? I was happy then. Like hell I was, but never mind."

Here the newspaper men laughed heartily. A beautiful, blonde young woman, dressed in a crimson bathing-suit, came along the floor, turning somersaults.

She sat at Mrs. Mortimer's feet, grinning like an insane kitten. She looked back over her shoulder at the party gathered round Sam Belladonna and screamed:

"Hey! You come along here and listen to Gloria. She's givin' Jack the works."

While Mrs. Mortimer continued to describe her early struggles, going into intimate details at which Junior giggled, the members of the party came rushing along the floor and squatted to listen, all laughing merrily and interjecting nonsensical remarks.

"Then," said Mrs. Mortimer, "when fortune shone on him, largely through my efforts, I noticed a gradual cooling in his passion for me. I overlooked his first infidelities and then I persuaded him to purchase Junior from an orphan asylum in Chicago, hoping that a sense of parental responsibilities would bring him back to me. You make me turn on the tears here, boys. You know what I mean?"

"We get you, ma'am," said one of the newspaper men with a wink, while the members of the party howled with laughter.

"Hey! Cut it out," said Mrs. Mortimer, as she applied her lighter to a cigarette deluxe. "I can't think if you mugs go on laughing. There followed a divine sequence of married bliss, under the influence of our common love for the little, prattling creature that had come into our midst. But alas, it was not for long. The demon of his passions had gotten too strong a hold over him. While he squandered his money on others, Junior and I have been finding it a hard struggle to make ends meet. Even so, I would have kept silent, were it not for this last outrage, when he has flown in the face of God Himself, with this creature whom he claims to be the goddess of love. Under the circumstances, there is no alternative for me but to ask the courts for a release from a marriage that has become a mockery."

"Hurrah!" cried the members of the party.

"How about Junior putting in some swell remark?" said one

of the newspaper men.

"Yeah," said Mrs. Mortimer. "You can put him down as saying, 'It's about time pop gave mom an' me a break.' See? Now, how about them pictures? Come along, Junior, we got to go an' get dressed for our pictures."

She and her adopted child dressed themselves in very shabby clothes and she did up both her own face and Junior's to represent suffering, poverty and Christian resignation. Then they were photographed in the kitchen, with Junior sitting at a common deal table, about to partake of a very meagre collation, which his mother was scraping from an old saucepan on to his plate. Then another photograph was taken of them, with Mrs. Mortimer sitting in a chair, with her apron to her eyes, while Junior tried to comfort her, with his arm round her neck.

"Side by side with them," said Mrs. Mortimer, "you put that picture that was taken on Jack's yacht last winter down in Panama, when he was down there with Lily Valentine. That'll show him up, see, living in the lap of luxury with his concubine, while poor me an' Junior are starving. Now, boys, have a drink."

"We have no time," cried the leader of the newspaper men. "This stuff is sizzling. We have to get it off our hands."

They rushed away and Mrs. Mortimer returned to her party.

CHAPTER XXXI

AT SIX O'CLOCK, CAREY PROCEEDED TO carry out Josh Donovan's orders. He rang for a bell-hop and, when the latter appeared, he gave the lad a ten-dollar bill and said:

"Go out and get me a flour sack and some wood ashes."

"Yes, sir," said the bell-hop. Then he stared and added: "What did you say, sir?"

"Get me a flour sack and some wood ashes," repeated Carey.

"But..."

"Don't you know what a flour sack is? It must be white. Then some wood ashes. Burn some wood and fetch me the ashes. Do you understand?"

After a pause, the bell-hop said he understood and went away. In a few minutes, however, Carey was called to the telephone, in order to explain to the assistant manager what he required.

"I am in earnest," said Carey. "I should jolly well think I am in earnest. If I don't leave this hotel within an hour, wearing sack-cloth and ashes, I am a dead man, and I am going to hold the management of this hotel responsible for my death. No. I can't explain. For God's sake get me what want I quickly."

In about twenty minutes, the assistant manager appeared, followed by the bell-hop, who carried on his arm a flour sack and in his hand a small vessel containing wood ashes. Rubbing his hands together nervously, the assistant manager looked at Carey and said:

"Are they what you wanted, Mr. Carey?"

"Precisely," said Carey, taking the flour sack.

He measured it against his body, like a person trying on a garment for length and said:

"A bit longer, perhaps, would be better, but I dare say that, in cases like this, one needn't be particular about appearances."

"I beg your pardon, sir," said the assistant manager.

"Oh, yes," said Carey, "and a pair of scissors. I've got none."

The assistant manager went away, looking very worried. When the scissors arrived, Carey brought the sack and the ashes into his bedroom. He cut three holes in the sack with the scissors, one hole for his head, the other two for his arms. Then he stripped himself naked, put on the sack and examined himself in the mirror. He burst out laughing.

"Perhaps a plain white sack would be more austere," he said aloud and with satisfaction, "but I rather like the maker's brand in front like that, especially backwards in the mirror. Quite in keeping with the local fetish for advertising. I might, in fact, be able to get a little money for this from the flour people. I should ring them up and try to get some."

The sack reached just below his knees and right across his stomach was written in red and black letters:

DUNZ HIGH GRADE

QUEEN OF THE PACIFIC
112 LBS
SELF-RAISING FLOUR

He was rubbing some wood ashes into his hair, when Green arrived at the apartment to take him to Bryant's house .

"Now, what the hell is the idea?" said Green in amazement, as he stared at the strange spectacle of a barefooted man, wearing only a flour sack, rubbing wood ashes into his hair. "What you been drinking?"

Carey laughed in a perfectly sane tone and indeed he looked quite gay.

"Don't you like my costume?" he said. "I think it's rather original, you know, sack-cloth and ashes."

"But this ain't a fancy dress hall," said Green. "This is a regular society dinner. See me? I've got on my soup an' fish."

"But your dinner jacket proves it's a fancy dress affair."

"How so?"

"You going as a gentleman."

"Aw! Snap out of it," said Green. "Christ sake, get dressed properly. And hurry up. There ain't much time. It's a long way to go, too, out to Santa Monica."

"Afraid I can't oblige you," said Carey. "I'm wearing this costume by special request."

"Whose request?"

"Can't tell you. I feel sure it's more than my life is worth. Wait for me in the sitting-room, like a good fellow, while I finish my toilet."

He pushed Green out of the bedroom and closed the door. He was in very high spirits and kept laughing to himself, while he tied a belt around his waist under the sack. Attached to the belt, he hung a bag, rather like the sporran on a Scotsman's kilt,

201

containing his money, his passport and a toothbrush. Then he joined Green in the sitting-room.

"All ready," he said. "Let's go."

"Well! I guess there's nothing to do but to humour you," said Green. "Maybe you're right and that this outfit is good publicity. One never knows. Though I reckon it's more than likely to make people laugh. We'll see in any case."

When the elevator attendant saw them enter his elevator, he was so astonished that he forgot to operate his lever.

"Come on, boy, wake up," said Green.

"Yes, sir," said the elevator boy, as he sent his elevator flying down to the ground floor.

As they marched up to the desk, where Carey nonchalantly deposited his key, they were surrounded by a crowd of people, that had been waiting for the appearance of "the big-time headliner of the moment."

Seven among the crowd were newspaper men and they shouted questions at Carey, but the sack-clothed celebrity marched through them, with his head in the air and his arms folded on his bosom like a monk, ignoring their questions. There were several blinding flashes, as cameramen, from points of vantage, snapped the scene. Then the newspaper men, despairing of getting a statement from him, dashed to the telephone booths and bayed into the instruments:

"BAREFOOTED BRITISH SCRIVENER IN MOURNING FOR IMPRISONED ANGELA DEVLIN WEARS ONLY HUNDRED AND TWELVE POUND SACK OF DUNZ QUEEN OF PACIFIC SELF-RAISING FLOUR TO BEAN FEAST IN HIS HONOUR CONVOYED BY PUFF GREEN."

They dived into Green's car, which was parked outside the hotel. It was an enormous Packard, driven by a Mexican-Indian chauffeur, who turned on the radio as soon as the car got into motion.

"In an interview given to-day to the public Press," droned the voice of the announcer, "Gentleman Jack Mortimer monocled executive of World Films, lashes Brian Carey for having stabbed him in the back with the poisoned dagger of ingratitude. In answer to the accusations of imprisonment of Angela Devlin contained in the Carey indictment, Mr. Mortimer has changed his plans with regard to Miss Devlin, whom he is allowing to go on the air to-morrow evening at nine o'clock in the Hollywood Bowl, under the auspices of Happiness Incorporated, through whose courtesy you have heard this announcement. When you are feeling blue and there's no silver lining in the dark clouds ahead, just step into the drug store at the corner and ask for Happiness. You will get it in twenty-five cent, fifty cent and dollar packets, each packet carrying the Happiness wrapper."

"What's that?" said Carey with a laugh. "Happiness?"

"It's a drug," said Green.

"Won't they be surprised when they find Angela is gone?" said Carey, with another gay laugh. "This is the most marvellous joke, really."

"What do you mean?" said Puff Green. "You really gone crazy?"

"Awfully good phrase that," continued Carey, "about being stabbed in the back with the poisoned dagger of ingratitude. I have quite changed my mind about Mortimer. I think he is really a man of genius. I'd have been frightfully sorry for having made that attack on him in the beastly thing Jean and I wrote, if I didn't know he hired you to get me to do it. I think it's all very brilliant. At the same time, Mr. Green, I think you are a pretty foul person. You don't mind my saying so, do you?"

Green said nothing, thinking the man was mad.

CHAPTER XXXII

TWO HUNDRED AND THIRTY guests had gathered at Mr. Claude Wiley Washington Bryant's house at Santa Monica to receive Mr. Carey. Owing to his enormous wealth and the polish which he had acquired at one of the leading English public schools and at Balliol College, Oxford, Mr. Bryant was the recognised leader of Hollywood society. Indeed, the upper classes of America had been shocked when he first took up residence there, at a time when the profits of the film industry were not yet sufficiently enormous to make film people socially eligible. But Mr. Bryant's social position was so secure that he could afford to snap his fingers at all and sundry. In fact, he said that he lived in Hollywood for patriotic reasons, in order to raise the tone and guide the activities of an industry that had such an influence on American thought and manners.

To judge by the crowd that had gathered for cock-tails in the magnificent gardens of his palace, he had not so far been very successful in improving manners. Gathered from all corners of the globe, they had nothing in common except a momentary notoriety in the film industry and a prodigious sense of their own importance, which expressed itself in the making of noise and in swaggering. There were present Jewish refugees from Nazi violence, cheek by jowl with Jew-baiting German Junkers, Russian *émigrés* of the Tsarist régime hobnobbing with American Communists, English aristocrats, destitute in their own country, earning fabulous salaries in Hollywood, through the perfection of their waist line, Austrian psycho-analysts, Arab Messiahs, Buddhist seers from India, tough cowboys from Nevada, dancers from the Argentine, dress-designers from Paris, financiers from Wall Street; in a word, an astounding collection, from among whom nobody but a foolish optimist like Mr. Bryant could hope to gather the leaven of a polite society.

He himself stood head and shoulders above the gathering in every sense of the word. Tall, handsome even, in spite of the dissipation shown in his fine, open countenance, immaculately dressed, he moved about the reception-hall of his palace, receiving his guests, with the graciousness of an accomplished diplomat. When Carey appeared in his sack, attended by the worried Mr. Green, Bryant displayed no surprise.

"This is Mr. Carey," said Green. "Mr. Bryant."

"Ah!" said Bryant, stretching out both arms to their full extent and taking both Carey's hands in his.

"Charmed to meet you, Mr. Carey. I think your costume is exquisite. All art has its roots in simplicity. I had no idea, though, that you belonged to the Surrealist school. I had put you down as a Romantic, with undeveloped Classical tendencies."

Carey laughed and thought:

"This is the prize madman of the lot."

At the moment," he said aloud, "I am definitely Realist of the School of Necessity."

"Ah!" said Bryant politely. "Is that the latest among the

European decadents? You must tell me about it. Meet Mrs. Bryant."

Carey shook hands with a ravishing creature from Tiflis, who had minute and exquisite hands, a face like. carving and an intoxicating voice. Mrs. Bryant said something in Russian, or some such language, and then Mr. Bryant led him through the hall, into the gardens where the guests were making themselves blind drunk at a reckless speed. There was a roar of laughter as Carey made his appearance and this annoyed Bryant A great deal.

"It's time to sit down to dinner," said Bryant. "People here unfortunately are so much on edge with the nervous vitality of the place, the tempo of living is so fast that they get easily intoxicated, with the result that too little attention is paid to conversation and food, as in more slow-moving Europe. However, it's exhilarating."

He signalled to three buglers who stood apart with their instruments at the ready. Immediately they put their instruments to their lips and blew the army call for dinner.

"Aw! Listen, Claude," said a drinker at a nearby cocktail-bar, "we ain't ready yet to put the bag on. Plenty of time."

"Hey! Fellahs," said another, "who's the funny-looking guy in the flour sack?"

"He must be that goddam Scotchman," said a tipsy woman, "who says he's the heir to the throne o'Poland. He goes around dressed someway like that."

"Order, please," cried Bryant. "I don't want Mr. Carey to get the impression that we in Hollywood are a lot of rowdy drunkards."

"Oh! It's Carey," they cried excitedly. "It's the guy that pulled a fast one on Jack Mortimer."

They crowded around Carey, the sensation of the moment,

and they no longer thought his costume funny, now that they knew who he was. Agents begged him to let them handle his business. Producers offered him jobs in their studios. Young women begged him to give them parts in his next production.

"This is all too fantastic," thought Carey.

After some difficulty, Bryant managed to save Carey from this crowd of enthusiasts and they marched down to a magnificent swimming-pool, around which tables were laid for dinner. In the pool itself there were two gondolas, of the kind that are used in Venice except that these ones were driven electrically and they served the purpose of carrying food from a large service table at one end of the pool, to the diners who were ranged round the other sides. In the centre of the pool, on a moored raft, there was a brilliant Mexican orchestra, brought by air that afternoon from Agua Caliente. Groups of gunmen stood around at points of vantage to protect the jewellery of the women and the persons of the more important magnates from kidnappers.

One of these groups was composed of Josh Donovan and two friends who resembled him, and they took up their position near the table of honour, at which Carey sat with his host. On a platform that commanded a view of the whole gathering, there was gang of journalists and photographers, all armed to the teeth with the weapons of their craft.

The dinner proceeded at what Bryant described as "the thrilling tempo" of Hollywood and then the moment for speech-making arrived. Mr. Bryant got to his feet and buglers blew another blast on their bugles, commanding silence.

"We have with us here to-night as our guest of honour," said Mr. Bryant, "a man who has been the victim of what I and those who think like me have been trying to eradicate from the art of the screen and from the life of Hollywood, which is the headquarters of that art."

He paused to listen to the applause, which broke out raucously. Carey glanced towards Josh Donovan and saw that individual watching him closely. From his position, Donovan had Carey under cover and made no effort to conceal the fact. Carey began to tremble.

"Hollywood," continued Bryant, "is the artistic conception of modern American life. The camera is the paint brush, the hammer and pen, with which Europe created art forms, which we in America are bound to surpass, if we save our national art from individuals and ideas that endeavour to make it a mockery of civilisation, by their vulgarity and buffoonery. Here we have the nerve centre of world culture, the point on the earth's surface at which new religions are coming into being, new conceptions of culture … "

At this moment he lost the point of his argument and his voice was drowned by an uproar caused by some Russian, who thought that the speech was an insult to the late Tsar. The buglers blew another blast on their bugles and the Russian was hurried away by two gunmen.

"Let Europe spit at us," continued Bryant, becoming excited. "Their affected contempt is a futile gesture, the gesture of a spiteful old cat. It is not Europe that we fear, but the elements within our own walls that turn us into ridicule by their vulgarity. I refer to individuals like Jack Mortimer, who imagines that Hollywood is a circus, in which the prize goes to the greatest buffoon. He represents the crudeness of infancy, which has to be disciplined, if the child is ever to grow into a responsible and civilised human being. And it is for that reason that I consider Mr. Carey's presence here to-night…"

At that moment, Josh Donovan made a sign to Carey and the latter got to his feet hurriedly. Bryant looked at him in surprise and Carey, with his eyes still on Donovan, held up his hand.

"I want to speak," he cried out.

"But I wanted to..." began Bryant.

"I must speak," cried Carey, trembling from head to foot." I do not agree with what our host has said. I am here under false pretences. I am not Mortimer's enemy. I have behaved very badly towards him and I want to apologise in this public manner for the foul attack I have made on him in *I Love Angela Devlin*. I have come here to-night wearing sack-cloth and ashes as a token of my shame at having behaved in this scandalous manner towards a man that befriended me."

He looked towards Mr. Donovan and the latter made a sign that enough had been said. But suddenly Carey felt a burning desire to rebel against Donovan's orders and he cried out:

"All I have said is a lie. I want to say..."

A shot rang out and Carey felt a bullet whizz past his head. Then all the lights suddenly went out. Carey continued to shout amidst the uproar that followed:

"In this crisis of human history, when the civilisation that man has created with great effort is in danger of being destroyed through the greed of the ignorant, you in Hollywood are debauching the human intellect..."

At that moment, he was struck on the back of the head by the butt of Josh Donovan's revolver and knocked unto unconsciousness.

CHAPTER XXXII

WHEN CAREY RECOVERED CONSCIOUSNESS, he found himself in a hut with Donovan and three other men.

"Where am I?" he said.

"Goddam lucky to be alive," said Donovan brutally.

"Come on. Pull yourself together. First time in years I missed. I just wanted to clip off one of your ears, though. Can't afford to have you bumped off just yet."

"You fired at me?" said Carey, remembering what had happened.

"I sure did," said Donovan. "I told you what to say, but you started off...Cheeky little runt!"

"What did he do, Josh ?" said a tall, fair man, who was lying on a seat, with his head resting on his hand.

"Started shootin' off his mouth,"said Josh. "The guy is nuts."

The tall, fair young man got to his feet and stretched himself. He was like a Viking, a magnificent specimen, with golden hair and skin, broad shoulders, narrow hips and cold, blue eyes that had in them the far-away look of the adventurer.

He was an airman called Con Willard.

"Let's get going," he said. "The guy is all right now. Give him the dope, Josh."

"What are you going to do with me ?" said Carey in great fear.

"If you keep quiet and obey orders," said Josh, "nothing rough is going to happen to you, but I warn you not to try anything funny again. I ain't going to stand for it."

They dragged Carey to his feet and brought him out of the hut. Then they all got into a car and drove away at a fast pace for about six miles. The car pulled in to the side of the road and halted. Donovan, who was sitting beside Carey in the back of the car, stuck a gun in Carey's side and whispered:

"Now, son, you're going to do exactly as I say. Get me?"

"I understand," said Carey.

"Take this gun," said Donovan, handing Carey an automatic pistol. "You needn't be afraid of it, because it's a fake gun. Jack Mortimer'll be along here presently. We're going to hold him up and you're going to go up to him, cover him with this gun and say: 'Here's where I get even with you, Mortimer. I've come to rescue Angela from your clutches. Hand her over or you'll croak. Do what you're told.' Then you turn to us and say: 'Go ahead boys. Follow out your orders.' Got all that ? Repeat it after me."

He made Carey repeat this speech until the latter had it by heart.

"Remember," said Josh, "that I'm going to be behind you all this while with a real gun, and the least sign of treachery on your part ... understand?"

"I understand," said Carey.

Suddenly one of the men whispered:

"Here he is."

"Pull her out," said Josh.

The driver suddenly pulled the car out across the road, forcing another car that approached to halt with a great scraping of brakes. At Donovan's impulsion, Carey got out, looking an extremely ridiculous figure in his sack, with an automatic pistol in his fist.

"Now, son," hissed Josh in his ear, "don't forget what you have to say if you want to go on living. Go ahead."

The others, also with guns in their hands, real ones, got out and surrounded Mortimer's car.

"Hey! What's this?" said Mortimer, sticking his head through the side window of the back of the car. His Filipino chauffeur and his bodyguard, who both sat in front, got out and put their hands above their heads. Carey rushed to the window through which Mortimer's head was sticking. He pointed the pistol at Mortimer, who put up his hands and seemed in mortal fear.

"Here's where I get even with you, Mortimer," said Carey. "I've come to rescue Angela from your clutches. Hand her over or you'll croak. Do what you're told. Go ahead, boys. Follow out your orders."

"I'm a married man," wailed Mortimer. "For God's sake, boys, take what I've got. Take anything you want, but don't hurt me."

Donovan pushed Carey into the back of the car with Mortimer and said to the Filipino:

"Get back into the car and drive home. Don't forget you're under cover."

The man obeyed. The bodyguard sat beside him, with his hands still held over his head. The other men followed in the other car. They passed through the gates of the ranch. As before, an electric bell rang violently, but the mastiffs did not rush forward. The artificial cow shone in the headlights of the car. They rushed up the drive and came to the men who were on guard outside the wall of the ranch-house. At a command from Mortimer, the men dropped their guns and put their hands over their heads. Josh ordered Mortimer out of the car. Mortimer got out with his hands over his head.

"You wait there," Donovan said to Carey.

The other car came up. The men got out of it and seized the gunmen, also the Filipino chauffeur and Mortimer's bodyguard. They bound them hand and foot while Donovan went into the courtyard of the ranch-house with Mortimer. Carey sat quietly in the back of Mortimer's car, holding his fake pistol in his hand. Dazed by the blow on the back of his head and the astounding things that kept happening to him, he did not question the strange drama that was now being enacted. Whether it was tragedy, comedy, or burlesque did not interest him. He felt that his only hope was to keep quiet and do what he was told. Nor was he surprised when he saw Mortimer come running out again, followed by Donovan, who carried somebody in his arms. Mortimer got in beside Carey once more. Donovan handed the person he was carrying to the tall blonde young man. Then he got into the driver's seat and drove away at a violent pace. The other car followed.

"Where are you taking me?" wailed Mortimer to Carey.

"How the devil should I know?" said Carey. "You probably know more about it than I do."

"Stop talking back there," said Donovan. "Keep that guy under cover, Carey."

About five miles farther ahead, Donovan stopped the car and ordered Mortimer to get out. The magnate meekly obeyed.

"You're going to burn for this, Carey," he shouted, shaking his fist at Carey.

The car shot ahead once more. After another few miles it

turned into a big field and came to a halt beside an aeroplane, whose engine was ticking over. The other car halted beside the first. Everybody got out. Willard lifted somebody in his arms out of the back of the car and ran to the aeroplane.

"Tie this guy up," said Donovan to the other two men who were with him.

"Okay, boss," they said.

They seized Carey and tied him securely. Then they carried him over to the aeroplane and dropped him into the back of the machine beside the other person. He looked at the other person and saw that it was Angela. Willard climbed into the cockpit and said:

"Okay, Josh, I'll be seein' ye."

"So long, Con," Donovan said. "I'll be stickin' around till you get back. Don't be long."

"I'll be right back," Willard said.

The plane taxied forward and then rose into the air. It circled and then, gaining altitude, it headed for the Mexican frontier. Willard began to sing. And well he might, for he had been paid twenty thousand dollars for this job, just for taking these two people beyond the frontier. His orders were to drop them in some remote place, from which they would not be able to escape in a hurry; and this Willard interpreted as an order to drop them some place in a condition that rendered them harmless; which meant dead, to his realistic mind.

That did not worry him in the least. He had been a crack pilot during the war and afterwards he became a pilot in the air mail service. He came to Hollywood some years later, to take part in a film dealing with the air service during the war. Like most stupid and sensual men, once he had tasted the luxury of life in Hollywood, he was unable to escape from it and return to the strenuous business of being a commercial pilot. When his brief contract expired he cast about for some lucrative means of employment. Being at that time irresistible to women and gifted with practically inexhaustible energy, he was the fashion for a time and lived in clover. Nominally he remained a pilot, operating his own private plane, but the flights that he made were generally to a shack in the mountains, where he entertained his passengers, who were invariably of the opposite sex.

By degrees he was forced into more suspicious undertakings, and he was at the end of his tether when this offer came from Donovan. Now, with his twenty thousand dollars in his pocket and enough gasoline in his machine to carry him into the wilds of Mexico, he felt happy. The important thing was to get rid of his two passengers.

As soon as he passed the frontier, he began to prepare for making a landing. Part of the preparations consisted in seeing that his automatic pistol was in order. He placed it beside him in the cockpit. Then he flew on, waiting for dawn to break.

Carey, in the meantime, had been struggling to free himself of his bonds. When he saw Willard examining his pistol, he realised that the man had evil intentions and his struggle with his cords became more earnest. At last he was able to free his hands. He quickly removed the cords from his feet and then, watching his opportunity, he reached forward and grabbed at the pistol that lay beside Willard. Willard was too quick for him. He turned round and clutched at the pistol, as Carey tried to pull it away. The two men grappled. The struggle was a short one, for Willard dealt Carey a powerful blow in the jaw that knocked the hapless man unconscious for a second time that evening. As he leaned back, however, to deliver his blow, he lost his balance and tumbled into the back of the plane on top of Angela.

The plane began to turn somersaults and hurtled towards

the earth at terrific speed. Willard did not lose his nerve, but crawled back into the cockpit and attempted to get the machine under control. For a moment it seemed that it was going to right itself, but at the very next moment, its nose struck a mound of sand and plunged right into it, with a terrific crash.

CHAPTER XXXIV

LEFT ON THE MOUNTAIN-SIDE, Mortimer gave way to one of those emotional crises which most human beings experience at one time or other in their lives. Certainly these crises are more common in infancy; but at that period they are less deep and they pass quickly, finding an outlet in tears, accompanied by howling. I refer, of course, to the urge of humanity, when oppressed by loneliness, due to defeat, sickness, or privation, to return to the womb from which it sprang. Such a return being physically impossible, man, who is above everything else an animal gifted with the genius of compromise, liquidates such crises by repeating aloud, in sorrowful tones, the word mammy.

So Mortimer ran along the road, with his trembling hands thrust out into the darkness, wailing for his mother like a lost child. And let such conduct not be considered ridiculous in a man of his great quality. Unless Shakespeare was a liar, the great Cæsar behaved during a crisis of sickness in an equally ridiculous manner. For it is written of Cæsar:

He had a fever when he was in Spain,

And, when the fit was on him, I did mark
How he did shake: 'tis true, this god did shake:
His coward lips did from their colour fly;
And that same rye whose bend doth awe the world
Did lose his lustre: I did hear him groan:
Ay, and that tongue of his that bade the Romaris
Mark him and write his speeches in their books,
Alas, it cried, "Give me some drink, Titinius,"
As a sick girl.

In fact, it is only through these manifestations of weakness that the great put themselves within reach of our feeble comprehension and give us the pleasure of knowing that they are human like ourselves and therefore worthy of our love. Nor are these momentary lapses to the disadvantage of their talents. They draw fresh force and courage from them. In fact, Mortimer, after he had run quite a long way along the road, babbling the word mammy, suddenly came to a halt, clenched his fists and cried out in a formidable tone:

"I must get on the wire. I ain't got a moment to lose."

In his excitement, he was about to order a secretary, or servant of some sort, to get him into telephonic communication with his ranch, when he looked about him and realised that he was behaving in a childish fashion. Immediately he plunged forward at a great rate, swinging his stubby arms and muttering to himself that this was not the time to lose faith in his plans.

"When a man says that the game of life is loaded against him," he said aloud, "that just means he ain't smart enough to make fate play all. For every move on the board there's another move that can beat it. Seems to me, I heard somewhere how a guy said that the good general can always turn defeat into victory. When he finds himself in the hands of the enemy, he just naturally turns around and says: 'Nerts! It's the enemy has fallen into my hands.' Why sure, this kid I picked up was carried off to God knows where, with that bum Carey. What's it got to do with me what happens to them? Nothing. I know nothing about them, so that don't have to trouble my conscience. Wasn't I kidnapped as well and left out here on the mountain to starve? Every man for himself. Hell! No. That ain't what's worrying me. Two people more or less, that don't matter, nohow. It's this Angela that's worrying me, this dame I pulled outa the cute little brain box I carry round with me. Can she make it? Can she fool'em same as she's fooled me? God! This is the biggest chance I've taken in my life. But I'm goin' through with it. Goddam it, I've got to go through with it. I can't turn back now. Yeah."

He uttered this last word at great length and in a loud voice and as the monosyllable died on the air, an automobile came rushing round the corner and caught the ruminating magnate within the glare of its headlights. The car halted beside him and the gruff voice of Josh Donovan called out:

"Okay, Mr. Mortimer, hop into the car. Everything's okay."

"Thought you were never coming back," said Mortimer, in a formal tone. "Step on it. Can't trust that guy. He might have put his foot in it already. He can't handle the police. They put the wind up him for good and proper reasons. Step on it, for God's sake."

They dropped him near the gate of his ranch and as he hurried through the gates dawn was breaking. A crowd of people rushed at him as soon as he appeared. They were newspaper men and detectives, who had been in occupation of the place since Dafoe announced the kidnapping some hours previously.

"Say, what's all this?" cried Mortimer, as they crowded

around him.

"How did you escape?" they cried.

"Escape from what?" said Mortimer, affecting ignorance.

"Haven't you been kidnapped?" they cried in amazement.

"Kidnapped?" said Mortimer. "Do I look kidnapped?"

"Excuse me," said a police officer, who appeared to be in charge of the others. "I don't understand this."

"Neither do I," said Mortimer truculently. "I want to know what's the meaning of this infringement on my rights as a property owner and a taxpaying citizen. What's the big idea?"

"Why," said the nonplussed officer, "we came here in answer to a report from Mr. Dafoe ... "

"That guy broke loose again, huh?" said Mortimer. "So he had me kidnapped, huh ? Now, will all you guys get home quietly and leave me in peace. I pay good money to have privacy here. No offence meant, but I only receive guests by invitation out here. Be seein' you."

"But, Mr. Mortimer, what about Miss Devlin?" cried one of the newspaper men.

"Since when did you become Miss Devlin's guardian?" snapped Mortimer. "If you're interested in Miss Devlin, why not tune in on your radio at nine o'clock to-morrow evening, or be at the Hollywood Bowl."

"But she left the house with you," said another. "She hasn't come back with you."

Thereupon Mortimer pretended to fly into a rage and yelled:

"What's this? A hold up? I'm going to get you guys off these premises pronto, if I have to call out the national guard to do it."

With that he ran up the drive towards the house, followed by the detectives and the newspaper men, who paid no attention to his threats. Dawn was now breaking but the great courtyard was all lighted up and there also was a crowd of policemen and reporters, who rushed forward asking him questions. He made his way through this press, around the swimming pool, in which three detectives were diving, on the lookout for clues. In the great lounge he found Dafoe, seated like a potentate in the foreground.

"What the hell is the meaning of this, Larry?" cried Mortimer.

Dafoe, wearing red silk pyjamas and a dressing gown of the same colour, sat at a table, on the far side of which there were three telephones placed in front of three reporters, who were busy talking into the instruments and writing on pads of paper. Policemen and others stood about. When he saw his employer, tears came into Dafoe's eyes, he stretched out his arms and he said in a voice that was broken with emotion:

"Can it be possible? I never expected to see you again in the flesh."

As he uttered these words, several cameras got into action, while the three reporters shouted into their instruments:

"At this moment, Mr. Mortimer has just returned safe and sound. He is now being embraced by his confidential secretary, Mr. Larry Dafoe."

"Cut that out," said Mortimer. "What's this? A charade?"

"Are you hurt?" cried Dafoe excitedly.

Mortimer affected to be completely mystified.

"Are you gone out of your mind?" he said. "What do you mean by calling in the police and starting all this racket about kidnapping?"

"But..." began Dafoe, pretending to be equally mystified.

"You can explain all that later," snapped Mortimer. Then he turned to the police and the reporters and added:

"Now, you guys, take a load o' this. I am giving out this statement in order to spare public feeling, which may be concerned needlessly about the safety of Miss Devlin. Here's what happened. I received information that there was going to be an attempt made last night, presumably at the instigation of certain interests which I shall not name, but whose identity must be obvious to the intelligent public, to kidnap Miss Devlin in order to prevent her going on the air to-night, and thereby give credence to accusations that have been made to the effect that she is a prisoner in my hands and subjected to various cruelties and maltreatments held reprehensible under the Constitution of the United States. I decided to substitute another girl for Miss Devlin, a girl that resembles her physically to a remarkable degree."

He then gave an account of his capture, of the kidnapping and of his being left stranded on the mountain-side.

"Unfortunately," he continued, "I had no time to take Dafoe into my confidence, as I did not wish to risk telephoning to him from my office, where I received the warning. While the substitute was being handed over, I tried by signs to make him understand that he was on no account to warn the authorities."

"So there has been a kidnapping after all," said one of the police officers truculently. "Who was it?"

"And where is Miss Devlin now?" cried a reporter. "This is all very mysterious."

"What's very mysterious about it?" shouted Mortimer. "The whereabouts of Miss Devlin are my business. I have given to the Press and to the public the exact amount of information that I feel is due to them both. I cannot risk a real kidnapping simply to please you gentlemen in your thirst for sensational news."

"But what about the girl that was kidnapped?" said the same police officer once more.

"But Mr. Dafoe here," said another, "described to us in detail how Miss Devlin was taken from her bed and carried off in her pyjamas and her dressing gown by a gang and..."

Mortimer put his hands before his face and affected to be overwhelmed.

"Okay, boys," he cried in a plaintive tone. "Have it what way you like. I have the responsibility on my shoulders of being the guardian of the most important living woman. I have done all in my power to save her from the annoyance of vulgar publicity, but the only result of my efforts seems to be the exact opposite of what I tried to achieve. I have tried by hiding Miss Devlin to save her from annoyance, but I have been accused, as a result, of crimes that might land me in the penitentiary, if they were proved against me. I have saved her only by taking on my shoulders the whole brunt of the publicity that her genius, her beauty and the power of her personality have caused. I have saved her thus far and I will go on saving her, if you guys give me a break. I am not afraid of my enemies."

Here he drew himself to his full height and added defiantly:

"I defy my enemies, both their slanders and their criminal attempts, but I expect that my friends, of the Press and the police, are not going to aid and abet them. Gentlemen, for God's sake, give me a break. I'm exhausted."

He slumped into a chair, dropped his arms between his knees and said:

"Larry, give me a highball. Oh! Why did you bring this down on me ? Didn't I tell you not to ... ?"

At this point he collapsed completely and then he muttered:

"Get me to bed, Larry. Clear these people off the premises. I must have a rest. I'll have further ... statement ... this afternoon."

The magnate was carried to his bedroom by two servants, while Dafoe persuaded the police and the reporters to vacate the premises. They went away mystified and grumbling and whispering that there was something strange afoot. Then Dafoe hurried to his employer's bedroom and locked the door. Mortimer was lying on his back sipping a highball.

"Sit down," said Mortimer curtly.

"What was the idea of turning on me like that ?" said Dafoe. "It was all my idea, wasn't it? You made those people believe I was a mug."

"And so you are," said Mortimer curtly, "if you think you're going to get the upper hand of me. I saw your game right along, although you might have thought I didn't."

Dafoe sat down slowly and said:

"How do you mean?"

"This friend of yours," said Mortimer, "Jesse Starr. Don't think I wasn't wise to it. Why, right along I had him in mind. That was my whole idea in picking up this dame in Ireland."

"That's a lie," said Dafoe angrily. "You never did think of it. It was I thought of it. It was only when you discovered, after I pointed it out to you that she was a complete flop, that she was too crude and that she had inhibitions about sex, that you listened to me."

"So what?" said Mortimer fiercely.

"I want to direct The Veiled Goddess," said Dafoe, "at a salary of five thousand dollars a week."

"You what?" cried Mortimer, leaping from the bed. "You impertinent goddam louse!"

Again Dafoe cowered into submission and Mortimer gave him another gem.

CHAPTER XXXV

A VIOLENT BUMP BROUGHT CAREY back to consciousness. In other words, he had been born again. He was struck on that part of his body which received the first salute to life, when the doctor had held him up by the heels and ... "Whack! Off you go into the world, son of man, with this foretaste of the treatment that is going to be meted out to you." And just as that first salute had brought the infant Carey to his senses and made him howl, so did the mature Carey regain his humanity when he was hurled out of the fallen aeroplane and bumped against the sand of the Mexican desert.

He sat up and felt himself all over, looking for wounds, fractures, and concussions. There were none. He only felt sore where he had been hit by the revolver butt and by Willard's fist. His buttocks stung, but that only roused him to activity, in the way that a malingering donkey is roused by the application of a nettle; he leaped to his feet and looked about him. He saw the wrecked aeroplane, half buried in the soft earth, and on the far side of the aeroplane, about twenty yards away, he saw Angela lying prostrate.

He ran to her, went on his knees and turned her over on her back. He examined her and found that she still lived. The discovery caused him unbounded joy. Forgetting that he had been an atheist until his body came in contact with the earth of Mexico, he clasped his hands before his upraised face and addressed the sky in these words:

"Most merciful God, I give Thee thanks most humbly for sparing her life and mine. Give us grace, Lord, never again to sin against truth."

Then, realising that God gives grace only to those that help themselves, he ran over to the wreckage and rummaged in it. The fore part of the machine was buried in the sand and Willard was buried with it. The only part of the unfortunate airman that was to be seen was his right leg, sticking from the cockpit. Carey spotted a locker.

"God is good," he said. "I might find something here."

He broke open the locker and found two flasks, together with some biscuits and preserved meat in tins; a supply of provisions carried by the dead aviator for cases of emergency. He took the lot back to where Angela lay. One of the flasks contained brandy and the other contained water. He forced some of the brandy between her lips. She shuddered, spat and opened her eyes.

"Are you hurt?" he whispered.

She looked at him wildly and then peered about her. She shuddered when she saw the wrecked aeroplane and the surrounding country. It looked desolate in the light of dawn. They were in a valley, covered with sand and occasional clumps of cactus and yucca trees. On every side great mountains rose, naked and savage. There was no sign of habitation and there was complete silence.

"Where are we?" she said.

"Never mind," said Carey. "We're alive. That's the important thing. Let's see are you hurt? Do you feel pain anywhere?"

"Only here," she said.

Luckily, she had fallen on the same part of her body as Carey had.

"Try to stand up, " he said.

"But how did we get here? " she said, as he helped her to her feet.

"In an aeroplane, " said Carey. "Don't you remember? Or were you asleep all the time ? "

"It's something that awful Dafoe gave me to drink, " she said, with another shudder. "I'm so weak."

"Lean on me, " said Carey. "The swine! What did he give you to drink? "

"I feel awful inside me, " she said. "I don't want to think about it. "

"Don't think about it," said Carey. "You're safe from him now, in any case. We'll go over to the shade of this clump of shrubs here and rest."

He picked up the flasks and the tins and led her away from the wreckage. After going some hundreds of yards, they came to a clump of desert shrubs.

There was a dip in the ground among the shrubs and he led her down into the dip.

"Let me take off your dressing-gown," he said. "Then I'll spread it on the ground and you can lie on it. "

Then he sat down beside her and took her head on to his lap.

"Tell me what happened," she said.

She was still in a daze. He told her what had happened on the previous evening. She began to pray and to thank God as he had done himself when he discovered that they were both alive.

"They wanted to kill us," she said.

"Yes, they did," said Carey. "But we needn't worry about it now. We have escaped from them."

"But they'll come after us and find us," she said.

"God! If I was only back in Ireland again I'd be a different girl. Wasn't I the fool to listen to that man, with his fine promises of what he was going to do for me? And he only keeping me locked up there in that house and Dafoe giving me queer drinks and the other young man watching me the whole time and they not letting you come near me either. Oh! Brian, I used to nearly die of loneliness for you."

"And I for you, too," said Carey.

Now it appeared to him that he had been madly in love with her the whole time that he was in Hollywood, for everything appeared to be different out here in the silence of the desert. Everything was natural and simple and it was easy to think. The mind was not confused. Things were in their right proportions. The problem of life was no longer terrible. Here he was with a girl whom he loved and there was no feeling of emptiness or incompleteness, to make him want to be anywhere else, or to do anything other than to love this girl and to care for her. The past was vague and repulsive like a nightmare dimly remembered.

"I wasn't really a bad girl until I met them," said Angela. "I was foolish and I used to be tempted to do things I shouldn't do, but I used to suffer for it afterwards, terrible torture I used to suffer, when I did bad things. But God used to forgive me. There was always God to forgive me. But after I met them, I didn't dare to ask God to forgive me."

"I felt the same," said Carey. "Although I didn't believe in God, I always was forgiven for the things I did that were wrong, until I met them, and then I felt that I was cut off from forgiveness. That is because we both committed the sin against the Holy Ghost."

"What sin is that?" Angela said. "Is it a terrible sin?"

"Yes," said Carey. "It is a terrible sin. It is the sin against truth and against love."

"Do you think we'll be ever forgiven for it?" she said.

"Yes, we surely will be forgiven for it," he said, "if we love one another, for that's the only way to be forgiven for it."

"Oh! Indeed, I will always love you," she said.

"I'm not afraid here, either, in spite of the desert and the mountains, for it's grand to be safe from them two. And that young man that used to be watching me and dressing himself up in my clothes and singing songs, so that I used to be terrified, hearing him sing with my voice, so that you couldn't see the difference. And when he dressed himself in my clothes, they used to make up his face, Mr. Dafoe, and another man that talked a foreign language, he was a doctor, too. This young man looked as like me as two peas, so he did, hair an' all. He had a girl's face, but he was a man all the same, when he wasn't dressed in my clothes. There was something terribly queer about him and he terrified me more than the others, although it was Mr. Dafoe that always gave me the drink and I used to be afraid not to take it, after the first time I refused and the other man, that said he was a doctor, gave me the same class of drink, pretending it was a sleeping-draught, on account of the way I couldn't sleep. Oh! God, Brian, don't let them get hold of me again, will you?"

"Have no fear," said Carey savagely. "They won't get hold of you again."

And as he soothed her, rocking her in his arms like a child, he felt a sense of pride and a power in him that made his youth return. All the bitterness and humiliation of his past life, and especially of the time that he had spent in Hollywood, were washed away by the appeal for protection uttered by the beautiful creature that snuggled within his arms. Then, indeed, he felt a pure love well up in him like a glorious song. It possessed his body and his soul in the silence of the desert.

"My treasure," he whispered, "have no fear. And don't worry about anything you have done in the past, because all that is dead now and it will soon be forgotten. Love washes away everything that is ugly, and the soul of a person that loves becomes pure like the soul of a new-born child. I have been far more wicked than you have been, but I now feel pure and innocent again and I'm not afraid."

"Oh! My love," she whispered, "I'll always worship the ground you walk on."

Then they slept for a while in one another's arms and when they awoke they ate some of the food that he had found in the aeroplane. Then they prepared to set off walking, to see could they find a way out of the desert. As they stepped forth from the clump of brushwood, they were startled to see a party of horsemen riding wildly down from the mountains on the east, towards the wreckage of the aeroplane. Carey drew her back hurriedly among the brushwood and they both hid, watching the crowd of horsemen approach at a fast gallop.

And then they saw that among the horsemen, who were all dressed as Mexicans, with great wide hats, there was a man wearing the cassock of a priest.

"We're saved," whispered Carey. "They're not bandits. They have a priest with them."

Taking Angela by the hand, he rushed out shouting to the approaching horsemen.

CHAPTER XXXVI

THE UTMOST CONFUSION REIGNED OVER the length and breadth of America and to a lesser extent over the whole civilised world, as a result of the reported kidnapping. Mortimer's denial of Dafoe's original statement came too late, as the magnate intended it should, to stop the first issues of the newspapers carrying the startling news. And of course, it was cabled all over the world and broadcast, causing panic even among the mandarins of Indo-China. And yet when the denial was printed it aroused popular fury.

First of all, the public was angry at being denied the thrill of taking part by proxy in the theft and possible violation of the most exciting living woman, with the consequent thrill of following the search for her, page by page, telegram by telegram, announcement by announcement, in the newspapers and over the radio, of revelling in reports that she was buried alive, dragged naked and manacled through tropical jungles, left to starve on an iceberg in the Arctic Sea, adrift in midocean on a raft with a couple of cut-throats, who are snarling at one another, while they prepare, with daggers, to fight to the death for her. It was like promising a child a cake and then refusing it.

The newspapers were particularly furious. Led by the *Pacific Eagle*, which the law had compelled to suspend publication of *I Love Angela Devlin*, they opened fire on Mortimer. The article in the *Pacific Eagle* was particularly damning.

"Let us examine the facts," said this journal. "Brian Carey, after the scandalous scene at Mr. Bryant's home yesterday, where he appeared in a costume that represented shame in the old world, and delivered a eulogy of Mr. Mortimer that was obviously delivered under compulsion, was dragged away at the point of the gun and has disappeared. This morning, at an early hour, Mr. Bryant issued a statement to the effect that, to his knowledge, Mr. Carey was abducted by some men from among those he had engaged as guards for his guests. Also missing is Con Willard, the airman from his home in Santa Monica. Has Willard gone on air trip? And are his companions Angela Devlin and Brian Carey? We are inclined to think that our surmise is partly correct.

"With the publication yesterday of the first instalment of the Carey story, which Mr. Mortimer has managed to suspend by the application of an injunction, the monocled magnate may have realised that the game was not worth the candle. Either he is a party to this kidnapping of Carey and the girl who purported to be Angela Devlin, a kidnapping in which a certain filibustering Irish organisation may have been implicated, or else his craze for publicity has carried him this time a little too far. And for the reason that Angela Devlin does not exist and never has existed except in the mind of Jack Mortimer. The whole business, to our mind, is but a vast publicity stunt to boost Mortimer's latest monstrosity *The Veiled Goddess*."

Taken in conjunction with the interview with his wife and her threat of divorce proceedings, this article stirred up popular anger to a wild degree. On all sides people were demanding that Mortimer should be brought to heel for his enormities, especially for attempting to seize control of the film industry by the greatest fraud in history. The telegraph wires were busy with messages that ran:

"THEORY WIDELY HELD HERE ANGELA DEVLIN DOES NOT EXIST. IRISH GIRL NAMED BIDDY MURPHY HELD USED AS DUMMY FOR JACK MORTIMER'S VEILED GODDESS OF LOVE. UGLY SITUATION DEVELOPING. MAYOR STATED CONSIDERING CALLING OUT NATIONAL GUARD. STILL NO LIGHT ON CAREY MYSTERY."

And then the world was startled early in the afternoon by a message wired from a remote part of northern Mexico by John F. Cooney, America's number one newshawk, the same individual who had been responsible for the incident in the armoured car. The message ran as follows:

"Hidden away in his stronghold among the mountains of northern Mexico, white-haired Bishop Rodríguez, valiant Crusader of the twentieth century, has just taken time out from fighting the Government with his brave peon followers, to bless one of the most romantic marriages of modern times. The bridegroom gave his name as Brian Carey. The bride described herself as Bridget Murphy, of Ballymorguttery, County Cork, Ireland.

"Flown down to interview Bishop Rodríguez, the thorn in the side of the Mexican Government's socialistic education schemes, I landed close to the wreck of the aeroplane in which Con Willard, the eloped couple's pilot, met his death. Two mounted peon soldiers led me up the mountain-side to the bishop's palace, a grass-roofed hut, in which the ceremony was

233

about to take place, before an audience of armed *Cristeros*.

"When the couple had been joined in holy wedlock, I asked Mrs. Carey whether she was Angela Devlin. Evidently terrified by her recent experiences, she fainted on seeing me and hearing the question. Her husband then made the following statement:

" 'The person known to the world as Angela Devlin does not exist and never has existed except in the imagination of Gentleman Jack Mortimer.'

"Mr. Carey refused to answer all further questions. When offered a lift back to civilisation in my plane, he retorted angrily:

" 'My wife and I have had enough of what you call civilisation. We prefer to live here in peace.'

"Before I left, I witnessed the departure of Bishop Rodríguez and his followers, accompanied by the newly married couple, to another hiding-place among the mountains. Carey's parting words to me were:

" 'I shall go on wearing sack-cloth and ashes until I have washed the stain of Hollywood off my soul.'

"His wife, however, sitting behind him on his mule, was dressed in an attractive suit of silk pyjamas."

This story drove the mob to a frenzy, and loud cries rang out on the Boulevard:

"Let's go out and lynch Mortimer."

CHAPTER XXXVII

OUT AT THE RANCH, IN THE GREAT LOUNGE of the Emir of Bokhara, the monocled magnate faced his terrified associates. Not only Myron Luther, Roger Kent, Mervin Clapp, Joe Boloni, Bud Tracy and Sam Gunn were there, but also Samuel Kruger and two other "higher up tycoons," flown from New York after the outbreak of the injunction war on the previous day. They were all in a state of hysteria and the smiling face of Mortimer, instead of reassuring them, simply convinced them that the man had gone out of his mind and was indifferent, not only to their, but to his own destruction.

"See what you've done?" cried Tracy. "I may as well pack up and go right now. You've ruined me in the picture business. Mixed up in this goddam racket of yours. Hope you get the chair."

"What's all this?" said Mortimer. "Why don't you guys keep your shirts on? What's all this hooey?"

"It ain't no hooey," said Roger Kent. "This guy Cooney, same guy that tried to photograph Angela in the armoured car going through New York, he ain't the sort of guy to jump at any phoney business. He found them all right."

"Yeah," said Mervin, "and that guy is going to get every ounce of publicity out of the biggest scoop of his life. Goddam luck! Went down there to interview this bishop, whatever his name is..."

"Ole Rodríguez," said Luther. "Well-known guy that's been up in the mountains for months fightin' the Mexican Government with a gang of peons."

"Nerts," said Mortimer. "He's got nothing. It's all goddam nonsense."

"Oh! Hasn't he? " said Kent. "Why, he described the whole business over the radio: how Angela and Carey crashed in the machine that Willard flew, how they were found by Rodríguez and his men, come there to meet Cooney for an interview, how Carey married Angela and is gone off with her."

"Human offal," said Gunn, pale with emotion.

"This is the end."

Mortimer laughed as if his sides would burst.

"So it's just a laughing matter to you, Jack," said Mr. Kruger. "All this dough gone down the drain, it's all a laughing matter to you, not to mind that mob down there."

"World Studios can close up shop right now," said Luther, "unless we can produce Angela Devlin to go on the air this evening."

"Swell chance we have of doin' that!" said Mervin.

"I'm ruined," said Tracy.

"Can't you guys listen to me?" said Mortimer. "Can't you let me explain?"

"Explain!" they all cried in hysterical derision.

"Sure," said Mortimer, sticking his monocle truculently into his eye socket. "Why, sure I'll explain. That guy didn't find Angela Devlin in Mexico. She'll go on the air all right."

"Who did he find, then?" they cried.

"That's what I'm going to tell you," said Mortimer.

"He's just trying to stall," said Gunn. "He knows she's not due to go on the air until nine o'clock this evening."

"Meantime he'll make a getaway," said Tracy.

"The guy may be nuts, but he can't make a getaway from me."

He approached Mortimer as if with the intention of hitting him, but Mortimer held out his arms appealingly and said:

"Pappy, I didn't think you had it in you. Honest I didn't. I didn't think you'd turn on me like that without givin' me a chance to defend myself."

He burst into tears. Tracy also became moved. He and Mortimer embraced one another emotionally and uttered terms of rough endearment. Then they parted, and Mortimer, with the speed of which he was a master, switched on his bond-salesman expression, and said a melting tone:

"Trouble with most people in this, as in every other business, is lack of imagination. Whatever may be said against me, and I dare say there's a lot that can be said against me and my methods, nobody that has ever been associated with me can say that I lack imagination. That right, Bud? That right, Myron?"

"You'll need a lot of imagination to straighten this out," said Luther.

"Give him a break," said Tracy. "Let's hear what he has to say."

"Right from the very beginning," continued Mortimer, "when I first conceived this Angela Devlin idea, I realised ... "

"So it was only an idea," snarled one of the tycoons from New York. "We've been chucking our money away for the sake of an idea."

"Yeah," said another of them furiously. "He has the neck to stand up here now and tell us that Angela Devlin is only an idea."

"Yeah," said Mortimer imperturbably. "And I'm telling you that she is, furthermore, the greatest idea since the first camera was cranked. But for the love o' Mike, don't interrupt me, or we'll never get nowhere."

"Go ahead," they said.

"I realised," continued Mortimer, "that at the beginning there must be two Angela Devlins. The real one came out of my imagination, inspired by a girl I saw in Ireland and whom I figured on employing. As the second, or the dummy one. The real one, my inspiration, was my conception of what the screen goddess of love should be, a being of physical purity and spiritual cleanliness, with a God-given personality, not based on the lure of sex, not on fierce passion, but on pure and ideal romance. The other had the qualities that we usually associate ..."

"Cut that out" said Gunn, rubbing his hands through his thick hair, an expression of agony on his nervous face. "Don't treat us like children or movie fans. We may be human offal but we're not children."

"Step on it, Jack," said Joe Boloni. "Cut out the sales talk. We're in a hurry. When I left town, they looked like settin' out on a lynchin' party. There's no time to waste. Can you produce the dame or not?"

"He's got two now," said Kent. "Did you ever hear anything so cuckoo in all your natural life?"

"All right," said Mortimer, changing once more to a tone of indignation. "If you guys won't let me explain, try an' see for yourselves, if you can, what I've done. There are times and this is one of them, when I feel like throwing in the towel and letting you guys get snowed under by your own ignorance. But before I do so, let me tell you, and you especially, Sam Gunn, you that's always shootin' off your mouth about art, that I have done something here which no artist that the world has ever known has done. Yeah! That dame found by Cooney in Mexico may bear some resemblance to the one I am now going to unveil before your astonished eyes. She may bear the same remote resemblance that something crude and unfinished bears to a polished work of art. But mine is the hand that did the polishing. I have worked in the short space of a week night and day to produce that masterpiece, to extract from the one all the qualities that attracted me in her and instil them into the other, a creation that was purely the product of my imagination. And now, gentlemen, I am going to unveil the Goddess of Love."

With that he bowed to them, like a showman and, taking little short steps, he trotted out of the room, through a side door near the divan. All the men gathered there looked at one another, wondering whether he was insane, or really going to save them and himself from the horrible dilemma in which they were placed, expecting at any moment to be attacked by a howling mob that carried ropes and petrol for a mass lynching.

And then they saw Mortimer reappear through the door. He stood aside, smiling in triumph. Then came Larry Dafoe, smiling in a strange, rapt way. He bowed slightly and with great dignity to someone unseen. Then with his left hand he made a gesture of invitation. Immediately, the audience saw, to their utter astonishment, Angela Devlin enter the room. And as Dafoe saw their astonishment, the rapt smile broadened until it covered his whole countenance. He licked his lower lip with his tongue, leaned back and gave vent to a silent, mirthless cackle.

And, indeed, he had every reason to be proud of his handiwork, for this Angela Devlin was in many ways superior to the original.

CHAPTER XXXVIII

IN ORDER TO CLARIFY THE SITUATION, if possible, it is necessary at this point to give some account of Jesse Starr, or Angela Devlin as he was to be in future. An American by birth, he had been brought up in England, where he distinguished himself, both at school and at the university, by his acting ability, chiefly in female parts. After returning to America he went on the stage, where he met with no success whatsoever, since he looked ridiculous as a man, owing to his extremely effeminate manners and appearance; he then came to Hollywood, where he drifted about the studios for a year, earning a precarious livelihood as a chorus boy in musical productions. Then he came in contact with Dafoe, who became charmed by the young man's personality. An intimate friendship developed between the two and Dafoe tried to interest Mortimer in the young actor. Mortimer was impressed by Starr's ability, for the young man was really brilliant, not only as an actor, but as a singer and dancer as well; in a word, he had the perfect combination of talents demanded of a successful screen star, who must, above all, be versatile. Yet it was impossible to use him, in the magnate's opinion, owing to his incurable effeminacy.

Even so, he was attached to the magnate's household and then Dafoe conceived the amazing idea of offering Jesse to the world as a woman, since he was unacceptable as a man. In a word, seeing how closely he resembled Angela physically, he suggested to Mortimer that Jesse should become Angela Devlin. And when Angela proved to be difficult and to be too violent and disturbing for the part intended for her, the troubled magnate agreed. With the aid of Dr. Karl Zog, Dafoe had worked the miracle with consummate success.

"By God!" thought Mortimer, as he watched Angela sail into the room, looking really like a screen goddess. "The man is a genius."

Then he turned to the others and cried:

"That's what I wanted to explain, fellahs. But now it's obvious to me that there was no need for an explanation. That pose, that expression, that indescribable quality of genius speak for themselves."

He spoke in the frenzy of a radio announcer during football game, in order to cover his anxiety about their reception of Angela. He saw them stare open-mouthed at her, their brows furrowed, their eyes puzzled. They all reacted in an identical fashion to her appearance. They were fascinated and at the same time repelled. It was the same Angela that they had seen before, the same girl that had enthralled them by her singing. And yet it was a different Angela, in spite of the similarity. This Angela had something that that the other one had not got, a strange wickedness lying behind the smiling innocence of her angelic countenance. Yes. She was truly an angel and a devil in one, a combination of good and evil in one that rendered her in some way barren and repellent, something that aroused all the passions simultaneously in a confused way. Bah! It was impossible to discover, their eyes said, what she lacked that the other Angela possessed, or in what way she was different.

Gunn was the first to disengage his tongue from the hypnotic spell imposed on it by her appearance and to give voice to the questionings and doubts of his eyes.

"She's fixed," he said. "That's what he's done. He's fixed her."

This was the cue for which Mortimer had been waiting and he leaped into the breach with a loud cry.

"She's not fixed," he thundered, "but adapted for the screen."

"Adapted for the screen," cried all the others in chorus.

"Adapted for the screen," thundered Mortimer once more, "with the closest possible regard for the original. All the salient features have been retained and something has been added which no screen star ever had before."

Leaning against the wall, with his hands folded on his bosom, Dafoe threw back his head once more and gave vent to a mirthless cackle.

"Yes," continued Mortimer, going up to Angela and taking her by the hand, which she offered to him with a queenly dignity. "Since the first day I came into this industry, I have dreamt of this moment, when I could salute on bended knee, with my lips, a star of stars that was entirely my own creation."

With these words, he went on one knee and touched Angela's right hand reverently with his lips. Then he arose and, still holding her hand, he continued:

"Gentlemen, this motion-picture business has often and with justice been called a racket, like any other, to exploit the public and drag from their unwilling hands the dimes and two-bit pieces that go to make up a seven-figure profit. Like everybody connected with this business, I have, during my career, sacrificed the best interests of truth in putting on the market what I thought was legitimate box-office bait. I have written genius across the face of mediocrity, turned tripe into caviar with a shot from the needle of bluff and held up the dictionary for an adjective big enough to drown the criticism of the world's suckers. For that reason, gentlemen, you will pardon me for being hardly able to speak with joy when I tell you that..."

Here he dropped Angela's hand, stood back, put his hand to his heart and cried out with the utmost fervour:

"For the first time in the history of motion pictures, a producer can claim to have created a star that has got everything, and when he makes that claim he speaks the whole truth and nothing but the truth. Gentlemen, have a good look at her and tell me if I lie. Has she got everything?"

Moved by the burning eloquence of his words, as well as by the diabolical fascination of Angela's countenance and figure, all those present cried out with one voice:

"She's got everything."

Then, at Mortimer's suggestion that they should set an example to the motion-picture audiences of the world, they each got down on one knee and touched her right hand with their lips, while Dafoe leaned against the wall, giving vent to his mirthless cackle. Now they were all, including Mortimer, in a kind of religious ecstasy, after having touched her hand with their lips and bowed their knees.

"Don't you feel," said Mortimer in a shrill voice, "as if you'd been lifted up and thrown down and knocked unconscious?"

"Goddam right," said Mervin. "I feel as if I had been hit by something."

"The script," said Gunn, "must be adapted to this

adaptation...I had no idea that life could be adapted to the screen, but now I believe I firmly believe that life can be adapted."

"We'll take her in solemn procession through the streets," cried Mortimer, "and let this be our answer to our enemies."

"It's a responsibility," said Tracy, "to direct an actress that can have this effect..."

"This adaptation," boomed Luther, "is going to go places that no original ever went."

"Are you guys going to come with me?" cried Mortimer. "We'll drive in solemn procession through the streets and show her to the people."

"We'll all go with you," they cried. "We'll follow Angela."

"Are you ready to come, Angela?" said Mortimer.

Then Angela spoke for the first time. In a voice of ravishing sweetness, that had in it the soft, melting tones of Ireland, as well as a deeper quality which was hard to associate with the female voice of any country, she said:

"I am ready."

Simple words, but they had the effect of making them all cry out in a kind of drunken shout, as if she had given voice to some awe-inspiring truth:

"How wonderful!"

Suddenly Dafoe's face became solemn. Then an expression of deep scorn and of hatred came into his eyes. He spat viciously and muttered:

"*Canaille!*"

CHAPTER XXXIX

THE MAGNATE, BEFORE HE SET FORTH, left no stone unturned to ensure that the procession through the streets of Hollywood would be a spectacular success. He conferred with the city authorities, with the radio stations and with the Press.

"What's the meaning of this outrage?" he said to the city authorities. "Is there no law to protect me against this campaign of vilification that is being conducted against me by my enemies? Can you guarantee me a safe conduct through this city, with my charge, Miss Devlin? Is a section of the Press going to be allowed to stir up popular feeling to such an extent that I can't take Miss Devlin to the Bowl this evening for her broadcast? Or am I going to have the protection that a citizen and the guardian of such a valuable property as Miss Devlin, who is a person of the greatest national importance, feels that he deserves?"

The authorities promised him all the protection in their power and the chief of police himself came out to the ranch to confer with him about the necessary arrangements. When the chief of police expressed his anxiety about whether Miss Devlin was really at the ranch or in northern Mexico as had been stated over the radio by Mr. Cooney, Mortimer said:

"See for yourself. Come and have a look at her."

And when the chief of police was taken in to Angela's dressing-room, where the star of stars was being dressed for the parade by Dafoe and Dr. Karl Zog, he felt as awed by the majesty of her beauty as any of the others who had seen her.

"She's got everything," he said. "I'll turn out every man under my command to protect her."

To the Press, Mortimer handed out the following statement:

"In order to allay public excitement and to quash rumours that Miss Devlin has been abducted and is now in Mexico, Mr. Mortimer has again changed his plans with regard to her. She will travel unveiled on her way to the Hollywood Bowl this evening. She will travel in an open car, thus giving the public their first opportunity of seeing her in the flesh. She will be attended by all the executive officers of World Films and by all those connected with the production of her first medium *The Veiled Goddess*. She will be attended also by an armed escort, as the authorities do not wish that any untoward event, considering the excitement of the public, should mar her first appearance."

The shrewd Mortimer had withheld his reply to his wife's attack until this moment. Now he struck.

"I offer to pay," he announced, "into the bank account of any charitable organisation that the judge wishes to name, the sum of one hundred thousand dollars, if Mrs. Mortimer can prove in a court of law, either that I have failed to make adequate provision for her and Junior, or that I have been unfaithful to my marriage vows. On the other hand, I disdain making charges against her, charges which are unfortunately only too easy to prove. Poor woman! I am convinced that she has been induced to make this dastardly attack on my character at this moment at the instigation of my enemies. I am, however, ready at all times to forgive and forget."

This statement, added to the announcement that Angela existed, was safe, and that she was going to be shown in procession that evening, turned the tide of public feeling completely in his favour. Long before the appointed time, the streets and all the roads from the ranch to the Hollywood Bowl were lined with a dense mass of people. Crowds of people came by air, by automobile and by train from cities one hundred miles distant. It was a truly astonishing scene.

At last everything was ready. The party got into their cars in the great courtyard of the ranch. Trembling with excitement, with his monocle in his eye, Mortimer stood up in his seat and cried out:

"God! This is the greatest moment in the history of the world."

They set forth, cheering loudly. Angela sat between Dafoe and Mortimer in the leading car, flanked by armed police on motor cycles. As soon as her car debouched from the ranch gates, she immediately came upon a multitude drawn up on either side of the road.

"Now listen, kid," whispered Mortimer in her ear as they moved along towards the city. "Go and get them or it's the end of us. Put everything you've got into your face and make it smile."

"She'll do what I tell her, Jack," said Dafoe leaning across and looking Mortimer in the face insolently.

"I'm her manager. And don't forget that I'm going to make you pay for the privilege of getting her to work for you."

Mortimer swore under his breath and muttered:

"By God! You're cunning. You've got me at last."

"Wrong, Mr. Mortimer," said Dafoe. "I've got Angela."

Before the magnate could retort, the shouting of the mob had suddenly become so loud that a single voice could not be distinguished and he himself was carried away by the mob hysteria. It was the same mob that had been howling for his blood a few hours previously. Now they were in a state of religious exaltation.

Incredible though it may seem, when Angela's car turned into the Hollywood Boulevard, the thoroughfare on either side was lined with kneeling women, all dressed in white, with a banner strung across above the road, bearing the inscription:

"The league of screen mothers dedicate their children to the pure and romantic love personified by Angela Devlin."

Farther down, on opposite sides of the road, there were two groups of young men, wearing flour sacks similar to the one Carey wore at the scandalous dinner-party. They also had a banner, on which was written:

"WELCOME TO THE CEMETERY OF THE LIVING DEAD."

Stranger than these, and other similar banners and groups of fanatics, was the effect that the sight of Angela's face had on the mass of spectators. Down the length of the Boulevard, as the people caught sight of her, their faces assumed her expression of barren ecstasy. All the faces that looked upon hers were immediately distorted from their natural shape by a passion that was neither good nor evil, but pertaining to something primitive and long forgotten by civilised beings.

And then, when she had passed and they could no longer see her face, they gave way to those excesses that are typical of people taking part in a religious revival. Some went into fits and rolled about on the ground. Others frothed at the mouth. Others, driven to lewdness of conduct, hurled themselves on those nearest to them. Some tore at their hair and rent their garments. Others wounded their bodies with whatever weapons came into their hands.

And the air was thunderous with a cry that rose from this mass, like the surging of a great sea against a cliff.

"She is," they cried. "She is. She is. She is."

This cry gained in volume with her progress, until at last its rhythm took possession of the whole mass and they swayed back and forth, intoning, again and again and again:

"She is. She is. She is. She is."

AFTERWORD

The very title of Liam O'Flaherty's novel, *Hollywood Cemetery* (1935), based on the author's varied experiences in that citadel of the film industry, suggests the question: what prompted such a radical departure of the author from the more habitual contexts of his work, rural Ireland and Dublin slums?

Son of a Fenian father and being an Irish-speaking Aran Islander (Inis Mór), O'Flaherty was sensitive to all dimensions of Irishness. He was also a victim of the ambiguous relation of his culturally colonized Irish fellow-citizens with their ancestral tongue. His early writings in Irish Gaelic, some of which were later gathered in the short story collection *Dúil* (Desire), were virtually ignored, when not rejected by the censor. If he were to realise his ambition to be a writer, he saw that the English language would have to be his medium. Following defeat of the Republic in the Irish Civil War 1922-24, he lived mainly in England, establishing himself there as a novelist and short story writer.

He travelled to Hollywood, California, in the spring of 1934, with an ambition to become a screen writer and to interest his cousin, John Ford in directing a film version of material that was to become his novel *Famine* (1937), then in gestation, and which he dedicated to Ford. Glimpses of Ford's working persona are presented, arguably, in the behaviour of the 'Jack Mortimer' character in *Hollywood Cemetery*. Thus, he had Mortimer say, anticipating the "Fake Ireland" aura of some of Ford's later work:

"You couldn't get an American audience to believe that a primitive Irish village is like what it is. No, sir, they want the real thing and the real thing is the genuine Hollywood product, made by the most highly paid expert in the business. Hey, Shultz, how many villages have we shot on this trip?"

"About fifteen," said Shultz.

"Was there a single one of those villages," said Mortimer, "that looked like an Irish village?"

"Not a darned one, chief," said Shultz. (p. 23)

The screen potential of raw Irish film talent would need careful cultivation:

"Here was this wild Irish rose," he cried in his most melting tones, "blooming unseen by a wild Irish river, when I come along and see her. What do I do? I take her along to Hollywood, teach her screen technique and offer her to the world as a modern goddess, as a film star. That's what I do. And she becomes a goddess, for the modern film star is a goddess, worshipped by the multitude, as they worshipped Venus of old." (p. 26)

John Ford (1894-1973) was born in in Cape Elizabeth, Maine. His father, John Augustine Feeney, was from Spiddal, Co. Galway and his mother, Barbara Curran, was from Kilronan, Inis Mór, Co. Galway and related distantly to Liam O'Flaherty. In 1914 John, Jr. installed himself in Hollywood, changed his name to John Ford, to become the legendary director of a stream of award-winning films.

O'Flaherty reasoned that the dramatic impact of a film

version of his novel *Famine* could not but be a major box-office success, given the size of the Irish American population, most of whose presence in the USA was due to that mid-19th century Hunger Holocaust in Ireland. How could not the imagination of this Irish American, future director of *The Grapes of Wrath* (1941), fail to be gripped by the cinematographic possibilities of a script that incorporated the suffering and the indomitable will to survive against overwhelming odds of his very own people? Yet, to the disappointment of O'Flaherty, instead of *Famine*, Ford aficionados were treated to his classic of stage-Irish buffoonery, *The Quiet Man* (1952), starring John Wayne and Maureen O'Hara. Ford may have reasoned, probably correctly, that the spectacle of death and unalleviated human suffering described in O'Flaherty's *Famine* could hardly be productive of as big a box-office take as an escapist stage Irish extravaganza such as the John Wayne - Maureen O'Hara green-tinted fantasy, based on a Maurice Walsh short story published in 1932, whose film rights had been bought by Ford.

The Quiet Man was almost universally lauded, especially in Ireland, and is *de rigour* Irish-American viewing on St. Patrick's Green Beer Day. An escapist film for an escapist people! In this context, *Hollywood Cemetery* is O'Flaherty's own illuminating answer as to why he departed from Irish themes on this occasion: to show how little hope there was of the US film industry making a realist film about Ireland, based on a realist novel. And while motivations may have been different between Hollywood and Gaelic League puritans back home, both ultimately favoured the anti-realist presentation of an Ireland that never was.

The acerbic comment of Philip Hamburger in *The New Yorker* magazine regarding *The Quiet Man*, namely that its director "appears to have fallen into a vat of treacle", perhaps better reflects the reaction of Liam O'Flaherty to his cousin's choice for his "Irish" film of the whimsical paddy-whackery of *The Quiet Man* rather than rather than the bleak naked truth of his own *Famine*. Might the "Mortimer" of *Hollywood Cemetery* have been the harbinger of John Ford's choice of material for his "Irish" block-buster?

Tomás Mac Síomóin
Sant Feliu de Guíxols, Catalunya
January 2019

ABOUT THE AUTHOR

Liam O'Flaherty (Liam Ó Flaithearta), 1896–1984, was one of the most distinguished and prolific writers, in Irish and English, of his generation and a major figure of the Irish Literary Renaissance.

Abandoning an early intention to join the priesthood, he joined the British Army under his mother's surname and was wounded the Western Front. After the war, he travelled to South America, Turkey, Canada and the Soviet Union, holding a variety of jobs before entering the United States illegally in 1920. He joined the Communist Party there, a move that determined the politics he supported for most of his life. He returned to Ireland in 1921, at the height of the War of Independence. His ideas for Ireland's future differed radically from those of Sinn Féin. Two days following the foundation of the Irish Free State, he and some followers occupied and held for four days the Rotunda building in Dublin, flying the red flag in a failed attempt at socialist revolution.

Shortly afterwards O'Flaherty made his way to London where he wrote short stories in Irish. However, this early work was badly received, prompting him to write henceforth mainly in English. His first novel, *Thy Neighbour's Wife*, was published in 1923 and was followed by a stream of novels, short stories, and poems. Many of his works were banned by the Irish Censorship of Publications Board. His writing combines a graphic and striking naturalism, acute psychological analysis, poetry and biting satire together with an abiding sympathy for the common man and anger against injustice. The powerful ideological substratum of the writings of this lifetime

Marxist is seldom noted or commented upon. Liam O'Flaherty died on 7 September 1984, aged 88, in Dublin. A memorial garden in his native village of Gort na gCapall, Inishmore, commemorates the life and work of this literary giant.

CPSIA information can be obtained
at www.ICGtesting.com
Printed in the USA
LVHW011754281119
638726LV00013B/1947/P